KING
OF
CRAZY RIVER

*Also by William Colt MacDonald
in Large Print:*

The Phantom Pass
Action at Arcanum
Alias Dix Ryder
Blind Cartridges
The Comanche Scalp
Ridin' Through
Two-Gun Deputy

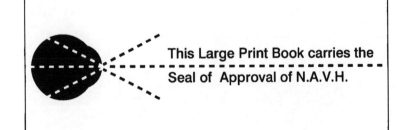

This Large Print Book carries the
Seal of Approval of N.A.V.H.

KING
OF
CRAZY RIVER

WILLIAM COLT
MacDONALD

WHEELER
PUBLISHING

Published in 2004 by arrangement with
Golden West Literary Agency.

Wheeler Large Print Western.

The text of this Large Print edition is unabridged.
Other aspects of the book may vary from the original edition.

Set in 16 pt. Plantin.

Printed in the United States on permanent paper.

Library of Congress Cataloging-in-Publication Data

MacDonald, William Colt, 1891–1968.
    King of Crazy River / by William Colt MacDonald.
      p. cm.
    ISBN 1-58724-573-6 (lg. print : sc : alk. paper)
    1. Ranchers — Crimes against — Fiction. 2. Revenge
— Fiction. 3. Large type books. I. Title.
PS3525.A2122K56 2004
813'.52—dc22   2003062188

KING
OF
CRAZY RIVER

National Association for Visually Handicapped
serving the partially seeing

As the Founder/CEO of NAVH, the only national health agency solely devoted to those who, although not totally blind, have an eye disease which could lead to serious visual impairment, I am pleased to recognize Thorndike Press* as one of the leading publishers in the large print field.

Founded in 1954 in San Francisco to prepare large print textbooks for partially seeing children, NAVH became the pioneer and standard setting agency in the preparation of large type.

Today, those publishers who meet our standards carry the prestigious "Seal of Approval" indicating high quality large print. We are delighted that Thorndike Press is one of the publishers whose titles meet these standards. We are also pleased to recognize the significant contribution Thorndike Press is making in this important and growing field.

Lorraine H. Marchi, L.H.D.
Founder/CEO
NAVH

* Thorndike Press encompasses the following imprints: Thorndike, Wheeler, Walker and Large Print Press.

CHAPTER 1

For the last time in his life, Big Vink Thorpe was making the stiff climb to the summit of Lookout Ridge. But, Big Vink didn't know that. As always, when he reached the top of the ridge he pulled the gray gelding to a halt. The horse was breathing heavily from its exertions. This short cut from the VIT outfit to the town of Morada was a task for any horse. Thorpe's bulky figure made the job doubly difficult. There was a longer wagon-trail from the ranch, a few miles to the south, which skirted the lower end of the Santos Hills, but mounted riders always negotiated the shorter way to town.

Thorpe removed his dusty black felt hat, mopped his face with a red bandanna, and stepped down from the saddle. Around and back of him on the flattened top of the ridge was a stunted growth of mesquite and prickly pear. He glanced down the precipitous slope up which he had come. Far below grew a tangled jungle of chaparral and catclaw and other South-West growths. To the untrained eye there seemed no trail up which a horse could find footing. At the bottom of the ridge the country flattened out slightly and became a broad expanse of rolling grass lands which stretched far to westward, where the Sangre de Santos Mountains raised jagged purple peaks in the hazy distance.

Off to the south, shimmering in the midday sun, crawled a narrow silvery ribbon which men knew by the name of Crazy River, the name being derived from the early Spanish, *Rio Demente.* There was a reason for that name, too, the stream having acquired the habit of changing its course every now and then over a period of time.

A chuckle broke through Vink Thorpe's firm lips as he gazed at the river. He ran muscular fingers through his thick iron-gray hair, replaced the hat on his head. "I reckon," he mused, half aloud, "I'll have to show Stinson that a king can be generous."

King of Crazy River they called Big Vink Thorpe, and a king he looked, every inch of him, despite the dust-stained corduroys, woollen shirt encasing bulky shoulders, and worn boots. Thorpe never had gone in for the fashionable clothing of the day. There was something in his rugged jaw, straight glance and arrogant bearing that told people they were in the presence of royalty, even though Thorpe refused to dress the part.

His gaze moved from the river, slowly northward until his eyes picked out a tiny smudge of dull brown, ragged at the edges. A herd of VIT cows. They were bunched, being worked. That would be the stray herd that had been combed from the deep recesses of the Sangre de Santos Range. Other, larger spots of brown were picked out against the distant gray-green floor of the wide valley. It seemed, when his eyes focused correctly, the whole valley was alive with Hereford cows. Thousands of cows grazing on hundreds of thousands of acres.

This was no new sight to Vink Thorpe: he never failed, on his way to Morada, to halt at the top of the ridge, not only to breathe his mount, but to make a survey of his domain. Somehow, the sight had never failed to thrill him. It was something, indeed, to be king of such a country.

"Not bad," he was wont to tell himself, "not bad — all things considered." This last, too, was always added.

Enemies he had made in building up this vast ranch. Were the fact known, he had probably made more enemies than friends. But the enemies, one by one, had disappeared, the friends remained. In the early, wilder days, gunpowder had been burned with relentless frequency.

A more vivid green, just north of the river, held Thorpe's interest for a minute. That was the cottonwood grove in which his home was situated — home and Eddie. Vink Thorpe's gaze blurred a trifle when he thought of Eddie. Eddie had been born in that house, and her mother had died there. Eddie, or Edith, at eighteen, grew more like her mother every day — more like her mother had been at that age, Thorpe's thoughts amended.

Thorpe's lips curved a trifle wistfully. His gaze quickly left the cottonwoods and swept along to northward, the movement taking in countless miles throughout the valley. From this height the valley floor looked flat as the proverbial pancake, but Thorpe knew from having travelled every foot of its rises and depressions that it was anything but that.

Far to the north, Big Vink's scrutiny halted again. Though there was no marking line, he knew that there commenced the Star-Cross holdings. Government land, the Star-Cross, leased at a few cents an acre for grazing purposes. What matter if Star-Cross stock did trespass on VIT property? There was enough, and more for all, Thorpe considered with a shrug. Besides, Hugh Norris, owner of the Star-Cross iron, was a decent sort. Why shouldn't Norris be allowed to make a start? — though Norris had been at it some years, now, Thorpe considered.

With these thoughts and others coursing his mind, Thorpe started to turn back to his horse. Quite suddenly he stopped, eyes narrowing on a number of tiny brown spots some miles to the south of the Star-Cross division line. Probably, about twenty cows there. To the left of the cows, a mile, Thorpe knew, ran a rise of ground that would shelter an interloper from anyone riding along the valley floor. Still farther to the south rode VIT hands. Thorpe frowned. They were too far away to see, or suspect, anything out of the ordinary. Miles away.

He moved a step nearer to get a clearer view around the thorny branches of a mesquite. He saw a rider move out toward that small group of cattle, saw one of the cows break from its companions with the rider in pursuit. Both, from this distance, seemed to be moving at a snail's pace, but Thorpe knew the running cow was calling forth everything the pony had to give.

Abruptly, the fleeing brown spot stopped. Thorpe saw the rider turn back toward a low line of brush where the northern end of Lookout Ridge rose in a slightly curving series of red granite buttes. The distance was too great to distinguish the rope, but Thorpe knew the cow had been captured and was being dragged behind the rider.

"I think," and Thorpe frowned, "I know that horse. Somethin' mighty familiar about it. Still . . . Maybe I'm mistaken. He's too far away for me to guess at any accusations."

The rider had dismounted, now. A moment later his body blended with the fallen cow's. Again, the two separated, the rider moving off a few paces. His body seemed to condense to smaller dimensions.

It was all clear to Thorpe. Though he could see no smoke nor flame, he knew as certainly as though he'd been on the spot, that the rider was crouched over the branding fire, heating a running iron.

The form of the unknown lengthened after a time, and again approached the cow. The two figures merged into one. Abruptly, the man straightened up. Thorpe saw him move toward his horse, climb into the saddle. The cow rose more slowly, then turned toward the rider. Thorpe saw the horse jerk to one side to avoid the cow's rush. After a few moments of maneuring the cow trotted slowly back to join its companions, the rider following at a more leisurely gait.

Thorpe considered the matter. "That *might* be one of my hands. If it ain't, that hombre was —" He broke off, moving swiftly toward the Winchester on his saddle. "An honest man will stand his ground," he mused. "A cowthief will hightail it."

He adjusted the sights of the rifle, then laughed at the futility of doing so. "Too far for a hit — anywheres nigh him, but he'll hear the report with the wind blowin' his way."

He levelled the barrel in the general direction of the suspected rustler who was again closing in on the small knot of cows. Thorpe's finger tightened about the trigger. The gun barked sharply, the report echoing back from the westward curving red buttes.

Thorpe lowered the gun, stood watching and wishing for his field glasses. It seemed several moments before there came a convulsive jerk on the part of the rider. Rather abruptly, the unknown turned his pony and disappeared in the brush near the buttes.

"Cowthief," Thorpe grunted. "Wish I'd knowed for sure."

He retraced his steps to the pony, slid the weapon into its scabbard, and was about to remount, when a voice reached him through the mesquite at his back, "Hit it?"

Thorpe, finishing climbing into the saddle, swung the animal around. He said, "Wasn't tryin' to hit him — too far away." He faced the man who had emerged from the thicket at the opposite side of the ridge, leading a horse behind him. "Figured I might meet you along here, someplace, Rance. You know, you got a sort of habit of always bein' on the job."

"That," Rance Duncan grinned, "is a damned good habit for the foreman of the VIT to have. I'm much obliged."

His slightly bowed legs in denim overalls and high-heeled boots quickly closed the distance between himself and his employer. Thorpe smiled down on him, and heard this lean, bronze-faced man under the roll-brim sombrero in indiscriminate gray saying, "Thought I heard somebody in the brush. I lit to move more quiet. Saw you preparin' to shake lead out of your barrel. Didn't speak for fear of spoilin' your aim." He waited for Thorpe to explain the shooting.

Thorpe said, jerking one thumb in the general direction of the spot where the unknown rider had been working, "See that small knot of cows down there? Didn't have any hands workin' 'em, did you?"

Rance Duncan craned his neck, then swung up to the saddle for a better view. He shook his head after a moment. "Not any."

"Figured as much. Feller down there playin' with a runnin' iron, looked like. He run when I fired."

"That's a certain amount of proof," Duncan conceded, "though it might have been any of the hands from the other outfits merely brandin' a critter that was overlooked last spring. If you don't want to give him the benefit of the doubt, it's still a certain amount of proof."

"Proof of what you've been sayin' ever since last fall?"

Duncan nodded. "We didn't get the gatherin' we should have."

"Pshaw!" Thorpe grunted good-naturedly. "What's a stolen cow now and then? We got plenty, Rance, and to spare. You're too parsimonious with my property."

"You're payin' me wages to look after your property," Duncan reminded. "I'll slope down thataway and see what I can find —"

"Forget it. That hombre, whoever he is, is too far away. By the time you got down there —"

"There'll be sign of some sort —"

"Forget it," Thorpe repeated. "I only shot to throw a scare into him. What's one cow more or less?"

"Losses count up," Duncan countered. "Many an outfit's been ruined by carelessness —"

Thorpe laughed heartily. "S'help me, Rance, that fate will never overtake the VIT while you're around. You been with me five years, now — you've been rodding the outfit three years. I don't know much more about you — personally, I mean — than I did when you was hired on. Where'd you pick up such a streak of industriousness? You're always level-headed, easy-goin' — but not too easy. Cripes! Don't you ever bust out?"

Duncan didn't answer right away. He had taken a sack of Durham from one pocket of his open vest. His fingers were steady as he rolled the tobacco into a neat cylinder.

"Me? Bust out?" he said finally. The words were touched with a soft Texas drawl. Thorpe had been liking Duncan's smile for five years now. It was a rather rare thing, that smile. Duncan went on, "Nope, I done all my bustin' out, long time back. I've learned my lesson."

"I never asked," Thorpe said quietly. "I ain't askin' now."

Duncan sobered, lighted his cigarette. Twin

15

plumes of gray smoke spiralled from his nostrils. "There ain't much to tell, Vink. I had a cow outfit of my own, once — and the money to operate. Thought I knew it all." A certain self-scorn lashed the words. "I started out to drink all the whisky in the world and play stud while drinkin' it. I failed pretty thorough at both jobs. What I didn't lose, cowthieves took. When I was broke, I figured I'd better learn how to operate a cow ranch before I made the same mistake twice. Yes, I've learned my lesson. I'm still learnin' — on the VIT — which don't give me no time to bust out."

He inhaled deeply on the cigarette between his long fingers. Thorpe's gaze travelled over the wiry form, saw, as though for the first time, a black-haired man who couldn't have been more than thirty. A black-haired man with a long, bony face, level gray eyes with quizzical crow's-feet at the corners, and a skin burned to a rich old mahogany.

Thorpe said dryly, "At last, I've found you're human. But I'd give my poke to see you bust out and get drunk — just once."

Did the gray eyes twinkle a trifle? Thorpe couldn't be sure.

Level-voiced, Duncan said, "I take a drink, now and then. But I've been through the mill." He said again, "I've learned my lesson."

Thorpe's eyes were meditative, "And

learned it well, son," he stated impulsively. "I know what you've been through. You see — well, I was pretty much of a fool once, myself. I —" He paused, changed the subject. "Don't think I'm criticisin', Rance. I reckon I never did know you, until now. You're so damn — damn" — he groped for words — "well, quiet, and sober, and" — for some reason the holstered Colts at Duncan's right hip made him add, "— and efficient. It's like I said a few minutes back, 'You got a habit of always bein' on the job.' "

Rance Duncan wasn't listening now. He sat his horse, searching the valley floor with hard eyes.

Thorpe guessed what was passing through his mind. "I already told you, Rance, that cuss hightailed it out of sight. If you're so dead set on driftin' down there and lookin' around, go to it. I'll give you a hint."

Duncan's questioning glance came back to Thorpe. "I'm waitin'."

"Now I couldn't be sure," Thorpe said carefully, "but I kind of thought I recognized the horse. You know that pinto Norris rides —"

"I reckon everybody does," Duncan nodded quietly.

"Well, takin' into consideration that my eyes is older than they used to be, the distance and so on — well, while I couldn't exact distinguish the markin's, just the same it looked that same paint horse. You see, it's

17

part hunch, along with what I saw."

"I know what you mean. Still, if it *was* Hugh Norris, he *might* have been sleeperin'. I don't just see how a VIT could be blotted into a Star-Cross."

"Shucks! Why worry about it? I'm pro'bly mistaken about the horse. If it was Norris — by the way, did you see him in Morada?"

Duncan shook his head. "Gus Oldfield's in town, though. Drove over from Capitol City last night. I wanted him to come out with me to-day, but he wouldn't —"

Thorpe chuckled. "You won't get Gus to talk cattle-buyin' until he's got some poker out of his system. He's lookin' for revenge from last year. I'm s'prised he bought any beef steers from me at all, after the way we cleaned him at draw. I had a letter three weeks back, sayin' he'd be in to-day. That's one thing that's takin' me into Morada — by the way, what did you do about Gillett?"

"Paid him his month's wages and told him to cut his string," Duncan said quietly. "He was in jail — as usual. I got Homer Yocum to let him go without bring him before the J.P."

"Hire another hand to take Gillett's place?"

"No, we can make out, until fall, without one."

"You're plumb tough on drunks, Rance."

"That ain't it," Duncan said earnestly. "I don't care how much, or how often, Gillett drinks, so long as he stays on the job. But this makes the third time now he's gone into town and raised hell. Nothin' for Yocum to do but put him in the cooler, when he goes to firin' that gun of his reckless like. He might hit somebody, or break a window or somethin'. I told Gillett I'd fire him next time that happened, and last night it did. He promised me yesterday evenin' when he left for Morada that he'd be back before midnight —"

"Mebbe he would have," Thorpe chuckled, "if he hadn't been in jail."

"Judgin' from the way he looked this mornin', he couldn't have moved a finger at midnight. No, Vink, there ain't no place on the VIT — not while I'm roddin' the outfit — for a man like Bert Gillett."

"You're the boss," Thorpe said shortly. "Run your crew your own way. I'm satisfied." He drew a long cigar from his vest pocket, offered one to Duncan and was refused with thanks. When the end of the cigar was glowing, he said, "Ward Stinson rode over to see me, just before I left home."

"Come to any agreement?"

"What agreement is there to come to?" Thorpe countered. "The facts are clear. Crazy River has shifted its course over a period of years. The river has always been the boundary line between us and the Forked-S. Those words are in the deeds — reckon they go back farther into the old Spanish grants. There ain't nothin' for me to say, when I come to think it over —"

"Except that," Duncan pointed out, "when the river shifted its course a quarter of a mile to the north, for a distance of some fifty miles across the valley, it lost you some acreage."

"Some," Thorpe conceded. "But I ain't worryin' about it. What's a few square miles compared to all the VIT owns?"

"What's Stinson worryin' about then?"

Thorpe chuckled. "He don't know I'm goin' to let him have that land, without any argument. He was all loaded for bear when he arrived. You know how he is, hates to lose a dollar or a square inch of land. I told him, serious like, that mebbe we should leave the matter to the courts to decide. Wanted to rib him a mite. With that, he hit the roof, figurin', I suppose, I'd beat him with my money. Seein' how he felt, I hurrahed him some more. Pretended to get peevish myself."

"It don't take much to put Ward on the prod."

"It sure don't," Thorpe agreed. "He'll probably be in town for the poker game to-night. I'll tell him, then, that he ain't got no fight with me. Shucks! I been neighbors with Ward Stinson too long to raise trouble about a few acres. Still and all, I do like to stir him up, just to hear him cuss. His profane vocabulary is some elegant and to be admired. Never seems to repeat himself."

Rance Duncan nodded. "I've heard him," he said dryly. "Funny thing the way he can cut loose when he loses his temper. Other times he's plumb sober."

"You called the turn, boy. Say, Eddie said she asked you last night to bring some needles from the store. Forget 'em?"

Duncan touched a vest pocket. "I didn't forget."

"No, you wouldn't." Innocently, Thorpe added, "I don't know what Eddie wants them needles for. Mebbe she aims to get sewin' on a bridal gown."

"Mebbe." Rance was non-committal.

Thorpe studied his foreman with twinkling eyes. "Monte Quillan dropped in for a call, 'bout an hour before I left. What sort of a husband would you say he'd make, Rance?"

Slowly, the color ebbed up beneath Duncan's tan. He said quietly, "Well, Monte's got a nice little spread in his 8Q-Barred-Out. He sure used his head in breedin' those Durham crosses —"

"I'm not talkin' about his cow knowledge," Thorpe interrupted. "I asked what sort of a husband —"

"That," Duncan said steadily, "would depend a good deal on what sort of husband Eddie wants. It's my personal opinion that she's a mite young —"

21

"Her mother was eighteen when I married her," Thorpe pointed out. "I wish Edith was alive to-day to sort of take this marriage business in hand. Natural, I want Eddie to be happy. You see, I'm expectin' Monte Quillan to speak to me about it any day now."

"The way I look at it, it's a matter between Eddie and Monte Quillan. Am I right?"

"C'rect as hell, old son," Thorpe smiled. He reined his horse around. "Well, I'm goin' to push along. It'll be four o'clock now before I hit Morada. If I don't hurry, I'll be too late for old Clem to catch the night stage with the store receipts —" then catching sight of a small canvas sack hanging at Duncan's saddle horn, "You got the mail, eh?"

Duncan nodded. "Clem had got it from the postoffice before I arrived. There's three days' mail here." He opened the sack, took out a small bundle of letters tied with a cord. Breaking the cord, he sorted over the envelopes, handing several to Thorpe.

Thorpe glanced at the letters bearing his name. "Shucks! Packin' houses, mail order houses — here's one from a gun company and another from a saddle firm. Them people sure like to write letters to sell me stuff. Here's a feed company advertisement —" He swore abruptly, tossed a large envelope, unopened, into the brush. "I ain't fool enough to buy gold stock in *that* company —" breaking off as his eyes encountered a letter bearing no return address. He turned the envelope over and over in his hands. "Hmm! Wonder who this is from?"

"Maybe it tells, inside the envelope," Rance suggested dryly.

"I'll bet you're right," Thorpe laughed. He handed back the other envelopes to be replaced in the sack, and ripped open the one in his hand.

Duncan wasn't paying any attention to his employer's movements, until he heard a half-suppressed exclamation, followed by a muttered oath. He looked up, and saw that Big Vink had gone white, and that his features were working with emotion.

Even while he watched, Duncan saw Thorpe's strong hand involuntarily constrict on the letter. There was a certain vehement strength in the action. It might have been a reptile Thorpe was crushing to death.

"Anythin' wrong?" Duncan asked quietly.

As though with difficulty, Thorpe brought his gaze to bear on Duncan, and in that moment Duncan read fear, stark unmitigated fear, in his employer's eyes. All the color was drained from the big man's face, he looked terror-stricken. His body slumped in the saddle. He looked at Duncan more steadily after a moment, but his look was that of a beaten man.

"God, Vink!" Duncan said quickly. "What's wrong?"

Thorpe's lips moved noiselessly. For a moment the words wouldn't come. He gulped and forced a ghastly smile, then quickly thrust the crumpled letter into a pocket, as though fearful that Duncan might see it.

The words falling from his ashen lips shook a trifle, "No — no — no, nothing's wrong, Rance. I — I — well, you see —"

"Dammit, man! Somethin' *is* wrong." A touch of the spur brought Duncan's horse nearer. For a moment he had thought Thorpe would fall from the saddle.

With an effort, Thorpe stiffened his form. "It's all right, Rance," he said hurriedly. "Nothin' to do with this letter at all. It's my heart. Old trouble that's bothered me on and off for years. I'm all right now. See you later."

Swinging his horse abruptly about, he went crashing across the top of the ridge and was soon lost to view as he descended the side toward town.

Rance Duncan looked after him a moment. "Somethin'," he told himself, "is hellishly wrong. Heart attack! Shucks! Vink is a rotten liar. It was that letter — just scared plain hell out of him. In all the five years I've worked for the VIT, he never showed fear thataway, and I've seen him in one or two pretty bad fights, too."

He could hear the sounds of Thorpe's horse moving recklessly down the east side of the ridge. Finally the sounds died out.

"Reckon he got down without a broken neck," Duncan muttered.

Something white on the ground caught his eye. It was the envelope that had enclosed the fear-arousing letter. With a quick, easy movement, the foreman leaned down from the saddle and retrieved the envelope. A swift glance showed Duncan three things: the address was written in a sprawling, ill-educated hand in ink; there was no return address given; though the cancellation stamp was blurred and smudged, Duncan thought it read either El Paso or El Toro. He couldn't decide which.

Duncan studied the envelope and finally placed it in an overalls' pocket. He sat his pony, undecided whether to follow Thorpe into town or not, and on second thought decided against it. "If he'd wanted me to go along, he'd have said so. . . . Pro'bly too late to do anythin' now, but I reckon I'll drift down and see if I can pick up any sign of that hombre Vink shot at."

Touching spurs to the pony's ribs, he moved warily down the steep slope heading in the general direction of the Star-Cross territory.

CHAPTER II

By the time Thorpe had passed the first buildings on the outskirts of Morada, he had regained considerable self-possession. After all, he told himself, there was no sense bein' stampeded this way. Money would clear up nearly any difficulty. Undoubtedly it would be an ugly business to handle, but still, it could be accomplished. Thorpe was thinking more clearly now. Plans commenced to formulate in his mind.

Once he even forced a smile at his own expense. Yep, he'd acted like a yearlin' colt shyin' away at sight of a throw rope. He wondered what Duncan had thought of his actions. Duncan. There was a straight-thinkin' man if there ever was one. Might be a good idea to take Rance into his confidence. Two heads were better than one. Yep, he'd see Duncan to-night, and — and in the next moment Thorpe dismissed that plan.

Inwardly he cursed his own inefficiency. Hell of a way for the King of the Crazy River country to act. This was his own problem. A king settled such affairs with no outside help — a real king. Why, this was his town — anyway, he liked to think of it that way. Hadn't he been elected mayor of Morada at every election held? Not that that meant a great deal, except for the honor attached. His mayoralty duties were next to nil. But, the town itself, that had been his idea. He had watched it grow, year by year, loaned money toward its development.

The general store at least was his personal property. Thorpe took a lot of pride in his store. It was the nucleus about which Morada had been formed, when the owner of the VIT had decided that Capitol City was much too far away to serve as a convenient source of supply for the Crazy River country outfits.

As his horse walked briskly along the centre of the dirt road, Thorpe glanced the length of Main Street. On either side a long row of adobe and frame buildings — some with high false fronts and wooden awnings with supporting uprights at the edge of the road — met his gaze. An almost unbroken line of hitch-racks, before which stood cow horses and vehicles, stretched on each side of the street. There were other thoroughfares, too, some with neat residences and white-washed picket fences. Yes, this was his town, his kingdom. Nothing serious could happen here, at this late date. Let the enemy come. Everything could be arranged.

Thorpe commenced to breathe easier. After all, it was the shock of the thing that had upset him. To think, after all these years . . .

It was suddenly borne in upon Thorpe's abstractions that his horse had come to a halt. He jerked up from the problems absorbing his mind, looked around, and smiled sheepishly. From sheer force of habit, the horse had, as was always customary, made its first stop upon arriving in Morada, on the left side of the street, before the tie-rail in front of Brad Wheeler's Morada House.

The Morada House hotel stood on the corner of Main and Hereford Streets. It faced on Main, though its side — or barroom — entrance was on Hereford. A roofed porch, lined with chairs and the customary loungers, ran from the side around to the front entrance of the hotel. A swift series of chuckles ran along the chairs, as Thorpe looked up, a rather blank expression in his eyes.

"Looks like you was concentratin' on something knotty, Vink," drawled Johnny Hines, owner of the Coffee-Pot outfit.

"Aw, the horse knows Thorpe's habits," commented a travelling liquor salesman, in a fancy vest and a diamond stick-pin. "Time for a drink, ain't it, Thorpe?"

Homer Yocum, Morada's deputy-sheriff, tossed a handful of peanut shells over the porch railing. "Vink," Yocum announced to the crowd in general, "is pro'bly figurin' how he can reduce taxes and cut my salary."

28

Yocum was a lank, dour-looking man with the melancholy eyes of a St. Bernard dog, and a funeral appearance that wasn't entirely due to his dusty black coat and trousers tucked into knee-length boots.

Thorpe grinned good-naturedly, as he climbed down from the saddle. "*Your* salary," he replied scornfully to Yocum's statement, "wouldn't even buy your peanuts, if you was paid for what you actually do."

There was some laughter at this. Yocum grunted through a crunching mouthful, "Anyway you look at it, Vink, it's a shell game."

Thorpe didn't answer this. He had just caught sight of a tall, dignified elderly man in a frock-coat, descending the steps from the bar-room entrance of the hotel.

"Hey, Judge," Thorpe called. "You're just the man I want to see."

He flipped his horse's reins over the tie-rail and moved hastily around the corner. Judge Alvord, the local Justice of the Peace, waited on the sidewalk at the foot of the steps, until Thorpe came up. The two men conversed in a serious undertone for several minutes. Finally, Thorpe nodded.

"Reckon you're right, Judge. That'll pro'bly be the best way. Then there won't be a chance for a slip."

One or two more sentences were exchanged, before Alvord turned the corner into Main Street. Thorpe looked after him a moment, as though deciding to call him back. After a few seconds his gaze was transferred to the ponies at the hitch-rack. No, no pinto horse there.

He turned back toward the saloon entrance. On the opposite side of Hereford Street, two women passing, with raised parasols, caught his eye. He bowed gravely, touched fingers to his hat, and ascended the wooden steps to the hotel porch.

At the top of the flight a man in puncher togs blocked his path. "Can I see you a minute, Mr. Thorpe?"

"Oh, hello, Gillett," Thorpe said awkwardly. He knew what was coming and dreaded it. "Well, speak ahead."

Gillett shifted uncomfortably. "I mean in private."

Thorpe took in the unshaven features, turned his head a trifle to evade the whisky-reeking breath. "No time like the present, Gillett. Speak out, man."

"It's about my job. I want it back."

"That," Thorpe said clearly, "is up to Rance Duncan. Talk to him."

"I already talked to him — this mornin'." Gillett bit his lip. "He says I'm through. Now, if you just understood how things stand —"

"If Rance says you're through, you're through, Gillett. I won't interfere with his job —"

"Meanin' you wouldn't even put in a good word for me? But, look here —"

"It's no good, Gillett," Thorpe said not unkindly. "I'm not aimin' to cross Rance. He runs my crew his own way —"

"You won't give me my job, then?" Gillett's face flushed angrily.

"That's the way it stands."

Gillett faced Thorpe a moment, face working with rage. Then he looked away, "S'help me, God, Thorpe," he muttered, "you'll be sorry for this some day."

Thorpe looked the man over coolly, shrugged his bulky shoulders, and passed on into the hotel. Gillett gazed after him, opening and clenching his fists convulsively. Suddenly aware that the loungers on the hotel porch were watching him, he slouched down the steps and around the corner.

Deputy Yocum brushed some peanut shells off his lap to the porch floor and turned to his neighbor on the right. "Did you hear what Gillett said?"

"Yeah, I did, Homer. Gillett looked plumb riled, didn't he?"

Yocum tossed a peanut into the air, deftly caught it in his open mouth. "If anything happens you'll be a witness. Folks in this burg never take much stock in my statements."

"Aw, I reckon nothin' won't happen. Gillett's just sort of broke out with a whisky rash. He'll get over it."

31

"Uh-huh. Like the stallion got over the fence — but he busted the fence all to hell. That Gillett's got a bad eye."

Inside the hotel bar-room, only three men stood at the bar. Two of them were residents of Morada, who nodded as Thorpe entered. The third was an individual of quick nervous actions in a dark suit and derby hat. A gold watch chain stretched across a high-cut vest that reached nearly to his stiff white collar. The owner of the derby swung around upon seeing Thorpe's reflection in the bar mirror.

"Vink Thorpe! You card-cheatin' old mossback. Figured you were about due. How's your liver?"

Thorpe gripped his hand, laughing. "My God, Gus!" he exclaimed fervently, "where'd you get the hard-boiled hat? Is that thing supposed to make you look prosperous? And a gold watch and chain! There must be a heap of money in buyin' cattle an' cheatin' poor cowmen out of their rightful profits."

Gus Oldfield laughed. "S'help me, Vink, I paid you a dollar more last year, per head, than my house could afford. You know, this beef buyin' ain't what it's cracked up to be. If I don't make the price right to you, I lose a good source of supply. If I don't pay less than you want to take, my company gives me a goin'-over —"

"You sure look elegant, so I guess you're

all right with your bosses," Thorpe said in mock admiration. "My God! To think you rode for the VIT only a few years back. Wait'll the boys see that hat on a horse. Betcha it will look like a sieve —"

"Aw, I brought ridin' things," Oldfield grinned. He grew serious. "On the level, though, Vink, I can't pay what I paid you last year. Things are growing tight." His voice lowered. "Just between you and me, I'm just scrapin' along."

"That's too dang bad. Well, we won't worry about prices now. You can fix that up with Rance, out at the ranch, tomorrow."

"Won't you be there?"

"I don't reckon, Gus. I got to go up to Capitol City."

"How's that?"

Momentarily, Thorpe's face clouded. "I got to see a lawyer about — about some business."

"Cripes! I didn't mean to be inquisitive."

"Hell! I know that. It ain't nothin' anyway — nothin' much, I mean." Thorpe forced a smile. "Anyway, to get back to that derby hat, I know damn well you didn't buy it from your poker winnin's in that game we had last year."

Oldfield grinned ruefully. "Let's have a drink on that. You sure cleaned me proper. I ain't felt like dealin' a hand of poker since, but I sure got somethin' in my bones that says I'm goin' to win to-night — there'll be a game, won't there?" a trifle anxiously.

"Nothin' else. That's what brought me in."
Thorpe gave an order to the bartender, "Spot
of Bourbon, Louie."

"Make it two," from Oldfield.

"Seen Matt and Brad yet?" Thorpe asked,
after a time.

Oldfield set down his glass, nodded. "Yes,
they're all set to play 'em high, wide and
handsome, to-night, if you'll take a hand in a
game. If Ward Stinson comes in, we'll have
the same crowd as last year."

"Stinson will be in, I reckon. Poker is his
rulin' passion." Thorpe chuckled, "Ward's
sort of peeved at me, though."

"What's wrong?"

"Little boundary line trouble. I reckon it
will be settled before Ward gets to carvin' my
heart out, though."

"Stinson can blow up easier than any man
I ever see. And be calm and regretful the
next minute. Good old scout, Stinson is."

"All of that — by the way, I ain't countin'
on any all-night session to-night, like we had
last year."

"Getting old, eh, Vink?"

"It ain't that. But I want to get an early
start to Capitol City in the morning. This
business of mine needs to be settled plumb
pronto, and I don't want to delay it by waitin'
for any stage. What say we get the game
started right after supper? We can play down

34

to the store. I aim to sleep there to-night —"

A loud laugh at the doorway interrupted the words. A blond, heavy-eyed giant in overalls and a slouch-brim sombrero barged into the bar-room. Despite his size there was a lithe, quick something in his movements. Left thumb hooked in his gun-belt, he came toward the bar, right hand outstretched:

"Well, look who's descended into our midst. None other but Gus Oldfield himself. Welcome to our city, Gus. Goin' to take any of my cows this year? . . . Hello, Vink! Is there any bounty on derby hats offered this season?" And to Louie, the barkeep, "Set up a whole houseful, Louie, and chalk it against the Star-Cross account."

"Glad to see you, Norris," Oldfield said, shaking hands with the owner of the Star-Cross. "I'll drink on you, but I'm darned if I can buy your beef."

"That," Hugh Norris laughed, "is Vink Thorpe's fault. Wish I could connect with some packin' house the way he does, instead of havin' to peddle my beef to anybody'll take it."

Thorpe had sauntered over to the doorway and looked out. No, there wasn't any paint horse in sight. He came back to the bar and joined Oldfield and Norris. Before the three had finished their drink, a man in batwing *chaparejos* pushed through the entrance. He was a rather handsome individual with brown wavy hair, a small moustache, and a scarlet neckerchief knotted at his throat. A first impression would have put him down as something of a dandy. On second glance, it could be seen he was capable, whatever his appearance.

He jangled a pair of silver-inlaid spurs across the floor. "Howdy, gents," he greeted, "anybody buyin'? Hello, there, Gus Oldfield. Heard you was in town."

"I just bought one, Monte," Hugh Norris chuckled. "Hurry up, mebbe Louie will let you get in on it before we finish."

"Good . . . Rye for mine, Louie. Hey, Gus, you figure to buy any 8Q-Barred-Out steers this year? I need money. Let you have 'em cheap."

"I'll betcha they're cheap." Oldfield was unconvinced.

"You," Norris grinned at Monte Quillan, "ain't goin' to have no more luck than me, Monte. I got turned down, too."

"I'm sorry, Quillan," Oldfield was saying. "This year I'm confinin' my buyin' to VIT stuff."

Norris shook his head gravely. "You'll learn your lesson some day, Gus, and come to the Star-Cross, when them VIT canners and bologna bulls have done ruined your best trade."

Thorpe laughed. "Trouble with you younger fellers, you're just jealous because an old coot like me corners the market. When you hombres really learn to raise beef critters —"

"I've learned," Norris chuckled, "but it don't do me no good. Now, my Star-Cross steers is just the same as VIT stock —"

"Just the same?" Thorpe laughed. "I might take that two ways, Norris."

Norris sobered abruptly. "Yeah, you could, couldn't you? But I didn't mean it that way."

Monte Quillan's swarthy countenance took on a rueful look. "Well, if Gus won't buy my beef, that's just my hard luck. Seems to be only one kind of folks want my stuff — them that don't pay for it. . . . Oh, by the way, Vink, Eddie wants you to bring her some — well, some sort of thread. She made a note."

He passed a folded slip of paper to Thorpe. Thorpe tucked it in a pocket. "I'll take care of it." Then added, "What do you mean, Monte, by 'them that don't pay for it'? Somebody rustlin' your herd?"

Quillan shrugged neat shoulders. "I'm jest talkin', I reckon — only I don't seem to get the increase I should."

Thorpe said quietly to Quillan, "Comin' over Lookout Ridge, I spotted some hombre workin' a cow. Thrun a hunk of lead in his direction, and he didn't lose no time makin' tracks. An honest man wouldn't have run."

"Huh." Quillan's face was blank. "You don't say. Know who he was? Recognize him?"

"Mite too far away for that. I kind of thought the horse looked familiar, though."

There was a moment's silence. Norris cut in on the conversation, "What you aimin' to do about it, Vink?"

"I'll decide when I get back from Capitol City. Got more pressin' business there first."

"Speakin' of horses," Hugh Norris said, "some son-of-a-bit-your-finger-off rustled that paint animal of mine. He plumb disappeared two days ago. If I catch the son that —"

"Well, don't blame me for it, Norris." Monte Quillan's face was red. "It just happens, though, that I'm ridin' a paint horse. One I been takin' the kinks out of, on and off, since last winter."

"I ain't blamin' you, cowboy," Norris laughed. "I know my horse —"

"I didn't notice you forkin' a paint pony, Monte," Thorpe said quietly, "when you rode into the VIT this mornin'."

"I was," Quillan hesitated, seemed a bit embarrassed. "Matter of fact, I wanted Eddie's opinion. I sort of figured to make her a present if she liked him, when he's thorough broke."

"Oh," Thorpe grunted. "I might have not noticed." He dropped the subject. "Well, reckon I'll go across to the store. Clem Lucas will be wantin' to get off on the night stage. It's five o'clock already," consulting a big silver watch. "I'll see you later, Gus."

38

"Right, Vink. Get ready for a beatin'. I figure to strip you right down to your boot taps."

"Just so long as I don't have to win that derby hat," Thorpe smiled, "I ain't worryin'."

CHAPTER III

Thorpe passed through the door and nearly collided with a slight, gray-haired man in cowman's togs. The man swung back against the door-jamb to avoid being stepped on.

"Excuse me, Ward," Thorpe apologized. "You was comin' in just —"

"Thought I'd find you in here," Ward Stinson said, a trifle grimly. "Vink, there's somethin' else I want to bring to mind about that boundary line. It says in the deed, plain as day, that —"

"Let's talk it over some other time, Ward. I'm kind of in a hurry now. Got to get across to the store. I'll see you to-night."

"We-ell —" Stinson hesitated. Before he could say more, Thorpe had repeated, "See you to-night," and brushed past him to descend the steps to the plank sidewalk.

The owner of the Forked-S — sometimes called the Snake — proceeded on into the bar-room, greeted Gus Oldfield with a perfunctory shake of the hand and said "hello" to Quillan and Norris. Ordering a drink of whisky, he downed it with a slightly shaking arm.

He removed his soft hat, mopped his forehead and sparse hair with a bandanna, and replaced the hat. "Seems like," he complained plaintively, "that Vink was in an all-fired rush. I wanted to talk to him."

"Mebbe," Norris chuckled, "he didn't want to talk to you."

"I'll bet he don't, neither," Stinson grouched.

"How you two comin' on that boundary line disagreement?" Quillan asked.

"We ain't got nowhere's," from Stinson, moodily. "I talked to Vink this mornin'. He said somethin' about takin' it to court. Now, that ain't necessary t'all, if he'll listen to reason —"

"I'd sure hate to buck Thorpe in a court of law," Norris chuckled. "I'd figure I was lost before the clerk started his 'hear ye! hear ye!' "

Stinson looked worried. "If I can only talk to him —"

Gus Oldfield said suddenly, "I figure Vink will let the law decide it."

"What do you mean?" Stinson asked sharply.

"Well," Oldfield said awkwardly. "Maybe Thorpe thinks it would be more fair, that way. I don't blame him. Anyway, he told me he was headin' for Capitol City in the mornin' to see a lawyer —"

"What!" Stinson almost yelled the one word.

"That's what I said," Oldfield nodded. He wasn't forgetting that Stinson would be an opponent in the coming poker game. With something to worry about, Stinson might not play his cards as carefully as he should. "Yep, Ward, Vink told me — said he was goin' early to see a law-sharp in Capitol City. Said there was something that had to be settled plumb *pronto*. Those were his words."

Stinson's lips moved ineffectually. From the collar of his woollen shirt to the top of his head he turned deep crimson. Then the explosion came: "Of all the lousy, two-bit, sidewindin', stubborn packmules I ever see," Stinson bawled. Rage overcame speech for a moment, then he went on, "Let the cowhocked big lump of beef take it into court. I'll fight him to my last cent. Law court! Cripes A'mighty!"

Stinson spat a long brown stream disgustedly. "S'help me, I'll show him! Law court! What he needs is a forty-five slug to take some of the mulishness out of him. He'll see! Ward Stinson don't take that kind of a deal from nobody!"

"Watch your temperature, Ward," Norris grinned. The others were silent, somewhat awed by the abrupt upheaval of Stinson's words.

"Watch nothin'!" Stinson raged, his face purple. "I'll watch my rights, that's what I'll watch, and God help any man that gets in my way. . . . Louie, give me a shot of Old Crow. I got to wash out the thoughts of a certain —"

"Take it easy, Ward," Quillan advised. "I heard Vink tell you he'd see you to-night. Don't jump to conclusions until you're sure of your ground."

That quieted Stinson to some extent. After downing his drink, he retired to a table in one corner to read a week-old newspaper.

On the hotel porch, Deputy Homer Yocum's gaze had followed Vink Thorpe down the steps. He watched while Thorpe paused a moment to look at Monte Quillan's pinto, then proceeded across Main Street. On the corner of Main and Hereford, Thorpe encountered a man nearly as tall as himself. The two stopped to talk a few minutes, Thorpe appearing to grow excited after the preliminary exchange of conversation. Finally, he passed a folded sheet of paper to the other.

Yocum tossed a handful of peanuts between his jaws. " 'Pears like," he mused, "Vink and Brad Wheeler have found somethin' serious to *habla* about. Wonder what that paper was. Letter, looks like. Hell, Brad is commencin' to look serious, too. What's the argument? There — Brad passed the letter back to Vink. Looks like Brad is tryin' to quiet Vink down." Another handful of peanuts went the way of their brothers.

"There — they're through talkin', now," Yocum added mentally.

Brad Wheeler left Thorpe to proceed along Main Street, while he walked swiftly across the road and mounted the Hereford Street steps to his hotel. His face was serious, and he rubbed one forefinger vigorously alongside of his bulbous nose.

"H'are, you, Brad," Yocum called lazily.

"Oh, hello, Homer. Thanks. All right. Thanks." Absentmindedly Wheeler passed on into the bar-room.

"Somethin' is sure botherin' Brad," Homer cogitated. "He always does his heavy thinkin' with finger to his nose."

"What's that?" Yocum's neighboring chair asked, not quite catching the deputy's mumbled thoughts.

Yocum crammed a handful of peanuts into his mouth. "I was wonderin'," he replied idly, "why Brad don't use his thumb. I would if I owned an elegant hotel like this."

"Huh? I don't get you."

"It don't make no difference," Yocum said wearily. He closed his eyes and tilted his head against the back of the chair.

Ten minutes passed. A short, squarely-built man of middle-age panted up the steps. Perspiration streaked his florid countenance. His trousers and vest were wrinkled, his hat a battered old felt. This was Matt Everett, owner of Morada's feed store. He looked

44

worried. Homer Yocum opened his eyes, straightened in his chair, and looked interestedly at the man.

"Hello, Matt," he called lazy greeting. "You look fagged."

"H-H-Hot day," Matt Everett said nervously. "Brad in the b-bar?"

Yocum nodded. "You been talkin' to Vink Thorpe?"

"Y-Y-Yes, Homer. Why?"

"Just wonderin'," Yocum drawled. "Saw him talkin' to Brad a spell back. Figgured mebbe —"

"F-F-Figgured what?" Matt Everett paused at the saloon entrance.

"Just figgured mebbe, that's all." Homer closed his eyes and tilted back in the chair again. Everett passed into the bar-room. In a moment Yocum opened his eyes slightly. This was commencing to look interesting. He wondered what was up. Matt Everett never stuttered unless something had upset him.

Yocum rose leisurely and looked into the bar-room. Norris, Quillan and Gus Oldfield still stood at the bar, drinking. Oldfield looked a little drunk. Ward Stinson sat in one corner, frowning at space. Brad Wheeler and Matt Everett weren't to be seen. They'd probably left the bar-room by the office — or lobby — entrance. Yocum returned to his chair, groped in a nearly empty pocket for more peanuts.

★ ★ ★

After leaving Matt Everett, whom he'd met on Main Street, a short distance from the hotel, Vink Thorpe proceeded on toward his general store, which stood on the south side of Main, midway between Hereford and Thorpe Streets. Excepting old Clem Lucas, his clerk, there was no one in the store when Thorpe entered.

A long counter ran the length of one side of the store. Two large windows and the double-doored entrance were at the front wall. Three sides of the room were lined with shelves which held canned fruits and vegetables, sacked foods, and miscellaneous goods. The middle of the floor was given over to boxes and barrels, a stack of brooms.

Across the rear of the store, a room had been partitioned off for a combination office and living quarters for the old clerk. Occasionally, on the clerk's nights off, Thorpe himself made use of the cot in the room, claiming it made a better bed than anything Brad Wheeler's hotel had to offer. Access to this room was had through a doorway at one side of the partition.

Thorpe entered his store slowly, nodded to the clerk, and commenced to pace the length of the store floor.

"Thought mebbe ye wa'n't comin', Mr. Thorpe," Clem Lucas said, in a thin, cracked voice, after a few moments. Lucas appeared to be seventy or seventy-five years old. He was stooped, thin to the point of emaciation, and walked with a queer shuffling step. A livid scar, the result of a railroad wreck, Clem explained when he could get anyone to listen, ran from his left temple down his cheek until it disappeared in his gray beard. The healing of the cut had given his features a gnome-like appearance, when one saw him from his left side.

A good many folks wondered why Vink Thorpe kept such an ancient clerk on his payroll, and to all such inquiries Thorpe always replied, "Why not? He may not be as spry as some fellers, but he's faithful and I don't have to worry about him runnin' off with some loose female. 'Sides," and here Thorpe always smiled, "he provides a certain amount of amusement for Morada. He don't never tire of tellin' about that railroad wreck he come through, and when he gets excited, the way his chin whiskers bob up and down is plumb fascinatin' an' entertainin'."

Lucas shoved his gold-rimmed spectacles up on his forehead, and studied his employer, who was now at the farther end of the store. "I said, Mr. Thorpe," he repeated querulously, "that I thought ye wa'n't comin'."

"Did you?" Thorpe replied. He brought his thoughts back to the present. "I expect you're waitin' to get started."

"C'rect," nodded the old man. "I got last

week's take-in all done up and ready. Nigh on to two thousand dollars, Mr. Thorpe. Quite a few folks settled bills —"

"Er — uh — Clem," Thorpe said. "I don't reckon to send the money up to the Capitol City Bank this week."

"You don't!" The old fellow looked put out. "What's the matter, Mr. Thorpe? You ain't gettin' ready to start your own bank in Morada like you've talked about?"

"Not just yet. I want Morada to grow a mite first, then get a railroad through here. We'll think about that bank, say a year from now, then you can have an easy job as watchman."

"But you ain't aimin' to have that money here all night?"

"Well, I may need it to-night," Thorpe explained, "or durin' the comin' week. I'll keep it in the safe."

"Heh! Heh!" the old clerk cackled. "So ye might need it to-night. Gus Oldfield was in here and he told me you was plannin' to play poker." Suddenly, his face fell. "Shucks, I —"

"Now, don't you fret none, Clem," Thorpe broke off, coming nearer. "You can have your weekly trip to the capitol, as usual. Figurin' to go to the Opera House, I suppose."

"Well," wistfully, "they do say as how Eddie Foy's to be at the Little Gem Opery, tomorrer night. You know, Mr. Thorpe, if it hadn't been for a mistake in show billin',

48

Eddie Foy would have been in that train wreck that —"

"Yes, so I understand," Thorpe cut in hastily. He had already listened many times to the account of the accident. "Well, now, you better run along, Clem" — consulting his watch — "it's nearly six. The stage is due pretty quick."

"Yes, sir. And when that Wheeler boy comes in tomorrow, we better have him stack them barreled goods that come —"

"And, Clem —"

"Yes, Mr. Thorpe."

"No playin' with the fancy ladies at the capitol, to-night."

"Heh! Heh! Mr. Thorpe, ye allus did know my weak points."

It was their stock joke, repeated weekly, before the old clerk started his twenty-five-mile trip to Capitol City.

Five minutes later old Lucas had doffed his work apron, replaced it with a coat and felt hat of rusty black, and shuffled off down Main Street, carrying a worn tan valise.

Thorpe followed him out of the store to the edge of the roadway. Five minutes later he watched the stage roll in and pull up before the Morada House, with a jangling of harness and screeching of brakes, on its daily stop from Breenville, sixty miles to the south.

While fresh horses were replacing the sweat-streaked animals which had brought in the coach, Thorpe scrutinized narrowly the passengers who alighted: two strangers who looked like drummers; Ernie Burks, of the Gun Repair Shop; Joe Myers, of the New York Emporium; and Letitia Preen, who operated the Ladies' Millinery Store. Thorpe, watching, saw old Lucas carrying on a brief conversation with Joe Myers.

Thorpe breathed a deep sigh of relief. He watched his clerk climb aboard, waved to him a few minutes later as the stage rocked past, the horses gathering speed at every jump. After a moment Thorpe turned back into the store. Picking up the canvas sack containing the past week's store receipts, he made his way to the room at the back of the store, entered and closed the door. It wasn't likely that any one would enter the store, now. If they did, they could call out.

To the left of the door, as Thorpe entered the room, was a single window, with beneath it a washstand. The back wall was blank, except for a narrow bolted door that led outside. In the centre of the room was a circular oak table of generous dimensions. At the right-hand back corner stood a huge iron safe, and across from the safe, against the front wall of the room, was a cot, on one end of which were neatly folded blankets. A hat rack, holding some of Lucas' clothing, stood near the cot. Against the side wall, between cot and safe, was a small wooden chest that belonged to Lucas, and held, Thorpe supposed, other belongings of his clerk's. A half-dozen straight-back wooden chairs were placed about the room.

Thorpe approached the safe, twirled the combination knob, turned the handle and pulled open the heavy iron door. On a shelf inside he placed the canvas sack of money, then took out a box of poker chips and a deck of cards which he carried over and placed on the table. A second trip to the safe produced a squat brown bottle, some whisky glasses, and a box of cigars. These were placed on the table beside the cards and chips. This done, Thorpe closed and secured the safe door.

A few minutes later he was on the street, having locked the store doors behind him. Heading in a diagonal direction across Main Street, he mounted the steps to the Morada House entrance. In the dining-room he found Brad Wheeler, Matt Everett, Ward Stinson and Gus Oldfield, the latter more than a little drunk by this time.

There was a good deal of laughter on the part of Oldfield during the meal. The others appeared to be thinking seriously on various knotty problems. When the meal was finished, the five men headed for Thorpe's store. Ward Stinson brought up the matter of the boundary-line dispute, but Thorpe, rather impatiently, put him off. Seating themselves about the round table in the back room of the store, Thorpe's guests waited while he lighted an oil lamp. There were but few more preliminaries to attend to before the game commenced.

The hours passed. The game waxed fast and furious. Poker hands were dealt and played, in a silence broken only by terse comments. The room swirled with tobacco smoke. And, now, Death prepared to deal a hand. Before another sun lifted above the horizon, even before the first morning breeze was to stir the dust of Morada's streets, Big Vink Thorpe was to play his final hand in that game which the Grim Reaper never fails to win. . . .

CHAPTER IV

Young Alonzo Wheeler, seventeen, lanky and snub-nosed, left his home in Thorpe Street, just off of Main, hurried on his morning's duties by a rather sharp-tongued mother. He wasn't — even his father, Brad Wheeler, admitted this — overly ambitious where manual labor was concerned. Histrionic ambitions, engendered by a performance once witnessed in Capitol City, had for long prompted Alonzo to go to New York City and enter his proper sphere on Broadway, either as actor or playwright. No doubt about it, Alonzo was an optimistic sort.

But Brad Wheeler had refused to advance money for any such uncertain venture, and young Alonzo was forced to save the price of the railway trip from such money as he earned for his services in the Thorpe store, such services including taking care of the store on Tuesday and a half-day Wednesdays when old Lucas indulged in his weekly holiday at Capitol City. Also, Alonzo lent a hand during meal hours and on Saturday nights when he was employed to help Lucas serve the increased flow of customers.

Alonzo yawned, as he turned the corner into Main Street. The sun was still high.

There weren't many pedestrians abroad. Here and there, Alonzo nodded a sleepy good-morning to a storekeeper sweeping out, or standing in a doorway. "I wish," Alonzo muttered, "old goatface could arrange to be away just afternoons. Wait until I'm famous along the Great White Way, I betcha I'll sleep until noon, anyway."

He scuffed his heels along the plank walk until he came to the store. Deputy Homer Yocum was waiting in front. The double-doors of the store were still locked.

"Wonderin' if you wasn't ever comin'," Homer growled. "Old Lucas is usual opened up —"

"What you want — peanuts?" Alonzo inquired.

"Peanuts," Homer nodded. "Ah' let's hurry it up."

"Aw, t'ain't more'n quarter past eight," Alonzo defended his tardiness. "I kinda thought Mr. Thorpe would open up. Reckon he must've stayed over to the hotel. When he sleeps in the store, he usual has it opened by the time I get —"

"Yeah, I know all that."

Alonzo produced the key to the double doors, and opened one of them. Yocum followed him inside. The air smelled stale and close. Yocum left the door open.

Alonzo moved around the counter to procure a paper sack. A few minutes later he placed the peanuts in Yocum's hand. Yocum seated himself on the box. For a few minutes the only sound was produced by a cracking of peanut shells. The deputy commenced to feel better.

"How come you got here late, 'Lonzo?" he asked. "Overslept, I suppose?"

"Yes, I been writin' on a play to be acted on the stage. Sat up until nigh 'leven-thirty last night. Ma give me fits for burnin' oil —"

"Write 'em, too, do you? Thought you was goin' to be an actor?"

"I can do both. I'm callin' my play the *Tarantula of Taos, or Deadly Dick's Dyin' Defeat.* You see, the hero rescues the heroine, at the end of the first act, from ten badmen and some scalpin' redskins —"

"Only ten badmen?"

"Well, you see —" apologetically, "the hero only carried five loads in each six-shooter —"

"How'd he dispose of the Injuns?"

"He wields his trusty Bowie knife to spill their gore," Alonzo explained dramatically.

Yocum looked severely at the boy. "Nice thing to be writin'. Don't you know the West has been settled —"

"But this is history —"

"What's your folks think of all this gore spillin' — at your age?"

"Ma don't know about what I'm writin'. She has a leanin' to pote-ry and thinks play-actin' is wicked. Pa — well, you know he never does open his mouth around the house. Ma's tongue is real sharp on occasion. Like last night, I guess he didn't dast stay to home. I'll betcha they had a bang-up game here —"

"Their Monday night poker spreads is usual all of that — especially when Gus Oldfield is in town."

Alonzo snickered. "I reckon pa was a might teed up last night. Ma was already in bed, when I heard pa sneak into the house. He stumbled against a table and woke ma up. I heard her call, 'Brad-lee!' like she always sounds when pa ain't in good standin', you know, sort of sharp and cuttin' like —"

"Yes," dryly, "I've heard yore ma speak to Brad at the hotel. What happened?"

"Paw stood stock-still without makin' a sound. I guess maw figured she'd heard the cat, or somethin'. Anyway, she went back to sleep. Then, I heard pa creepin' into my room. He fussed around a minute, pro'bly wonderin' if he dast crawl in with me. Reckon he changed his mind, 'cause I heard the front door open and close real quiet, after he left my room. I reckon he'd sleep in our hotel all the time if maw would let him."

"Y'ought to be ashamed," Yocum stated severely, "talkin' about your paw's and maw's intimacies that-away."

"You ought to be ashamed for listenin', then," Alonzo retorted defiantly. "But I ain't surprised. Ma always said Homer Yocum couldn't be beat for havin' his nose in other folks' doin's."

"As deputy-sheriff of this commonwealth," Yocum stated with some show of dignity, "it's necessary that I know what's takin' place. Give me another dime's worth of peanuts."

The order was complied with, and Yocum headed for the street to lounge against a post in the shade of the wooden awning, his neck still a trifle red back of the ears. Alonzo rehearsed a few lines of his play, then reluctantly procured a broom and commenced to sweep the floor. Struck by a sudden thought, he put down the broom. Last time there'd been a poker game he'd found four-bits under the table. Maybe this time. . . .

He walked unhurriedly toward the back room. The door stood slightly ajar. Alonzo pushed it open, then stopped abruptly.

"Oh, good mornin,' Mister Thorpe. I didn't know you —"

The words ended in a sudden yell of stark terror.

Alonzo backed hastily away, then turned and ran toward the front door as fast as his legs could carry him. "Homer! Homer Yocum!" he bawled frantically.

The deputy-sheriff was already entering the front door, having heard the boy's first wild yell.

"What's the matter with you, younker? You

practisin' your stage play?"

Alonzo gripped Yocum's sleeve, his teeth chattering, his face a sallow yellow. "H-H-Homer — he's — he's dead. His eyes was — was wide — wide open — and I thought —"

"Stop it!" Yocum's voice was sharp. "You hurrahin' me, 'Lonzo?"

Alonzo gulped, as Homer shook him. "Honest I ain't, Homer — he's deader'n dead —"

"Who's dead?"

"Mister — Mister Thorpe — in that room." Alonzo levelled a shaking finger at the back of the store.

Yocum looked narrowly at the boy a minute, then swung past and headed for the back room. Alonzo waited near the front door, his mouth open, lower lip trembling. He saw the deputy step into the room, then slowly back out. Yocum's face was a study in emotion when he again faced the boy.

"You're right, 'Lonzo," he said huskily. "Look here, Rance Duncan's over to the hotel. Go get him, *pronto*. Then, slope down to Doc Parker's. Bring him on the run. It's too late for Doc to do anythin', but —"

Alonzo was already on his way toward the Morada House, glad of an opportunity to spread the news of his discovery. Yocum closed the store door and waited inside. Two or three men, drawn by Alonzo's excited movements, approached the doorway. Yocum

58

shook his head at them through the glass, and refused to open up.

Rance Duncan came pounding across the street. Yocum held the door open. Rance entered. The door was shut and locked again.

"Young 'Lonzo says —" Rance commenced.

"He told the truth," Yocum nodded. "I figured I'd better send for you, seein' you was Vink's right bower."

"Where is he?" Duncan asked.

Yocum jerked one thumb over his shoulder. "Back room," he said.

Duncan entered the room with Yocum at his heels. No doubt about it: Vink Thorpe was dead. The big man was seated at the poker table, head sunk on his chest. His eyes were wide, staring. A dark brown splotch on his left breast told the story. It required but a single glance to tell Rance Duncan that his employer had passed on.

His voice shook a trifle, "An' only yesterday he told me I always had a habit of bein' on the job. This is once I failed him."

"Don't take it too hard, Rance. It ain't your fault —"

"Who done it?" Rance cut in, his voice hard.

Yocum shrugged his shoulders. "You know as much as I do, Rance. We'll give a look around. Don't disturb things no more'n possible."

Duncan's eyes lingered on the still form in the chair. Thorpe's right arm dangled at his side. His left, with fingers still crimped about five playing cards, lay on the table before him, the pasteboards face up.

Automatically, Duncan read the five cards: eight of clubs, eight of spades, ace of clubs, ace of spades and ace of hearts.

"Aces and eights — three of a kind and a pair," Duncan commented. Something clicked in his memory. Aces and eights. What was it? The thought eluded him. He was too stunned for lucid ratiocination.

"It sure wasn't a winnin' hand for Vink," Yocum said soberly.

Duncan shook his head, resumed his inspection of the table. A nearly empty bottle of whisky stood within reach at Thorpe's right. Poker chips were scattered across the surface. At the opposite side of the table, across from the dead man, lay a loosely-bunched deck of cards. Nearby was an empty whisky-glass, standing near the edge of the circular oak. At this place, a chair was pushed back about a foot from the table. The other chairs in the room were placed back against the walls. A burned-out oil lamp stood on the safe. On the floor around the table there was nothing but a few cigar butts and tobacco ashes.

Duncan glanced up and through the open window in the wall opposite the dead man. Beyond a narrow passageway, his eyes met the blank wall of the Thorpe store's neighbor on the east, Toralbert's Hardware and Gun Store — mostly guns. No, no window there through which a gun might have been fired.

Yocum followed Duncan's glance. "Figure the skunk might have stood in that passageway, between these two buildings, and fired a shot through this window?"

Duncan slowly shook his head. "It might be, but somehow I got a hunch this was an inside job — done by somebody Vink was acquainted with."

"How you figurin', Rance?"

Duncan explained. "From the sign I read around this table. To me, that part's right clear. Looks like somebody come in here, after the poker game broke up last night. You'll note most of the chairs are stood back, and the whisky-glasses put on that washstand over there. This killer come in, and pulled a chair up to the table, across from Vink. There's an empty glass at his place, the bottle is near Vink. Looks like Vink poured the murderin' skunk a drink."

"I'm followin' you." Yocum meditatively chewed a peanut. "Then, what happened?"

"The murderer," Rance continued, "dealt Vink a hand of cards. I suppose he dealt himself a hand, too, but we can't tell that. Aside from Vink's hand, the pasteboards are bunched. Anyway, while Vink was looking at his cards, the skunk shot him."

"I wonder —" Yocum started, then broke off.

"What?"

"I was just wonderin' if there could have

been any arguments over that poker game last night. A heavy loser might have returned here — after the others were gone — and got Vink to play one more hand, or somethin' of the kind. We'll say that aces and eights proved to be the winnin' hand. The feller got mad, plugged Vink, and then ducked out through that window —"

"Was the store doors locked this mornin'?"

Yocum nodded. "I had to wait for young 'Lonzo to let me in. Say, who's got keys to those double doors?"

"Vink had one, old Lucas had another, and 'Lonzo had one he used to open up with, them days he run the store. Unless the doors was open when the murderer arrived, Vink might have let him in. I imagine Vink would lock those doors after the game broke up."

"That reminds me of somethin'," Yocum said slowly. "Last night, after 'Lonzo turned in, he heard his father fussin' around his room." Yocum supplied the details of the morning's conversation with Alonzo.

Rance frowned. "Lord, Homer! I'd hate to think that Brad —"

Yocum caught the unfinished thought. "So'd I," he nodded. "Vink and Brad has been friends for — anyway, everybody thought they were friends —" As though reluctant to finish the words, he changed the subject, let his gaze stray around the room. "I note Vink's gun and belt hangin' over there," he motioned to a hook on one wall, "provin' that Vink wasn't expectin' trouble when this murderer come in."

Duncan nodded grimly. "God, Homer, this is a hell of a thing."

"You're right. Vink was a white man."

Duncan cast a glance at the safe. The door stood half open. He moved across the floor, looked on shelves and in drawers. There was no sign of money to be seen.

"Safe cleaned out?" Yocum asked.

"Looks thataway. 'Course, old Lucas would have took the past week's store receipts up to Capitol City to be banked. Still, unless Vink was plumb cleaned out in that poker game, there should be some money around. . . . Wait until I go look in the till."

Duncan moved out to the store. In the till behind the counter, he found about ten dollars in change. That was all. As he turned to rejoin Yocum in the back room, there came a heavy pounding on the door.

Looking through the upper glass-half of the doors, Rance saw Doctor Parker standing there, with Alonzo Wheeler close by. Duncan went to the door, opened it. He saw that a small group of citizens had gathered before the store. While Alonzo was busy telling of his discovery, Duncan let the doctor into the store and again locked the door.

"This is tough business, Duncan," Parker said.

"It sure is, Doc. Come on back. We ain't touched a thing."

The doctor followed Rance. He was a big, raw-boned man in his late forties, sandy-complexioned, with large bony hands covered with hair and freckles. He was inclined to be pompous. His manner was officious, brusque. It could be seen he placed a good deal of importance on his own opinions. He had set up in business in Morada about three years before, claiming to have come from the East, though he had never mentioned the exact section of the East from which he had arrived. Beyond learning that he was a capable physician and surgeon, Morada had never gained any definite information concerning Doctor Guy Parker.

He listened abstractedly to Yocum's story and Rance's deductions. "You may be right, Duncan," he said tersely. "It may be an inside job." Then, gazing down on the dead man a few minutes he added, "Well, there's nothing I can do for Thorpe — except in my capacity as coroner. I'll call an inquest, shortly. Duncan, what time did this poker game break up?"

"I ain't certain," Duncan replied. "I got into town around nine o'clock. Sort of figured I might ride back with Vink, if he headed for home. I dropped in here at eleven. Vink said then they didn't intend to play much longer, as he wanted to turn in and get an early start for Capitol City —"

"See anything at the time to arouse your suspicions," Parker asked narrowly. "Did everything look all right?"

Rance nodded. "I didn't pay any particular attention. Why should I? All the players were Vink's friends — anyway, I thought they were. I didn't stay but a minute. Vink had forgot his horse at the Morada hitchrack. Asked me to take it to the livery. Said he might write one or two letters here, then turn in on Lucas' cot for the night. I left, then, took Vink's horse and mine to the livery stable. After that I went to the hotel, got a room, and went to sleep."

"What brought you into town last night?" Parker asked crisply.

Duncan shook his head hopelessly. "Just plain hunch, I reckon. I got an idea that Vink might need me. When I saw him here, playin' cards, calm like, I figured I was wrong."

"Have anything to base your hunch on?" Parker asked.

"Mebbyso. You see, I met Vink on Lookout Ridge yesterday, a few minutes after he'd taken a shot at a suspected rustler. Vink didn't mention any names, exactly, but he did think he recognized the paint horse the feller was ridin —"

"By the way," Yocum broke in, "Hugh Norris was saying yesterday that somebody had stole his pinto pony. It happens, too, that

Monte Quillan is riding a pinto. I'm tellin' that for what it's worth."

Duncan nodded and went on, "In the mail I gave Vink, up on Lookout Ridge, was a letter that sure jarred him plenty —"

"Know what was in the letter?" Parker asked quickly.

Rance shook his head. "I just know that Vink looked scared, if a man ever did."

"Speakin' of letters," Yocum said. "I saw Vink talkin' to Brad Wheeler yesterday afternoon, at the corner of Main and Hereford. I saw Vink pass what looked like a letter to Brad. Brad read it and handed it back. They was sure arguin' serious about somethin'."

"Brad act mad?" Rance asked.

"Well, I wouldn't go to say he was mad. It was Vink that acted upset. Brad seemed to be talkin' more placatin' like — like he was tryin' to quiet Vink down. Brad come back to the hotel a little later, and in a little while Matt Everett come lookin' for Brad. Matt was right agitated about somethin'. Just on a hunch I asked Matt if he'd been talkin' to Vink, and he said yes. Which same occurrences leads me to believe that Matt, Brad and Vink was mixed together in that letter."

Duncan said slowly, "I'd sure hate to think Matt or Brad had anythin' to do with Vink's death. Those three have been friends for years."

"Here's another way to look at it," Yocum

said. "Yesterday I heard Bert Gillett talk threatenin' to Vink . . ." He explained the episode in detail, concluding, "John Rhys, sittin' next to me, heard it, too."

Rance's face went hard. "I never thought of Gillett as a killer, but he'll bear lookin' into. He drinks too much for his own good. Otherwise, he's a good worker. Have you seen him around town this mornin'?"

Yocum shook his head. "It was pretty early for anybody to be on the street. Gillett was drunk yesterday afternoon. Prob'bly sleepin' it off this mornin'."

"Or slopin' off," Duncan amended, "if he did it."

Doctor Parker said, "Well, there isn't much I can do until I've made a thorough examination. Then, I'll impanel a coroner's jury and hold an inquest as soon as possible —"

"I'm goin' lookin' for Gillett —" Rance commenced.

"Just a minute, Duncan," Parker said. "Remember you haven't any actual proof against Gillett. If you can find him, we'll take his testimony at the inquest. But it's up to my jury to decide whether or not he's guilty. I suggest that you don't take the law into your own hands —"

"I'll suit myself about that," Rance said grimly.

"That's up to you. But don't go off half-cocked."

Rance's voice was steady, "I ain't, Doc. Only, I'm askin' that you hold this inquest plumb *pronto*. If we've got to cut red-tape let's get our knives sharpened as soon as possible."

"I know my own business," Parker said testily. "Everything must be done according to the law. By the way, have you sent anyone to notify Thorpe's daughter yet?"

Rance shook his head. A lump came into his throat, "I figure Eddie will hear about it, soon enough, as it is. I don't want to be the one to break such news. I'd like to get this inquest over first, and get Vink laid out decently before —"

"You're right, of course," Parker nodded. "I'll do this: I'll impanel my jury at once and bring the men around to view the remains. When that's done, I'll make a thorough examination. When I'm through, the undertaker can come and take Vink away. That suit you?"

"It'll help," Duncan conceded. "If you can only get this inquest to rollin' —"

"Meanwhile," Parker interrupted, "you and Homer circulate around town. See if you can find news of Gillett, or of anyone else who might have had a hand in this business."

Parker drew down the open window, locked the catch. The three men prepared to leave. The key was still in the front door. Duncan and Yocum preceded the doctor outside, then Parker locked the door behind him and started off down Main Street.

CHAPTER V

By this time quite a crowd had gathered before the Thorpe store. Duncan and Yocum looked quickly over the crowd. In the fore ranks stood Brad Wheeler, Ward Stinson, Matt Everett and Gus Oldfield.

Brad Wheeler asked brokenly, "My God! Rance, is it true?"

Rance nodded. "Too damnable true, Brad." He looked into Gus Oldfield's bloodshot eyes. Gus said, "Too damn bad," and looked away.

Rance shifted his gaze to Ward Stinson. The gray-haired man muttered, "Tough. We'll miss Vink. I wish —" He paused.

"You wish what?" Rance added quickly.

Stinson shook his head, shifted his cud to tobacco. "I wish we'd knowed it was goin' to happen. We might have done somethin'."

Matt Everett stuttered as usual when upset. "Is it r-r-right, Rance, that Vink was sittin' there playin' cards when it happened?" Everett had a queer habit of glancing from the corners of his eyes at anyone to whom he was talking.

"Who told you that?" Rance countered.

"A-A-Alonzo, here," Everett jerked one

thumb in the boy's direction.

"It's so, it's so," Alonzo nodded vigorously. "I didn't stop to see what the cards were, though."

"B-B-But the game had broke up," Everett protested.

"Somebody," Rance said grimly, "went back and started another game, looks like. You fellers happen to remember what cards Vink held on his last hand?"

"I do," Ward Stinson said. "Vink took a nice little pot away from me with two pair — kings and nines."

"That proves my statement, I reckon," Duncan said. "When he was killed, Vink held aces and eights."

"A-A-Aces and e-e-eights!" Everett sputtered. "Did you say aces and eights, R-R-Rance?"

Rance nodded. "Ace of spades, clubs and hearts, eight of spades and clubs — say, what's the matter with you, Matt?"

Everett's face was ashen. He couldn't apparently find his tongue. Finally, "Why — why — it's just that —"

"Don't you get excited now, Matt," Brad Wheeler cut in, a trifle sharply, Rance thought. "You see, Rance, Matt is sort of upset —"

"I'm listenin' to Matt," Rance snapped. "What about aces and eights, Matt?"

Everett glanced sidewise at Wheeler, his

70

eyes dropped. "It's just made me think somethin' —" he commenced.

"Don't you, Matt!" Wheeler interrupted authoritatively. Again, that warning tone.

"You keep out of this, Brad," Rance said sternly. "If Matt has any information that might help us find the murderin' skunk, I want it. And don't forget you'll all be questioned when Doc Parker calls his coroner's inquest. If you know anythin', you better throw a straight loop. Now, Matt, what was you sayin'?"

But Wheeler's words had had their effect. Everett had regained his composure, "Why, it wasn't nothin' at all," he said slowly. "I just happened to think I'd heard aces and eights called 'the dead man's hand.' "

Rance eyed him sharply, but Everett wasn't meeting the glance. Rance swore under his breath, then, "All right, Matt. But remember, if you were goin' to say somethin' else, and then withhold information, you'll be obstructin' justice. That goes for you, too, Brad."

Wheeler didn't answer. A few moments later he and Everett left the crowd and walked rapidly in the direction of the Morada House, where they disappeared around the corner of Hereford Street. Duncan noticed they were talking seriously, but by this time other things had intruded on his mind. He remembered, now, that aces and eights were

71

often termed "the dead man's hand" in the Western country.

But what in hell did that have to do with the matter? Rance shook his head. And why had Matt Everett been so upset? The dealing of the hand had probably been due to pure chance. Yet, in the face of Everett's attitude, Rance couldn't quite convince himself that this was so.

Several men in the crowd had been talking to Yocum, asking questions relative to the murder. Duncan looked the men over a few minutes, then asked, "Anybody here seen Bert Gillett this mornin'?"

No one answered. Finally, a man at the back of the crowd said, "I seen Gillett and Hugh Norris in the Cowmen's Rest Saloon last night."

"What time was that?"

"Closin' time — around twelve-thirty. I was there when Tim Barnes shut up."

"Gillett and Norris leave when you did?"

The man nodded. "They was both right behind me. Last I saw of 'em they was standin' at the hitch-rack talkin', after Tim locked his door and went to his own home. I headed for bed, then. Don't know where Gillett and Norris went."

Rance asked further questions. Norris hadn't been seen in town that morning, either. The probabilities were he had gone to his ranch the night before. The question was, had

Gillett accompanied him? There wasn't any particular reason why he should, unless Norris had offered him a bed for the night.

Yocum said, "I reckon, Rance, I'll get my pony and slope out to the Star-Cross." He crammed a handful of peanuts into his mouth and started through the crowd.

Rance followed him. On the rim of the crowd he caught up. Rance said, "Mebbe you should have some help, Homer. If Gillett was there and inclined to be ugly —"

"I don't reckon on that," Yocum replied quietly. "If Gillett done this killin', I got a hunch he'd beat it out of the country *pronto*. In that case, mebbe we can get a line from Norris where he went, or what direction he was headin' when last seen. If Gillett *is* at the Star-Cross, he'll come quiet rather than raise a suspicion. Or he may be glad to come and offer an alibi. That's guesswork, of course. You move around town and see what you can pick up. It's only a twelve-mile ride to the Star-Cross. I should be back shortly after noon — say, one o'clock."

Yocum rocked off down the street on his angular legs, heading in the direction of the livery stable. Duncan rejoined the crowd. He said to Gus Oldfield and Ward Stinson:

"Anythin' happen last night, durin' the game, that would lead us to a clue?"

Gus and Ward exchanged glances. Stinson said, "Nothin' I know of."

Gus Oldfield added, "Not a thing, Rance. Why?"

Rance asked, "Who was the heavy winner and heavy loser last night?"

Ward Stinson answered that. "I won a mite," he admitted, "though Vink was a big winner. He cleaned up right and left. I reckon Matt Everett broke about even. He plays 'em close. Brad lost more than he likes to drop. Gus, guess you was hardest hit, wasn't you?"

Reluctantly, Oldfield confessed he had lost more than usual. He forced a weak smile, "Vink always did have the Indian sign on my poker."

"What time did the game break up?" Duncan asked next.

"About twelve," from Oldfield.

"Might have been later," Stinson said. "Not much, though."

"Where'd you go then?"

Stinson said, carefully choosing his words, "Vink came to the door and locked up. Matt Everett said 'good-night' and headed down Main to his boarding-house. Me'n Brad and Gus went back to the hotel and had a drink. Then we went to our rooms and turned in."

"Brad stayed at the hotel, too, eh?" Stinson nodded. Rance frowned but said nothing of Alonzo's story, then asked, "Hear any shots last night?"

Oldfield shook his head.

Stinson said, "Nary a sound. I reckon we all went to sleep the minute we laid our heads down. We'd been drinkin' all evenin', of course. Vink got bottles from the safe, twice. For that matter, a shot wouldn't arouse this town, once it was asleep —"

"Did Vink shut the safe door again, each time?" Rance cut in.

Stinson shook his head. "I remember it was standin' open when we left."

"How come you noticed that?"

Stinson answered frankly, "I was thinkin' what an easy job it would be for a stick-up. Mentioned that fact to Vink. He said he wasn't worryin' about any bandits in Morada. Just the same, I'll bet robbery was the motive behind the killin'."

Duncan considered that for a moment. "Well, the safe is cleaned out, if that's what you mean. How much did Vink win last night?"

"I don't know exact," Stinson said promptly. "I remember toward the end of the game, Vink remarked he was around fifteen hundred ahead. It was a fast game, Rance. But I wasn't thinking about Vink's poker winnin's. Last week's store receipts —"

"The store receipts," Rance cut in, "likely went to Capitol City with old Lucas, just as they've done every week for the past two years, anyway. Lucas always catches the Monday night stage, takes his day off,

Tuesday, in Capitol City, and returns to Morada on the noon stage Wednesday —"

"That money didn't go this week," Stinson said bluntly.

"Huh?" Duncan looked surprised. "What makes you say that?"

"I got it from Joe Myers —"

"What's Myers know about it?"

"You know Joe Myers, that runs the New York Emporium —" Stinson paused, looked through the crowd, then called to a short, dark man standing a few yards away. "Joe, come here and tell Rance what you told me about that money."

Myers pushed his way over to Rance. "There isn't much to tell," he said. "I always go down to Breenville to visit my daughter and her husband on Sunday, and come back Monday night on the stage. Lucas is always waiting to get on when I 'light. Well, last night he was there like always. I spoke to him and said, 'Taking the money up to the Capitol City Bank as usual, eh, Clem?' And he said 'no' just like this, 'No, no money with me this time. Mister Thorpe ain't sending it this week.' And then he got into the stage."

"Thanks," Rance nodded, absent-mindedly.

This was a new phase of the matter. Why hadn't Vink abided by his weekly custom of sending the money for deposit? It couldn't have been he was holding the money against

76

contemplated poker losses. Vink's cheque on the Capitol City Bank was good any place in the country. Another thought struck him: it was the end of the month, accounts had probably been settled. There must have been around fifteen hundred dollars taken in the past week. Maybe more.

On the other hand, perhaps Lucas had lied to Myers. Vink may have sent the money as usual. There was a chance that Lucas was already out of the state, making a clean getaway with the money. That, though, Rance found hard to believe. Lucas had worked in the store going on two years. There'd been plenty opportunity before this, if he'd been a thief.

"When's the inquest goin' to be held, Rance?" Oldfield broke in on Duncan's thoughts.

"Doc Parker ain't announced that yet. Soon, I reckon."

Rance Duncan was wondering if it might not be a good idea to hold over the inquest until Lucas could be reached. And in the same moment rejected the idea. He wanted all that business over and done with before Edith Thorpe knew her father was dead, if possible.

"There ain't no use of you hombres hangin' around here any longer," Rance said to the crowd. "Meanwhile, if any of you know anythin' that should be told, give your information to Doc Parker or me."

At that moment Monte Quillan came pushing through the crowd. "Anythin' new been learned, Rance?" he asked.

Rance shook his head, shortly, "I'm askin' questions, not answerin' 'em, Monte. I hear you're ridin' a pinto horse now."

"What about it?" Quillan looked belligerent.

Rance shrugged his shoulders. "It ain't worryin' me, Monte. Mebbe it should be worryin' you."

Quillan's face flushed angrily. "I know what you're hintin' at, Duncan, but you ain't pinnin' nothin' on me. Just because Vink took a shot at a rustler yesterday that rode off on a paint horse is no sign that —"

"How do you know," Duncan asked quietly, "that Vink recognized that paint animal — or thought he did?"

Quillan hesitated. "Well, now, I don't know why I put it that way," he said lamely. "Come to think of it, Vink didn't specify any sort of animal when he told about it in the Morada Bar yesterday. But there was some sort of talk about paint horses. I remember Norris said his had been rustled. I guess I just sort of jumped to conclusions that the cowthief rode a pinto —"

"Jumpin' to conclusions, Monte," Rance observed, "is sometimes bad business —"

"Now, look here, Duncan, you don't need to go suspicionin' me on anythin' — see? I was at the VIT, visitin' Eddie, when Vink pulled out for town. Didn't leave until nigh an hour later. You can ask Eddie —"

"How come you stayed in town last night?"

"Figured to ride back to VIT with Vink this mornin'. I had a private matter to talk over with him —"

"Didn't you know Vink was goin' to Capitol City this mornin'?"

"Well, I heard some talk about it in the Morada Bar, but I thought I might see him before he left, or maybe make the trip with him, just for company —"

"You in the habit of leavin' your outfit that long?"

"That's my concern, but my crew is capable. I wanted to have a talk with Vink. As far as that pinto is — well, I wanted to give that pinto as a present to — well, somebody." The words stumbled uncertainly over his lips.

With Edith Thorpe in mind, Rance didn't press the question. No use bringing the girl into this, if she could be kept out. Doubtless, one of the VIT hands had seen Quillan leave the Thorpe ranch and would be able to remember the time.

Rance said, "Where'd you stay last night? I was in the Morada Bar. I don't remember seein' you."

"Slept in Matt Everett's feed barn, if you got to know," Quillan said sullenly. "I'm savin' my money, and don't feel like spendin' it on hotels. Matt knowed I went there. I asked him early in the evenin', before he went to the store to play poker. I meant to get up early this mornin' and see Vink, but I overslept." A sneer entered his tones, "Anythin' else you'd like to know? Maybe you're curious as to why I'm savin' money, too."

"Don't be a fool, Monte," Rance said quietly.

Quillan edged back through the crowd which had commenced to break up. Duncan watched him cross the street and head east on Main Street. In a few minutes Duncan, too, left the front of the store and headed in the same direction. His first stop brought him into the Cowmen's Rest Saloon, where Tim Barnes, the jovial, red-faced proprietor, told him that Hugh Norris and Bert Gillett had been in his place until closing time the previous evening.

Leaving the Cowmen's Rest, Duncan sauntered around the streets of Morada for the next hour or so, asking questions here and there. At the end of this time he had to admit his search for clues had proved fruitless. Two men he encountered thought they had heard a shot, but couldn't be sure. Nor could they state with any exactitude the time of the shot. They'd been in bed at the time.

CHAPTER VI

It was about noon when Duncan entered the Morada House Bar and engaged Louie, the bartender, in conversation. There was no one in the bar at the moment except the two of them. For some time the foreman of the VIT questioned Louie closely regarding Vink Thorpe's visit to the bar-room the previous day. Next, Duncan probed for information regarding talk after Thorpe had taken his departure.

Finally, having exhausted Louie's possibilities, Duncan ordered a beer and stood at one end of the bar, his mind revolving with speculation. He had nearly finished his drink when Brad Wheeler and Matt Everett entered from the office entrance of the hotel. Their faces looked troubled. Suddenly, Brad Wheeler looked up and noticed Duncan.

"Hello, Rance. I didn't see you there. What's new — anythin'?"

"I reckon not, Brad," Duncan said steadily, "not if you won't come across."

"What do you mean?" Wheeler bridled. "You suspicionin' me?"

"I'm suspicionin' everybody connected with Vink Thorpe," Duncan told him flatly. "Yesterday, Brad, you had some sort of argument

81

with Vink about a letter —"

"Hell, no! We wasn't arguin'. We did talk some —"

"What was in that letter?"

"I don't know as it's any of your business."

"I'm figurin' I got a right to ask. Certainly, Doc Parker, as coroner, will want to know."

Wheeler rubbed his nose thoughtfully. "Now, look here, Rance," he said in placating tones, "that letter was a private matter between Vink and me."

"And Matt Everett, too, I reckon."

Everett looked away. Wheeler said, "Matt had nothin' to do with it, nor did the letter have anythin' to do with Vink's getting killed."

"I ain't so sure of that, Brad," Rance said coldly. "Mebbe you'll be made to talk at the inquest."

Wheeler snapped, "That's another matter, but no inquest will get anythin' more out of me. Good God, Rance! You know I was Vink's friend for years. You might just as well suspect Oldfield or any of the rest of the men who played — for that matter, I just happened to think that Oldfield didn't return here with us, right away, last night —"

"What's that about me?" Gus Oldfield entered from the office of the hotel.

"Mebbe you can tell me yourself, Gus," Duncan said. "As I understood it before, Matt Everett returned to his boardin' house after the game broke up. The rest of you were supposed to have returned here. Now it comes out, Gus, that you didn't return with them."

Oldfield looked belligerently at Wheeler, then back at Duncan. "What if I didn't? I'd been drinkin' sort of heavy. I admit I stood on the corner of Main and Hereford for a time, getting some fresh air."

"How long did you stand there?" Rance snapped.

"Possibly five minutes."

"Anybody see you that you know?"

Oldfield considered. "No, I guess not. The town was pretty well closed up by that time. . . . But, hell, Rance, Brad will tell you that I come in while him and Stinson was finishin' a drink."

"That's true enough," Wheeler said haltingly, "but —"

"Brad," Oldfield flamed, "you tryin' to insinuate I had anythin' to do with this murder?"

"Well, I don't know's I'd go that far. I don't want to get anybody in wrong, but so long as Rance is suspicionin' me, I reckon he ought to have all the facts."

"What are *all* the facts?" Duncan demanded.

Oldfield swore at Wheeler. Wheeler got red, but held his temper. "It's this way, Rance," he said. "Gus lost pretty heavy last night. He had to give Vink three cheques to cover losses at three different times. They sort of had an argument about it — leastwise, Gus wanted to argue. He said he couldn't afford to lose that money. He wanted Vink to return the cheques and take an I. O. U. to be honored later. Well, you know how Vink was. He always did like to hurrah a feller. It's my personal opinion he meant to give Gus them cheques to-day. Gus was pretty well lit and inclined to be quarrelsome. Vink was gettin' a big laugh, ribbin' him."

"That right, Oldfield?" Rance asked.

After some evasion, Oldfield admitted it was. "But, hell, Rance, do you think I'm the kind of a skunk that would go back and shoot Vink Thorpe, just to get my cheques?"

"Frankly, Gus," Rance said coldly, "I never thought you was. Have you took any steps to stop payment on those cheques —"

"Why should I?" Oldfield was plainly puzzled.

"There's two answers to that. One is, if you had 'em, you wouldn't have to stop payment. Howsomever, if you ain't got 'em, you might do somethin' about it. You know, of course, that the safe was cleaned out."

"There was some talk of that kind around town," Oldfield nodded. "But I never thought to stop payment —"

"Better think it over, then."

"By Cripes! I will. I'll get a letter off at once." He turned and headed for the office doorway.

"I wonder," Matt Everett looked sidewise at Duncan, "if Oldfield is bluffin'. It would be easy enough to write his bank —"

"Don't be too ready to cast aspersions, Matt," Rance said coldly. "Even if some crook got those cheques he might be afraid to try and cash 'em. 'Stead of thinkin' so much about Gus, you and Brad better get your heads together and tell what you know about that letter."

"Don't know anythin' about any letter," Everett was stubborn.

"I'll tell you somethin' else, Rance," Wheeler said. "Vink had the letter in question, but he didn't have it when Doc Parker went through his pockets."

"Didn't know Parker did," Duncan frowned. "Why, I was there —"

"Not when he come back with his jury, you wasn't," Wheeler pointed out. "I met Parker and the jury after they'd looked at the body, and left the store. I asked Parker if he found any letters, or anythin' of the kind, but he said he didn't —"

Duncan swore under his breath. "Parker talks too much sometimes."

"I'm agreein' with you there," Wheeler said — a bit triumphantly, Duncan thought. "He ain't been in this country long enough to get acquainted with our ways. This bein' his first murder inquest, he's kind of uncertain of his ground."

"That's the trouble with all this red-tape," Duncan growled. "Takes too long to cut and is plumb entanglin' when a feller wants to get on the move."

Ward Stinson appeared at the saloon entrance, came in, nodded to the others, and ordered a drink. When he put down his glass, Rance said, "Ward, I understand you made some sort of angry remarks in here yesterday, when you heard that Vink was intendin' to consult some lawyer."

"What sort of remarks?" Stinson asked cautiously.

"Well, it seems you were riled over this boundary business. I understand you made a statement to the effect that God help any man that got in your way, because you aimed to fight for your rights. And that what Vink Thorpe needed was a forty-five slug to cure his mulishness."

"Who told you that?" Stinson demanded angrily. He glanced toward Louie, the barkeep, who immediately busied himself polishing glasses.

"Did you say that, or didn't you?" Rance persisted.

"Can't say I remember, for sure," Stinson evaded. "Look here, Rance, you tryin' to prove it was me killed Vink Thorpe?"

"I'm tryin' to find out who did. Did you have any words with Vink last night?"

"Certainly not," Stinson growled. "We

might've crabbed at each other a mite the way we do sometimes, but —"

"How about that, Brad?" Rance asked.

Wheeler looked uncomfortable. He turned to Stinson, "Look here, Ward, you got to admit you was plumb pettish last night when Vink refused to talk about that boundary line business. You kept pesterin' him after every hand, didn't you, now —"

"Maybe I did," Stinson conceded reluctantly, "but by the Jumpin' Joseph, Brad, that boundary line argyment w'n't no killin' affair. I ain't a murderer."

"I'm hopin' not," Rance said, not entirely convinced.

"I don't like the way you say that, Rance," Stinson protested hotly. "I ain't under suspicion, am I?"

"I reckon you are," from Rance, coldly. "Everybody is that —"

Stinson burst into an explosive series of oaths, ending with, "Well, by the seven bald steers of Moses and Pharaoh if that ain't the gonswaggled damndest thing I ever hear! Hell's bells! Why suspect me? Any blind pink-eyed bat would know where to look, previdin' he wa'n't still wet behind the ears. What makes cow country troubles? Cowthieves! That's what! Vink come in yesterday, I understand, with some talk about takin' a potshot at a cowthief, an' recognisin' a hawss. Find out whose hawss that was, and you've cotched your man. Why, by the Jumpin' Joseph of Solomon's Temple, if you ain't the dumbest —"

"I ain't overlooked that rustler, Ward," Rance said wearily. "It was a paint horse Vink saw. Norris rode one. Quillan forks one, now."

"You suspectin' them two?" Wheeler asked curiously.

"I'm pointin' out facts," Rance evaded, "to show that nobody is free of suspicion, until we've found the killer. What do you expect me to do? The facts are plain for anybody to see: Brad, here, and Matt, had a talk about a letter that agitated Vink considerable. They refuse to state what it was —"

"Oh, Cripes!" Wheeler growled. "Have a drink on the house and forget that letter. . . . Louie, set 'em up."

"I don't know anythin' about that letter, Rance," Everett protested. "You're talkin' through your hat."

"Mebbeso," Rance said, and gave his order to the bartender. "But I'm still talkin' facts. Here's some more: Gus Oldfield loses more than he can afford in that poker game. He doesn't come back to the hotel with you other fellers. This mornin' Vink is found dead, and the cheques that Gus gave are gone — along with other money."

"Well, mebbe Gus done it," Stinson said slowly, "I can see —"

"Don't be too ready to blame Gus, Ward," Duncan cut in. "There's the facts relatin' to you. You had an argument with Vink about your boundary line. You was heard to make war-talk, after you'd heard Vink was goin' to see a lawyer —"

"Wouldn't that make *you* mad?" Stinson's temper rose again.

"Not mad enough to kill," Rance said quietly, "but I ain't you. You don't even know, do you, that Vink was goin' to see this lawyer about that boundary line —"

"Don't know what else he'd want to see him for —"

"Maybe that'll come out later. But anybody can see, Ward, how hot you get when the matter's mentioned. We all know you got a hot temper. For that matter, Oldfield is trigger-tempered, too. I'm not sayin' you done it, Ward, but can't you conceive how a hot-tempered hombre might blow up and do somethin' he'd be sorry for later?"

"Look here, Rance," Wheeler said suddenly, "what right you got askin' questions and hurlin' accusations, right and left? You ain't a law officer —"

Rance put down his glass untouched. "I reckon, Brad," he said steadily, "that Vink gave me that right when he made me his foreman. It's my job to look out for Vink's welfare as well as his property, and so help me Hanner, I aim to do it! I'm not at all sure this coroner's inquest is goin' to produce anythin' definite. I'm pickin' up information on my own, so I can start in where the inquest leaves off."

"You better mind your own business," Wheeler said testily, "and leave things to the coroner."

"Maybe you could bluff the coroner, Brad, but you can't bluff me. You're holdin' out information. You ain't come clean. Where did you go when you come back here last night?"

"Dropped in here for a night-cap, then went to bed," Wheeler said promptly.

"I hate to call you a liar, Brad."

"No man's goin' to call me a liar," Wheeler flamed. "By God, I'll —"

"I'll prove it," Rance said quietly. "Brad, after the others had gone to bed, you went home. You entered your house. You went into 'Lonzo's room. Later, sometime, you came back to this hotel. Now, are you a liar, or aren't you?"

Wheeler's face had gone white, then crimson. "Well, well — I — sort of forgot that," he said slowly. "That don't count."

"T'hell it don't," Rance flashed. "Brad, somebody Vink knew killed him. There's three keys to the store. Vink, old Lucas and 'Lonzo each have one. I'm not sayin' you did, Brad, but you could have got 'Lonzo's key, slipped into the store, shot Vink and returned the key to 'Lonzo's pocket — all before you returned here."

Everett and Stinson were looking at Wheeler with questioning eyes now. Stinson said, "So help me, Brad, I thought when you went into your room, last night, you were in for good. I didn't know you went out again."

"Anyone who stayed in this hotel last night could have gone out through the office entrance," Rance pointed out. "There's no stage through here after six o'clock. There's no clerk in the office after that time. Any late guests are taken care of by the barkeep, so long as the bar is open. We all know that. . . . How about it, Brad; are you a liar, or ain't you?"

"Reckon I am, Rance," Wheeler smiled in sickly fashion. "I did go down to the house last night, but I come straight back here. I didn't take Alonzo's key. I was aimin' to sleep here first, then I got to thinkin' my wife might worry, so I went home. After gettin' in the house, I was afeared I might wake her, so I come back here. How do you happen to know about it, anyhow?"

"Alonzo was awake when you come in," Duncan explained. "He told Yocum about it. Yocum told me. I'm tellin' you hombres these things in the hope you'll come clean for me. Any information I gather will be passed on to Doc Parker. I'm accusin' nobody, but I'm suspectin' everybody."

CHAPTER VII

The creaking of saddle leather outside broke in on the conversation. Going to the door, Rance saw Deputy Yocum dismounting. Behind him were two riders — Hugh Norris and Bert Gillett. Norris looked grave. Gillett appeared sullen, resentful.

"I'm in here, Homer," Rance called. "Come on in."

The three entered the bar-room. Norris was first to speak. "Look here, Rance, you and Homer are all wrong about Gillett. I was with him every minute until we left town last night — and after, too. I'm plumb sorry to hear about Vink, though."

"That's somethin' we're agreed on, then," Rance nodded. "The fact remains that Gillett made war-talk to Vink yesterday. Ain't that so, Gillett?"

Gillett shook his head, muttered something in the negative.

"I couldn't get much out of him, Rance," Yocum said disgustedly. "He was willin' enough to come in, though."

"Did he act surprised?" Rance asked.

"Yeah, sort of — I dunno, though. He wasn't none too cheerful."

"How about it, Gillett," Duncan asked, "you did have a talk with Vink yesterday, didn't you?"

Gillett raised his eyes to Duncan's face, then dropped them. "Yeah, I did," he admitted sullenly.

"What about?"

"I don't know as it's any of your business, Duncan, but I was askin' for my job back."

"What did Vink say?"

"Told me it was up to you," Gillett muttered. "But I —"

"What answer did you make, then?" Rance snapped.

Gillett's pale blue eyes shifted uneasily. He rubbed his hand thoughtfully on his bristly chin. "Hell, I don't just remember," he evaded. "Thorpe walked away, and —"

"Didn't you say," Rance persisted, " 'So help me, God, Thorpe, you'll be sorry for this some day'?"

"Duncan," Gillett flamed suddenly, "you can't hang this killin' on me. What right you got questionin' me? You ain't a law-officer, and I ain't under arrest —"

"You're li'ble to be right sudden under arrest, Gillett, if you don't tell what you know," Rance snapped. "Deputy Yocum and another man heard you make that statement."

"All right, mebbe I did," Gillett conceded reluctantly. "I'd been drinkin', and was plumb peeved. But I wouldn't kill

Thorpe, mad as I was —"

"Look here, Rance," Norris broke in. "What right you got ridin' one of my men —"

"Your men — ?"

"That's what I said. I hired Bert Gillett last night. You can't talk that way to —"

"I'll talk the way I want to, Norris," Rance said grimly, "in tryin' to learn who killed Vink Thorpe. Gillett may have hired on with you, but that don't excuse him from bein' questioned. Howcome you hired him?"

"Reckon that's my business," Norris grunted, "but if you got to know, I needed a hand. Nothing wrong with Gillett, is there? No reason for not hirin' him? He worked for you ever since calf round-up. If he hadn't been a good worker, I don't reckon you'd kept him that long. Or have you" — a sneer accompanied the words — "taken the morals an' obligations of the whole Crazy River country on your shoulders?"

"Take it easy, Norris," Rance said quietly.

"Nobody's goin' to run rough-shod over a Star-Cross man — not while he's on my pay-roll. What if Gillett did make that statement? Me, I'd done the same in his condition. But, listen to me, Duncan, you ain't got a thing on him. He was in my company every minute last night. He slept at the Star-Cross, after we left town. So he's clear — see? Clear as hell!"

"Are you, Norris?" Rance asked.

"What me? Clear? Hell, yes!" Norris laughed loudly. "What do you mean, Duncan?"

"We won't go into it now," Rance said steadily, "If you're clear, it's all right. If I learn you aren't, I'll be comin' with my gun smokin'. Get that straight, Norris — with my gun smokin'."

"That," Norris said, suddenly sober, "sounds like war-talk."

"It's meant to be," Rance said, "if the cards fall thataway."

"Have it your own way." Norris shrugged careless shoulders. "If you want Gillett arrested, say so. If not, I'll have him on hand, any time he's wanted."

Rance nodded. "That's all I'm askin', Norris. Your word clears him — for the present."

"What do you mean — for the present?"

"Exactly what I said. There's more than one man under suspicion in Morada, Norris. You're included —"

"Why me?" Norris laughed harshly.

"Mebbe you'll find out later."

At that moment Oldfield re-entered the bar-room. Stinson asked, "Write your letter, Gus?"

Oldfield patted a pocket of his coat. "Got it right here. I'll send it on the night stage."

Running feet sounded on the steps outside. Monte Quillan came dashing in, his face a study in perturbation. He looked wildly about the bar-room, then caught sight of Duncan.

"Rance!" he exclaimed wildly, "Rance!"

"What's up, Monte?" sharply.

"Eddie's ridin' into town. Somebody's got to tell her."

Duncan eyed Quillan steadily for a few moments. Quillan's eyes dropped and a slow flush crept up his cheeks. "Well," he mumbled, "I don't want that job."

"Seems to me that *you* —" Duncan commenced, then broke off. Brushing past Quillan, he stepped out of the bar and descended the steps to Hereford Street. He was just in time to see Edith Thorpe walking her pony along Main, her gaze fastened on the saloon entrance of the Morada House. Catching sight of Rance, she raised one arm in greeting.

Duncan gulped, flung up his right hand in answer. Well, it was up to him now. Edith Thorpe had turned her pony to approach Duncan. Even as the space closed between them, Rance was thinking — and not for the first time — that Eddie Thorpe was a deucedly attractive girl. There was a boyish fresh something about Eddie Thorpe, with her healthy tanned skin and blue, blue eyes. Her slim figure was encased in a comfortable divided riding skirt, mannish flannel shirt and high-heeled riding boots. A green neckerchief encircled her slim throat, and a stiff-brimmed buckskin-hued sombrero covered her thick, wavy reddish-brown hair.

The horse had stopped. Rance stood looking up at the girl, groping for words. Edith broke the silence:

"What in time have I done now, Rance?"

"Huh? What you mean, Eddie?"

"Well, folks act sort of funny. Usually everybody's right friendly, but this mornin' they just about speak, and that's all. Some of 'em pretended they didn't even see me. Hurry right along, like I'd spoiled somethin' — like that time I put chilli pepper in the church supper —" A delicious throaty laugh escaped her lips at a four-year-old memory.

"Gosh! That was funny, wasn't it?" Duncan wasn't laughing, though. "Why, there's nothin' wrong with folks, Eddie. That's just your imagination. Now, see here, what —"

"Imagination my right eye!" Eddie retorted. "Even Monte Quillan went haywire. He was cutting across Main, right in front of me. I called to him, and he started to run. I'm wondering if his morning drink is more important than I am. I'm sure he heard me —"

"Monte Quillan," Rance exploded, "is a skunk —" He caught himself.

"A–A what?" Eddie's eyes widened. "A skunk — ?"

"I said," Rance coughed uneasily, "Monte Quillan is *sunk* if he thinks he can treat Eddie Thorpe thataway."

The girl hadn't noticed that Duncan was

97

slowly leading her horse along Hereford Street, where he could reach First Street, which ran parallel to Main. Rance wanted to get the girl away from the eyes of the curious. A protective instinct he himself didn't understand was responsible for Rance's actions. Eddie suddenly became aware that her horse was in motion, and that they had passed the Morada Hotel.

"Rance, where you leading my pony?"

Rance kept going without looking back at the girl. He gritted his teeth, wondered what to say next. Finally, "What brought you to town, Eddie?"

The girl sobered a trifle. Thought that something must be wrong commenced to enter her consciousness. "Why, I came in for some thread. I told Monte yesterday to have Dad bring it, but Dad didn't come home last night. But I'd run out of thread. I wanted some ribbon, too. You know, I'm making a dress for that dance Monte's going to take me to next week —"

"I reckon, Eddie," Rance said huskily, "you won't want to be goin' to that party now."

"I should say I won't," stiffly, "not after Monte acting this way — say, Rance Duncan, where you taking me?"

They had reached the corner of First Street. Here there were but a few scattered residences and, beyond, open country. There were only two or three people in sight. Rance turned the corner. "We'll swing back to Main, at Thorpe Street, and from there to Ma Melissa Jones' house —"

"Rance, have you lost your wits? I'm after thread. I don't want to go to Mrs. Jones' Boarding-House. What is this, a joke?"

"No, it ain't, Eddie." For the first time Rance had a ready answer.

"Well, what —" Eddie's voice shook, as understanding came. "Rance, has somebody been hurt, or — is Dad —"

Rance stopped and came back, standing close to her right stirrup. He was finding it hard to meet Eddie's eyes. The girl's lower lip quivered. Rance reached up, patted her hand. "You guessed it, Eddie. I didn't know how to tell you. I figured to take you down to Mrs. Jones'. She's a comfortin' and understandin' sort. You can't go back home, now —"

As long as he lived, Rance Duncan never forgot the expression on the girl's face. Her eyes grew misty after a moment, but, to his vast relief, she didn't break into sobbing. Suddenly she jerked the horse around. "Where is Dad? I'm going to him!"

"Not now, Eddie," Rance said steadily. He caught the horse's bridle, held it quiet. Eddie wanted the whole story. Rance gave it briefly, slipping over the more gruesome details. "You can see him later," Rance finished. "Monte's coming after you — later. He had

— had some other duties to do. That's why he couldn't stop when you called him."

The girl didn't answer. Rance commenced to lead the horse along First Street, talking steadily as he walked. He never remembered his words afterward. He only knew he was holding the girl from a collapse. At Thorpe Street he turned the corner. From behind came a muffled sob. Rance swallowed hard. He spoke low-voiced over his shoulder:

"Hang on to your nerve, Eddie. Take your reins. I'm lettin' go the bridle, but I'm right with you every minute. We'll be crossin' Main pretty quick now. Don't let folks see you wilt."

And later, "Here we are, girl."

The horse had stopped in front of the Jones' Boarding-House. Eddie blinked back her tears, climbed down from the saddle. "Thanks, Rance," she said unsteadily, "I might have made a mess of things, if you hadn't been with me."

Rance tied the horse to a post, walked at the girl's side up the walk to the boarding-house. He didn't know what he was going to say to Ma Melissa Jones. That he left to Fate, and Fate took care of the matter. Ma Jones was an understanding sort.

As they reached the door, it swung open. Ma Jones' portly figure stood framed there. Her motherly arms went out, "You pore lamb," she said kindly, "c'mon in and let me care for you a spell."

Rance didn't hear what else was said. He was suddenly aware that the door had been shut in his face. Mentally, he thanked the powers that be for such folks as Ma Melissa Jones. He walked out toward the road, his face wet with perspiration. He mopped his forehead. "God! I don't want no more jobs like that."

He led Eddie's pony down to the corner of Thorpe and Main and gave it in charge of the proprietor of the Morada Livery.

As he left the livery he saw Monte Quillan hastening toward him. Hot anger swept through Rance Duncan.

"And him courtin' Eddie, and folks already lookin' to the day they start to team in double-harness," he muttered resentfully. "Fine way for him to act — first time he gets a chance to do somethin' for his girl, he throws the job onto me. Damn his measly —"

At that moment Quillan came up. His eyes weren't meeting Duncan's. "Much obliged, Rance," he said uneasily. "Did she — did Eddie break down?"

"She did not," Rance snapped. "Eddie's pure steel — too good for —" He checked the hot words, then, "Look here, Monte, Eddie's goin' to want to go to the undertaker's to-night. You know whose job that is, don't you?"

"Reckon I do," Quillan muttered.

Rance nodded shortly. "Don't let that girl lose faith in you, Monte." His temper would no longer be checked. "You call at Ma Jones' for her to-night, Monte, and take her there."

"You tellin' me —" Quillan commenced testily.

"I'm *orderin'* you," Rance jerked out. "You do it, or so help me God, Monte, I'll break every bone in your body!"

Without giving Quillan time to answer, Duncan swung grimly around and strode back toward the centre of town.

CHAPTER VIII

Three cups of black coffee at the Delmonico Chop House didn't stir Rance Duncan's thoughts to the activity he had hoped for. He couldn't eat, didn't want to eat. He sat at a table in one corner by himself. If other diners asked questions he replied with a short "yes" or "no," but refused abruptly to be drawn into conversation.

Once he took from his pocket the envelope which had carried the mysterious letter about which Brad Wheeler refused to speak, and examined it thoroughly. If only the postmark wasn't blurred, he thought. It might give him some sort of clue. Finally, he gave it up, his mind revolving with speculation, and replaced the envelope in his pocket. He had decided not to say anything about having the envelope. If Brad Wheeler could withhold information, so could he.

The thought came to him it might be a good idea to examine the passageway between the Thorpe store and Toralbert's Hardware and Gun Store, the Thorpe building's neighbour to the east. The window of the room in which Thorpe had been killed opened on this passageway. The murderer might have made his escape by this window.

He rose from the table, paid for his coffee at the long counter which ran the length of one side of the restaurant, and emerged into Main Street. Heading west on Main, he crossed Thorpe Street, and continued on toward the Thorpe store. Just before stepping into the passageway between the Thorpe and Toralbert stores, he gazed quickly along the street. Duncan didn't want any of the curious hanging around while he searched for any evidence that might exist.

Duncan stepped quickly into the passageway and, stooping slightly, commenced to scrutinize the earth beneath the window of the Thorpe building. Every inch of ground for a space of several feet was carefully gone over. True, there were footprints there, of all shapes and sizes, but nothing definite on which Duncan could pin any hopes. The passageway between the two buildings was often used as a shortcut through from Main to Santone Street, the parallel street south of the principal thoroughfare. Consequently, the dusty earth was thoroughly trampled.

Duncan growled disappointedly, moved along the passageway to the rear of the Thorpe building. Several yards from the rear wall of the store stood a long narrow shed with a corrugated iron roof, which served as a store-house for goods. It had no windows and one small padlocked door.

Between the store and the store-house Duncan found hoofmarks and footprints, from which nothing in particular could be deduced. There'd been no rain and little wind for several days, so the prints might have been there for some time. Occasionally, customers hitched their mounts there. From this point Rance moved out to the alley running back of the Thorpe store-house. Here also there was little of importance to be seen. The alley was littered with piles of rubbish — cans, old bottles, papers. Hoofprints and wagonwheel ruts ran the length of the alley.

Duncan came back to the stretch of ground between the shed and the store building, and again bent to a close scrutiny of the earth. He moved around in a stooping position, trying to pick something definite from the maze of prints, but that definite something seemed to be lacking.

And then, just as he was about to give up hope, something shiny caught his eye. Stooping close, he retrieved a small metallic cylinder of brass. It was an exploded cartridge shell of forty-five calibre, designed for use in a six-shooter.

Duncan straightened up, studied the shell, then abruptly frowned. Exploded shells weren't an unusual find — especially forty-five calibre six-shooter shells — but this one was different. Duncan's frown deepened.

He studied the base of the shell intently,

his attention concentrated on the print of the firing-pin. Usually, a firing-pin imprint was a perfectly round and somewhat blunt depression in the metal base of the exploded shell. The imprint in the shell Duncan held was sharp and anything but circular.

"Damn if this ain't a funny one," Rance muttered. "I thought I knew somethin' about guns, but I never knew one was made that would leave this sort of print on a shell. Me, I better check up on my knowledge."

Finally he shook his head, slipped the shell in a pocket and headed back toward Main Street. "Looks like," he mused, "the murderer plugged out his empty shell when he was makin' a getaway. 'Course, there's a chance this ain't from the murderer's gun, but somehow I got a hunch . . ."

His thoughts ended as he stepped into Main Street to find Doctor Parker standing on the walk before the Thorpe store. A few people were standing across the street, looking his way.

"What's up, Doc?" Rance asked.

"Oh, hello, Duncan —" turning around. "I didn't see you before. Where'd you come from?"

Duncan was non-committal. "Me, I just been nosin' around."

"Learn anything new?"

Duncan told him of the various conversations he'd had that day, ending with,

"There's suspects for you, Doc."

Parker looked critically at him. "I'm afraid, Duncan, you're too ready to base your suspicions on insufficient evidence."

"Admitted, but if we can get additional proof —"

"We'll have to have considerable more, before I can instruct a jury to indict any of the men you've mentioned. Gillett's alibi seems airtight."

"Suppose Gillett and Norris were working together —"

"You haven't any proof of that. Just because Norris hired Gillett is no sign — here's another thing, Duncan, don't expect too much from Wheeler concerning this letter you keep harping on. That letter, as Wheeler says, may have contained personal business matters, known only to Thorpe and himself. Wheeler is too reliable a citizen to be mixed up in anything —"

"You'll make him talk at the inquest, won't you?"

"We'll see, when the inquest comes off." Parker was short.

"When will that be?"

"Just as soon as we can hold it, after Clem Lucas gets here —"

"You aimin' to wait for him, now —"

"In the face of information I've picked up from Joe Myers, to the effect that Lucas didn't take with him the store receipts, I think it best to wait —"

"You heard about Lucas not takin' the money, eh? Hell, Doc, I figured to get this inquest over and out of the way —"

"I think, Duncan," Parker said stiffly, "that so long as I'm coroner, I'll be the one to say how and when and where —"

"Sure, Doc," Duncan nodded disappointedly. "I ain't tellin' you your business. But, shucks, Lucas won't be in on the stage until to-morrow noon —"

"He'll be in to-night, I hope. We'll hold the inquest first thing to-morrow morning. I've arranged with Deputy Yocum to go after Lucas. Yocum's leaving for Capitol City at once. At Capitol City he's going to hire a buggy and drive Lucas back. Yocum will leave just as soon as he's seen you, and get fresh horses along the way. He'll make good time."

"Too damn bad Lucas is too old to fork a horse. They'd make better time — What was that you said about Homer wantin' to see me?"

"Yocum," Parker explained, "was disinclined to leave Morada without a deputy. He suggested that he appoint you to fill in the office in his absence. I didn't want to send an outsider to get Lucas. The old man may have information I don't want spread around. Either you or Deputy Yocum, in my opinion, are the logical men to go after him. I was sure you wouldn't want to leave Morada at a time like this. You have no objections, I hope."

"To bein' deputised? No, sure not. The only objections I have is to postponin' this inquiry. Gives folks that much longer to get together and dovetail their stories. Howsomever" — noting the stubborn look that had crossed Parker's features — "you're the boss."

He motioned toward a knot of men lounging across the street, their eyes glued in his direction. "What they hangin' around for?"

"Curiosity, I guess," Parker replied. "There was quite a crowd here about five minutes before you showed up."

"Por que?"

"The undertaker just removed Thorpe's body. You know how folks like to hang around."

Duncan nodded, added, "Finished your examination, eh?" and at Parker's affirmative reply asked, "What did you find? Forty-five slug killed Vink, I suppose?"

"It was the size of a forty-five," Parker said. "Battered up a bit, of course, but I think I'm safe in calling it a forty-five. The bullet passed through Thorpe's heart in a slightly upward direction, glancing off a rib, and eventually lodged in the spine. Judging from the course the bullet took, I'm of the opinion that a smaller man than Thorpe fired the shot."

Duncan smiled. "Vink," he reminded, "was a right big man, so that's not hard to figure. You're pretty big, but Vink was bigger than you even. You know, Doc, the killer might have held his gun low — say, just over the edge of the table."

Parker frowned. "I hadn't thought of it that way. . . . Death was almost instantaneous, of course. I figure Thorpe died between one and one-thirty this morning. Maybe a short time before or after. That's as near as I can judge."

Duncan's eyes narrowed. After a moment, "Doc, Brad Wheeler tells me you didn't find any papers, or anythin' —"

"Nor money, either," Parker cut in, "except about ten dollars in change, in the store till. If you're thinking about that letter Brad Wheeler is supposed to have seen, I didn't find it. The only papers I found on Thorpe were a couple of receipted bills. His keys were intact. There was a little change in one pocket. So far as money is concerned, the safe had been cleaned out. Duncan, you're placing far too much importance on that letter."

Rance smiled thinly. "All right, Doc. I won't say another word about it — to you."

"That's up to you." Parker's words carried an edge. "Well, I've got to be getting along." He nodded shortly and strode off down the street, his back stiff and erect.

Duncan headed in the opposite direction. At the next corner he spied Deputy Yocum riding along Hereford Street.

"Hi, Rance!" Yocum stated.

Duncan waited until the deputy pulled up at his side.

"I been lookin' for you," Yocum stated.

"So I understand. Parker tells me I'm to be deputised."

"All right, ain't it?" And at Duncan's short nod, Yocum said, "C'mon we'll drift down to my office. I'll swear you in, and see can I find a badge. There ought to be a couple layin' around my desk."

They arrived a few minutes later at the combination jail and deputy-sheriff's office. It was a squat, oblong building of adobe, with the office occupying about one-third of the front floor space. In the back wall of the office was a door leading to the cells, which were at present empty.

A spur-scarred deck near a window at one side of the office and four straight-back chairs constituted the only furniture. Here and there about the walls were fastened a few reward notices for wanted men, a couple of packing-house calendars, and a topographical map of the state. Suspended on wooden pegs driven into the walls were a shot-gun and two Winchester rifles. At one side hung three pairs of handcuffs.

The oath of office was administered to the

accompaniment of noisily chewed peanuts, after which Yocum rummaged through his desk and found an extra deputy badge for Duncan.

Duncan put the badge in his pocket. "I won't put this on right away. Folks have a habit of keepin' their mouths shut if they think they're talkin' to the law."

"Shucks! Parker will spread the news."

"Mebbe he'll be so damn wrapped up in this postponed inquiry, he'll forget to. Parker's a good doctor, but when it comes to a showdown he displays all the speed of a broken-hocked cowhorse."

Yocum nodded, added dubiously, "I don't know how Windy Cannon is goin' to take your appointment. He'll like to blow up when I tell him. He's great on holdin' down expenses. But when I reach the capitol, I'll explain that —"

"You tell Sheriff Cannon for me," Duncan cut in, "that I ain't askin' no pay. And I'll stand my own expenses, too. I'm right glad to get the authority that goes with this badge. It might come handy before this murder business is cleared up."

Yocum looked relieved. "It'll be all right with old Windy, then. He'll be only too glad to turn in a report on how his administration held down expenses, even with an extra deputy. Anyway, he better not kick. This is an emergency. Only he always likes to do the appointin' himself."

"If Windy Cannon gets proddy you tell him he'll lose himself a lot of votes next election. This is bein' done on Vink Thorpe's account, and Vink has a heap of friends in Crazy River County."

"I reckon you're right. . . . Say, Rance, what do — you think of this idea of postponin' the inquiry until I get old Lucas here?"

"You know what I think of it."

"You'n me both, cowboy. Well, I best be slopin'."

"Wait a minute, Homer. Let me see your gun."

Wonderingly, Yocum drew his six-shooter and handed it over. Rance thumbed back the hammer, scrutinized it a moment, then gently lowered it. He handed it back with the observation, "When did you start usin' a .44–40?"

"Quite some spell back. I can use Winchester ca'tridges, see — say, what you got up yore sleeve, Rance?"

"My arm, Homer. Jokin' aside, mebbe I'll tell you later. I just wanted to see was your firin'-pin the same as mine."

"Shouldn't be no material difference. Why?"

"Mebbe I'll tell you later," Rance repeated. "You'd better get started. What time you figure to get back with Lucas? You might have to go to the Opera House to get him. He's loco as hell for the shows."

"Maybe I can make it before he goes to the theayter." Yocum consulted his nickel-plated watch. "Three-thirty now. I'll make the ride to the capital inside three hours. I'm aimin' to get fresh horses at Aubrey and Haslam Tanks. With luck I can get Lucas on his way by seven-thirty — and make changes the same way on the way back. Shucks! I should be back with him before midnight."

"You will," Rance reminded, "providin' he's there. You know he might have taken that money with him, regardless what he told Myers, and he *might* be out of the state by this time."

"That's somethin' I can't believe," Yocum shook his head, "not old Lucas. He's been plumb faithful too long now. If he'd ever planned to run off with Vink's money, he had plenty of chance before now."

"We're agreed to that." Duncan smiled: "Got plenty peanuts to carry you on the trip?"

"I reckon," Yocum nodded seriously. "I can get more in Capitol City."

"Better get slopin' then, Homer."

Duncan moved out to the hitchrack. Yocum locked the door of his office, handed the key to Duncan and climbed into the saddle. "See you some more, cowboy," he nodded. The horse jumped into a fast lope and disappeared down the street.

CHAPTER IX

By nightfall, everyone in Morada knew that Rance had been deputised, even though he carried no visible evidence in the form of a badge pinned to his vest. He had been able to get no further information from those with whom Thorpe had been in contact the previous day. Each man to whom he talked now shut up like the proverbial clam, or evaded his questions.

Rance had just finished supper when Monte Quillan came into the Delmonico Chop House. Monte started toward one of the counter stools, but Duncan motioned him over to the table. Somewhat reluctantly Quillan took a chair across from Duncan.

"Now, there's nothin' I can tell you, Rance —" he commenced.

"I'm not expecting you to," quietly. "I'm aimin' to tell you, Monte. . . . I was down to Melissa Jones' a short spell back to see Eddie."

"Looks like she's takin' it nervy," Quillan said awkwardly.

"You don't need to worry about Eddie's nerve, Monte. Now, look here, I've been to the undertaker's. Everythin's all right now —

as all right as can be. I ain't tellin' you Vink looks natural, like folks usually say in such cases. Dead men — especially friends — never do look natural to me. That's a habit folks got into the way of sayin' —"

"You aimin' to make a speech on the deceased?" Quillan asked, somewhat sarcastically.

Duncan held his temper. "Take it easy, Monte. I'm tryin' to get along with you. You been figurin' a right spell to marry Eddie, ain't you — ?"

"That," Quillan said, "is my business."

"I suggest," Duncan told him dryly, "that you 'tend to business better'n you did this mornin'. Now, wait a minute — don't go flarin' up. There's no need of you'n me circlin' around each other like a couple of strange Injun dogs. I'm admittin' I sort of blew up this mornin'. If you're a man, you'll admit I had reason to."

"Maybe so," Quillan conceded sullenly. "But what goes on between Eddie and me is —"

"Your own business, naturally. Hell, Monte, I don't want to cut into your affairs. But folks know you've been callin' on Eddie for a right smart time now. They're expecting things of you. Don't throw that girl down, at a time like this. She's enough broke up as it is. I told her you'd call to take her to the undertaker's to-night — right after supper. Make it early, before too many folks are there."

"Those are my intentions," Quillan stated stiffly. "I —"

"I'm glad to hear it —"

"I dropped in for a few minutes," Quillan finished, "right after you left, to tell her I was sorry about it, and that I'd call for her. Later to-night I'm goin' to ride out to the VIT and get some clothes for her, from that Mex woman. She asked me to tell Uhler and the rest of the boys, too — unless you already sent word."

"I didn't. Been just too damn busy. I'll appreciate that, Monte. If you'll just look after Eddie's needs for the next few days, I'll be much obliged. I reckon to have my hands full. Eddie'll be dependin' on you. Vink always thought well of you. Leastwise, I never heard him say he objected to you marryin' his daughter. I wouldn't want you to disappoint his memory."

Quillan's eyes snapped. "You figurin' to take Vink's place?"

"So far as I can in lookin' out for Eddie."

"Seems to me you're loadin' yourself with responsibility. Has Eddie asked you to do that?"

"Eddie didn't have to ask me," Duncan said evenly. "There's some things I know. I've been hopin' you'd accept your duties the same way. Until Eddie asks me to quit — or until there's somebody to watch out for her — I'll continue to go along as is. That plain?"

"It's plain you feel that you should tell me what to do," Quillan snapped. "That ain't necessary, Duncan. You mind your business and I'll mind mine. That clear?"

"That's all I'm askin' — where Eddie's concerned," Duncan said slowly, and repeated, "That's all I'm askin'."

Quillan started some angry statement, then stopped, his face cloudy. A waitress came to take his order. Duncan rose from the chair, nodded shortly to Quillan and headed toward the front of the restaurant.

It was dark when he stepped outside. He looked at his watch, then walked toward the centre of town. Rectangles of light shone from windows and doorways. He paused at the corner of Hereford Street, crossed over and climbed the steps to the Morada House porch. Save for himself, the porch was deserted now. He settled into a chair.

A half-hour passed. Occasionally a pair of cowman's boots clamped along the sidewalk, or a rider jogged his pony along Main Street. Voices reached Rance faintly from the Morada Bar. A cowhand from the Coffee-Pot outfit emerged from the bar after a time and sat down near Duncan. Duncan didn't feel like talking. He rose, descended the steps and sauntered along Main Street.

In front of Chet Beeson's Tonsorial Parlor a small Mexican boy stopped Rance, "You are the Senor Duncan — no?"

"You called the turn, *muchacho*. What's up?" The boy was barefooted and dirty, clad in ragged overalls. He couldn't have been more than nine years old.

"I have for the Senor Duncan the *nota* —"

"You got a note for me? Let's have it, son."

The boy passed over a folded bit of paper, his dark eyes wide on Duncan. Duncan unfolded the note, bent closer to the light shining from the barber shop window. Printed in lead pencil, Duncan read:

"Duncan. You're too damn nosey. You best go slow or yore libel not to go anyplace. This is for your own good and Edith Thorpes best welfare. Mind yore own business.

A friend."

Duncan glanced from the note to the boy. "Who gave you this?"

The small Mexican shrugged skinny shoulders. *"Quien sabe?"*

"Come on now, son. I want the truth."

"Es verdad, senor. . . . Is the truth." The boy's English was unequal to the occasion. He broke suddenly into rapid Spanish.

"Whoa! Go slower, son. Mebbe I'll get you. *Repetir."*

The boy repeated the words. Duncan listened carefully, translating as rapidly as his Spanish would allow:

"You say a man stopped you in the alley

back of Matt Everett's feed barn. Too dark to see who he was, but he gave you a half *peso* to find me and give me this note?"

The boy's black head bobbed violently. "Too black of the night," he added slowly. "May-bee" — and his teeth flashed white in a grinning mouth — "eet was *El Diablo* — how you say? — thee Ol' Nick, no?"

"Nope, I don't reckon it was the devil, son. An' you don't either, or you wouldn't be here. Howsomever, if you don't know, you don't know. Listen, if you can tell me who he is, I'll give you a dollar. One whole peso, see?" holding up the coin.

The boy's face contorted with anguish. Again the swift Spanish: Wasn't it a calamity? How could he tell? The man spoke roughly. The night was too dark to see his face. He had given the note with instructions for delivery, then turned and hurried eastward along the alley, before vanishing into the dark.

That was all the small Mexican knew. Duncan saw he'd have been more than willing to talk. The promise of a dollar had intrigued him mightily. Duncan smiled, held out the silver coin to the boy.

"If any more hombres give you notes, son, you follow 'em and see where they go before you deliver 'em."

"*Si, si, senor. Muchas gracias.* Nex' time I'll gon see for sure —"

"That's fine." Duncan cut short the boy's

thanks, and turned back to the light from the window to again examine the note. When next he looked round, the boy had vanished.

Duncan folded the note and stuck it into his pocket. "If that ain't a warnin', I never saw one," he mused. "Printed, so I wouldn't recognize handwritin'. That means somebody I know. Words spelled wrong on purpose, to throw me off the track, but the mis-spellin' wasn't consistent. . . . Edith Thorpe's welfare. Hmm. S'help me, if any harm comes to that girl —"

He broke off, considering, "What could anybody have against her? Hell! Eddie never harmed anybody. Damn that Quillan! He better ride close herd on Eddie. I reckon he will, though. He's plumb gone. . . . That young greaser said he got the note from a feller back of Matt Everett's. Hmm. Still, that don't mean Matt gave it to him. Funny way to sign such a note — a friend. I'll bet he's a friend," scornfully. "Oh, well . . ."

Rance again proceeded along the walk. The rest of the evening he put in sauntering around town. Time dragged heavily, despite the myriad thoughts that coursed his mind. He almost hoped there'd be a drunk to be picked up for disturbing the peace, or something of the kind, but nothing happened to break the monotony.

Once he saw Monte Quillan and learned that Monte had taken Eddie Thorpe to the undertaker's, then back to Melissa Jones' Boarding-House. Monte reported somewhat coldly that the girl hadn't broken down. She had asked what Duncan was doing.

"And you told her, I suppose," Rance said grimly, "that I was doin' my best to run the town and everybody in it."

Quillan had taken that soberly. He shook his head. "I told Eddie," he said, "that you were doing your best to learn who killed her father. I don't stab folks in the back, Rance. If you think I do, you got me wrong. I'll admit you rile me a mite when you —"

"When I tell you to look out for Eddie, eh?" grimly.

"Exactly. I know enough for that."

"That's fine. Keep up the good work."

Quillan flushed. "She's gone to bed now. Ma Melissa's 'tendin' her needs. I'm leavin' to ride to the VIT. Do I have to get your permission?"

"Don't be a total fool, Monte."

That had ended the conversation. Later, he saw Quillan ride out of town.

CHAPTER X

Ten o'clock came, then eleven. Duncan commenced to watch for sounds of the buggy carrying Yocum and old Lucas. Gradually the town quieted down. There were fewer people on the streets. One by one, lights blinked out along Main Street. Morada was going to bed. Only a few lights shone from windows here and there, and these, too, were finally extinguished. A definite hush settled over the town.

There wasn't much of a moon, and that was partly obscured by drifting clouds. The stars didn't help much. Rance walked along Thorpe Street, turned, went on Main. His boot heels resounded hollowly on the plank walks.

In front of the Thorpe store he halted and rolled a cigarette. Looking across to the corner of Main and Hereford he noted the Morada House was dark. That meant it was after midnight. He wondered what had happened to delay Homer Yocum. The deputy should have arrived by this time.

Rance's mind recurred to the warning note as he ran the tip of his tongue along the edge of the cigarette paper. Somebody trying to scare him out, or was it just the work of a

123

crank? Duncan couldn't believe it was the latter.

He searched for and found a match. It scratched noisily in the quiet of the darkened street. Fanning his lungs deeply with the smoke, Rance broke the match in two and tossed the pieces into the road. He leaned back against one of the supporting posts that held up the wooden awning of the Thorpe store, and smoked the cigarette half through before deciding to move on again.

"I reckon," he told himself, "it might be a good idea to drop into the Chink's restaurant for a cup of coffee. Nope, he'd be closed. Tim Barnes' Cowmen's Rest will be shut up by this time, too."

He ground out the cigarette butt under his heel and stood undecided. "Wonder where in time Homer is. Let's see, twenty-five miles over and twenty-five back —"

Something thwacked violently into the hitch-rack post at Rance's right. At the same instant he saw a streak of fire dart from the Morada House corner. The roar of a forty-five shattered the quiet of the empty street!

Rance vaulted over the hitch-rack, started at a run across the road, jerking his gun as he moved. He turned the Morada House corner. No one there now. He paused a moment, ears strained to catch the slightest sound. He heard the door bang open. That was back of him, some place. He didn't stop to see. Running footsteps reached him.

Rance dashed along Hereford Street. At the alley back of the hotel he paused. From fifty yards down the alley there came a sudden clatter of tin cans and the pounding of booted feet.

Rance lifted his gun. The weapon jumped in his hand, roared savagely. He thought he heard a yelp of pain. It was too dark to see anything. The footsteps sounded fainter now. Rance jumped into full pursuit, tearing swiftly along the alley, trying to avoid the heaps of rubbish that obstructed his path.

Again he raised his gun. At that moment his right spur became entangled in a discarded bedspring. He crashed down heavily, the gun flying from his hand. His head struck a piece of rock half-embedded in the earth.

For a moment Rance was too stunned to move. Slowly he fought to his feet. The breath had been knocked from his body. A swelling throbbing at one side of his head.

"Hell of a deputy I turned out to be," he swore disgustedly.

There weren't any footsteps to be heard now. He groped in the darkness for his gun, found it a yard away. He proceeded on eastward along the alley until he'd emerged on Thorpe Street. There wasn't a soul to be seen.

As Rance turned into Main, a man rushed

up to him, "What's up?"

Rance studied his face. It was one of Morada's citizens with whom he was slightly acquainted. "Nothin' much," Rance said quietly. "Some hombre took a shot at me."

"Catch him?"

"Does it look like it?"

"Thought I heard two shots. I was just turnin' in when I heard the first one —"

"Reckon my shot missed. Anyway, I didn't stop the feller. Didn't see anybody turn off Thorpe Street, did you?"

The man shook his head. "Nope. I came from the other way — over on Hereford. Cut down this way thinkin' —"

"You're wastin' your time, now. He got away slick. Might as well go back to bed."

"Reckon you're right. Got any idea who it was — ?"

"Nary an idea." Rance glanced across the street toward Matt Everett's Feed Store. It was dark. Oh, well, it would be: Everett lived at Jones' Boarding House. Tim Barnes' saloon across Main was dark, too.

"Well, good-night. I'm goin' to turn in."

"That's a right idea," Rance nodded. "So-long."

A dozen or so other citizens had gathered by this time, and they, too, departed for their respective beds. For the second time that night, lights commenced to snuff out along the street. Morada grew quiet again.

"Looks like," Rance mused, "folks are payin' more attention to gun shots since Vink was killed. . . . Wonder who threw that shot at me? Mebbe he'll try it again."

He headed back toward the Thorpe store, took up his position as before. Now he was alert for the first movement within the scope of his gaze. But nothing happened.

A half-hour passed. Duncan looked at his watch in the yellow light of a match, and yawned. Where was Homer Yocum? As though in answer to the question there came a soft *clop-clop* of horses' hoofs at the far end of town. The sounds grew nearer. An axle squeaked protestingly against lack of grease in the wheel hubs.

Rance moved out to the centre of the road as the vehicle, with Yocum's saddle-horse tied behind, took form in the gloom and slowed to a walk. "Got here, eh, Homer?"

"That you, Rance?" Yocum's voice came through the darkness. He swore, then, "Yeah, we're here. A heap later than I expected. Travelled some slow. Clem's sick."

Duncan could make out a huddled form beside Yocum now. He led the team to the hitch-rack and tied it. Yocum jumped down from the buggy and came around to the other side.

"Too bad, Clem," Rance was saying. "What's wrong?"

"Nothing radical," the old fellow croaked.

"These pesty rheumatics act up an' get me down ever' so often. Good thing Homer come to fetch me, I guess, though it's bad news he brought, Rance."

"Plenty bad," Duncan agreed grimly. "I suppose Homer told you, you're wanted to testify at the inquest tomorrow. Think you'll be able to stand it?"

"If it kills me," Lucas said quickly. "I owe that much to Vink Thorpe. A kinder man never drawed breath. I —" The words broke off in a groan, as Lucas started to descend from the buggy.

"Let me give you a hand," Duncan advised. He helped the old man get down, then placed a supporting arm around him. "Look here, Clem," he said, "you can't sleep in the store to-night. I'll go across and rouse up the hotel —"

"Nope, I'd sooner stay in that back room. Mister Thorpe's been took away, ain't he?" And at Rance's affirmative, Lucas went on, "I've slept there nigh on to two year now, and my cot's comf'table —"

"But, Clem," Yocum protested. "You won't want to stay there where —"

"Don't make no difference t'me. I ain't afeard of Vink hauntin' old Lucas. By grab, Rance, if the unholy varmint what killed him can be discovered, I'll help pull the hemp noose that breaks his neck —" He broke off, wincing. "Dang these ol' pins of mine. Always a-failin' me when I need 'em most. Jes' give me an arm, Rance. I'll make to get into the store, 'thout bein' carried. Homer got me a bottle of linament. She burns right smart, but does the trick. Be right as a cricket, t'morrer. . . . Homer, will ye do me the kindness to fetch my valise?"

They progressed as far as the double doors of the store. Lucas produced his key and managed to unlock. Rance went ahead to light a lamp. In the back room, where Thorpe had met his death, he lighted a second lamp. Then he returned to help Lucas in.

His sympathy went out to the old man as they proceeded toward the back room. Every step seemed torture. "Don't ye ever get rheumatics, Rance," Lucas advised. "They're the devil's own invention."

"I'll try not to, Clem."

The back room was reached. Lucas sank gratefully to his cot. Tiny beads of perspiration stood out on his forehead. He gave a long sigh of relief, and a wan smile curved his pale lips. "Don't know's I ever noticed before how long that store was."

Yocum put down the valise. "Anythin' we can do for you, Clem?"

"I reckon not, boys. Jus' leave me be. I'll be able to stir around come mornin' . . . Rance, Homer says I'm to be questioned 'bout the store money?"

"That's right, Clem. Joe Myers says you told him —"

"Nope, I didn't take that money, Rance. Fust time in two year Mister Thorpe didn't send it with me to put in the bank. Nigh on to eighteen hundred dollars, too — seventeen hundred and thuty-six dollars and eighty-four cents, if my memory serves me c'rect. I tell ye, Rance, Mr. Thorpe should have started a bank of his own like he's been plannin' to do. Like's not he'd be alive to-day if that money hadn't tempted some blackguard —"

Rance nodded. "So you really didn't carry that money with you, eh, Clem?"

"As Gawd's my witness, Rance, I didn't."

Duncan saw he was speakin' the truth. There couldn't be any doubt about that. He said, "Haven't any idea what made him change his mind about sending it, have you, Clem?"

"Nary a one, Rance. He didn't explain. I 'spect ye was suspicionin' me of runnin' off with that money, wa'n't ye, now?"

Duncan was a trifle shamed as he admitted the truth of Clem's question. Yocum said, "Hell, Clem. We been suspicionin' everybody connected with Vink in any way. But you're clear with us. All we want is your testimony, to-morrow mornin'. You better roll in now. Can we do anythin' for you?"

"Well, if ye'll take my shoes off, it'll save me bendin' over. I can make to get undressed from then on. Gosh dang these rheumatics. I feel like I was a hundred years old, 'stead of just seventy-odd. . . . Homer, if ye'll open my valise and get out my night shirt, I'll be obliged."

They finally got the old man tucked between blankets. "Leave thet lamp a-burnin' low, Rance," Lucas requested. "Like's not I'll stir around after I'm rested a mite and give my laigs a rub with thet linament. I'll see ye to-morrow. Good night."

Duncan and the deputy departed. On their way through the store Yocum stopped only long enough to fill his pockets with peanuts before blowing out the lamp.

On the street he said to Rance, "Clem's sure got it bad."

"Rheumatics is tough when they hit violent," Rance answered. "I've known folks to be bed-rid for years with 'em. It must have been a long ride."

"Plenty. I had a bottle along to sort of ease Clem over the rough spots, but he don't take to strong drink. Got teetotaler ideas. Hell, I was commencin' to think I never would get him started from the hotel in Capitol City. He'd been in bed all day. The manager of the hotel said he was sick when he arrived and went right to bed. From what they tell me, Lucas was yellin' for hot bricks early this mornin' — no, it's yesterday mornin' now — to ease the pain. He like to break down when I told him about Vink. He's a gritty ol' cuss, though. Mebbe —" Yocum broke off and laughed.

"Mebbe what?"

"You see," the deputy explained, "I sort of had to help Clem get started, I'd hired the buggy, and he was tryin' to get up from bed. Well, I got a bottle of horse linament and rubbed Clem's legs plenty. Lot of cayenne in that linament. Clem pro'bly figured he better make the start before I rubbed all the skin off. Anyway, I got him here, and now Doctor Parker ain't got no excuse to postpone that inquiry any longer."

"Did you see Sheriff Cannon?"

"Yeah. Told him about your appointment. He didn't have as much to say as I'd expected. Fact is, he told me I'd done the right thing."

"Plumb unusual for Windy Cannon."

"Wasn't it? Windy was kind of preoccupied though. He's all stirred up tryin' to locate some horse thief. You know how serious he takes little things. He didn't have much time to bother with me. Give me strict instructions — and you, too — to run down Vink's killer. . . . Anythin' new?"

"I'm sorry Clem had to be sick and delay you."

"Any particular reason?"

"Some coyote took a shot at me. If you'd been here we might have caught him. I didn't want to take chances of walkin' into a trap, alone —"

"T'hell you say!"

"I got a warnin' note before the shot, too. Here —" Rance showed Yocum the note and explained the circumstances attendant upon the shooting. He held a lighted match while Yocum perused the paper.

"Well, I'll be goddamed!" Yocum exploded at last. "Ain't got any idea who that's from, eh?"

Duncan shrugged his shoulders. "I've asked plenty nosey questions to-day, but it might be none of them I questioned. For that matter, I can't be sure the feller who sent the note is the one that shot at me."

"Yeah, it might be a quincidence."

"A what?"

"A quincidence — you know, when two things happen simultan'ous without bein' related."

"Oh — a coincidence."

"That's it. . . . You might have winged the skunk that shot at you. I'll keep my eyes peeled to-morrow for fellers that limp or have their arms bandaged. If you hit him serious, Doc Parker will likely know about it —"

"That's to be seen. What you aimin' to do, now?"

"Take this buggy down to the livery and get the horses put up. Then, I'm goin' to turn in. I'm plumb weary. Twenty-five miles in the saddle and twenty-five back in a lurchin' buggy is a day's work."

"I know that."

"You better come down to my office. I got enough blankets. I'll roll up on the floor. You can have the cot."

"I'll take that buggy to the livery for you. I figure to stay up for a spell."

"Howcome?"

"Sort of keep an eye on Lucas."

"What do you mean?"

"Somebody took a shot at me. That same somebody might not want Lucas to testify tomorrow. It would be easy to throw a shot through that window while he's asleep."

"Uh-huh, I see what you mean. Not a bad idea. I'll stay up with you —"

"You'll go on to bed, that's what you'll do. You're fagged. Go catch your shut eye. You can relieve me later if you like."

Yocum yawned. "Guess you're right at that, Rance. All right, see you in a couple hours." He faded into the gloom of the night. . . .

But the hours until dawn passed without incident. By the time Homer rose and went out to find Duncan the vigil had produced nothing untoward.

"Didn't see a thing, eh?" the deputy asked, when he found Duncan standing in front of the Thorpe store.

"Not a think. I looked in Lucas' window a couple of times. Once he was asleep. The second time he was up, rubbin' his legs with that linament. I watched until he went back to bed. The old cuss sure walks like he was crippled plenty. Hope he'll be able to testify."

"It's tough. I reckon old age brings on all sorts of ailments."

"If peanuts can prevent, old age won't affect you none."

"Aw, go to grass. Better run along and grab two-three hours' sleep. I'll wake you up in time for the inquest."

Duncan yawned widely. "It's a good idea, feller. I'll see you later, then."

CHAPTER XI

The coroner's inquest was held that morning, and as Rance had predicted failed to indict any individual for the slaying. The many conversations Duncan had held with various men connected in one way or another with Thorpe were brought out during the giving of testimony, but Doctor Parker's verbal probing failed to produce anything new.

When questioned regarding the mysterious letter which Thorpe had been seen to show to Brad Wheeler, Wheeler swore there was nothing mysterious about it, that it had concerned a private business matter between the two men, and could the letter be produced the jury would see he spoke the truth. But the letter was missing.

Regarding the nature of the business, Wheeler begged to be excused from testifying, on the basis that he himself might go through with the plans disrupted by Thorpe's death. He hinted at a contemplated sale of his hotel to acquire funds with which to start a banking business in Morada, though making no definite statement to this effect, on the plea that he didn't want rival interests to anticipate his plans. The jury and coroner, remembering his friendship for Thorpe and impressed by his apparent frankness, excused him from further testimony, especially after he had denied flatly that Thorpe had grown excited when the letter was discussed.

In view of Wheeler's standing in the community, Yocum's contradictory testimony regarding the letter and what he had seen pass between Thorpe and Wheeler was given little heed.

Rance testified to such information as he had, but withheld information relative to his possession of the mysterious envelope and cartridge shell he had found. Matt Everett denied all knowledge of the mysterious letter's existence.

Clem Lucas was on hand, still limping, and produced Parker's biggest disappointment when he was unable to say why Thorpe had not sent the store receipts to Capitol City for deposit as was customary.

Through Judge Alford's testimony it came out that Vink Thorpe had never had a will drawn. It was on the matter of making a will that Thorpe had talked to Alford that day on the Morada House corner.

Alford testified that Thorpe had been very insistent upon leaving a will that would be "unbreakable — plumb water and air-tight," were Thorpe's words as Alford remembered them. In view of Thorpe's caution in the matter, Alford had suggested that Thorpe go to Capitol City and employ an up-to-date young attorney to draw such a paper.

As Alford had pointed out at the inquest, "Two heads are better than one. Besides, I've been retired from active practice for a good many years. New laws are made, new publications brought out. In short, conditions change. It was my idea that a younger man might do a better piece of work — a tighter piece of work — than myself. I promised Vink that I could look over the papers when they were drawn, and add anything that might be possible. Thorpe agreed with me that was the best way to handle the matter, and planned to go to Capitol City the following morning."

Alford's testimony had come as considerable of a shock to Ward Stinson, who had already reluctantly admitted that Thorpe's contemplated visit to a lawyer in Capitol City had aroused his ire.

When all the testimony was in, Parker had charged his jury to indict anyone to whom sufficient evidence pointed as being the murderer. At the same time Parker had reminded the jurors that, in his opinion, there was insufficient evidence for an indictment, Hugh Norris' testimony having thoroughly cleared Bert Gillett of suspicion, despite Gillett's threat.

The upshot of the matter was that after a two-hour conference the jury returned a verdict to the effect that Vincent I. Thorpe had met his death "at the hand of an unknown, or unknowns," with the motive for the crime attributed to the robbery of the money Thorpe was supposed to have had in his safe. Nor was any importance placed upon the poker hand Vink Thorpe held at the time of his death. To the coroner and jurors it was a minor detail, not to be given serious consideration.

With the unsatisfactory — to Rance Duncan — verdict in, it was now necessary to produce further evidence before anyone could be arrested and brought to trial for the crime. And that, it appeared to Duncan, was up to himself and Homer Yocum. With this thought in mind, Duncan asked permission to retain his authority as deputy-sheriff for the time being.

At the close of the inquest Rance Duncan walked down Main Street with Doctor Parker, whose office was across from Yocum's office and jail.

Parker said, "You aren't satisfied, are you, Rance? Are you thinking Thorpe knew he was going to be killed — or at least that his life was in danger — and for that reason was anxious to have a will drawn?"

Rance shook his head. "If Vink had thought he was in danger, he'd have made preparations. Why, he didn't even have his gun on at the time . . . Nope, I ain't satisfied. Not none. I'd have liked to seen you go into that letter business with Brad Wheeler, and forced him to tell —"

"Pshaw, Duncan. I couldn't do anything more. I'll tell you what I think: Thorpe has spoken frequently about starting a bank here. Doubtless Wheeler planned to go into it with him. That letter may have been from a third source of capital they'd been counting on. Wheeler may still plan to go through with the idea, but doesn't want it known until he can arrange for capital in the necessary amount. That would be only natural, and I think we have no right to question into his private affairs." He paused, then, "Look here, Duncan, do you think Wheeler killed Thorpe?"

"I didn't say that," non-committally. "At the same time, if your jury had indicted Wheeler and brought him to trial, he might have been made to tell what that letter contained."

"And suppose he refused to tell, even then. There's no real evidence against him. No jury would bring in a conviction, simply because he went to Alonzo's room last night. Everybody knows he's henpecked. It's only natural he'd change his mind and be afraid to stay home. In case of a trial the best you could expect for failure to reveal the letter's contents would be a charge of contempt of court — carrying probably a fine. And what does that amount to? Do you think the county would thank me for the expense of a trial? Taxes are bad enough as it is. There

140

isn't a single iota of proof against him. With the letter missing we haven't a thing on Brad Wheeler."

"Mebbe you're right." Rance shrugged his shoulders and frowned. He changed the subject. "I noted Matt Everett's hand was bandaged. You do it?" and at Parker's affirmative nod, "What happened?"

Parker smiled, "Always suspicious, aren't you, Duncan? Well, this time you're a mile wide of the mark. Matt had a rather nasty rope burn across the back of his right hand —"

"Rope burn? Since when has Matt took to ropin' — ?"

"Now, Rance, snap your mind out of cattle for a few minutes. It wasn't that kind of roping. I didn't pay any great attention when he was telling me about it, but it seems he was hoisting something with a rope and pully this morning before the inquest. Anyway, the rope slipped and burned his hand. I've had those kind of burns to treat before. They're painful."

"I'll bet they are." Rance looked thoughtful. "Say, Doc, did it look like the sort of burn that could be made by a bullet grazing the flesh?"

Parker frowned. "Well, now that you mention it, Duncan, that might be so. But, gosh, I think you're shooting wide of the mark again, aren't you? Who would shoot at Matt — say, I heard somebody shot at you last night, and you returned the fire. Is that correct?"

"Nobody lied to you."

"Duncan, you don't think Matt Everett —"

"I didn't say that, either," Rance smiled thinly.

They were just passing the Morada House corner. Rance said suddenly, "Reckon I'll stop here, Doc. See you later."

"Looking for more evidence, I suppose." The doctor's smile hinted at a sneer.

Duncan nodded, "I'm goin' to continue to look until I find some, too . . . *Adios*."

Parker continued on his way. Duncan turned and headed in the direction of Matt Everett's feed store. Various men along Main Street tried to engage Rance in conversation relative to the findings of the inquest, but Rance refused to be detained.

A customer was occupying Everett's attention when Rance entered. Rance dropped into a chair near the door and waited until the man had finished ordering and departed. Then:

"What did you think of the inquest, Matt?"

Everett looked up from an account book on his desk at Rance's right, glanced from the corners of his eyes at Rance. "Reckon it was about all we could expect," he said warily.

"I'm still wonderin' about that letter, Matt."

Everett's usually red face grew redder than ever. "I-I-I think you got the wrong idea, R-R-Rance. You think I k-k-know somethin'

142

about that letter, b-b-but I don't."

Duncan had never resented Everett's habit of never looking directly at the person to whom he was talking. Doubtless, Rance thought, the habit was due to self-consciousness. But, now, the VIT foreman wished he could see straight into those eyes and read what was taking place in the man's brain.

Rance said casually, "I note you got your right paw wrapped up. What happened to it?"

Everett's eyes slipped away. "B-B-Burned it on a rope," he tried without success to say calmly. "H-H-Hoistin' a bale of hay into my barn. The dang rope s-s-slipped and burned me proper, before I could s-s-stop it."

"That's tough," Rance yawned. "Well, I suppose I better be gettin' on my way." He rose lazily from his chair, thrust one hand into a pocket and drew out the empty cartridge shell he had found at the rear of the Thorpe store. "Ever see a gun hammer leave that kind of a mark on a shell, Matt?"

Matt glanced sidewise at the base of the forty-five shell. For once his glance widened. His eyes fairly bulged. Quite suddenly he went a sickly yellow color. He was too shocked to stutter now. Words came to his lips, but he couldn't speak. His eyes were still on the firing-pin mark when he shook his head in denial.

Rance knew the man lied. He thrust the

shell back in his pocket. "That," he said, "is more evidence, Matt."

"W-W-Where did you g-g-get it, R-R-Rance?"

"If I told you, you'd know as much as I do." Rance laughed softly. "You forget I'm a legalized deputy now, Matt. I ain't supposed to tell where I get my evidence."

A customer entered the store. It was an effort for Everett to rise from his desk and attend to the man's requirements. Rance was standing near the desk now. His eyes narrowed as he followed Everett's form the length of the store. Several blank letterheads were scattered about the desk. Rance looked at them, then picked one up.

His lips curved as he read the neat black printing at the top of the sheet of paper: Morada Feed Store, Matthew Everett, Prop.

Rance glanced quickly at Everett, who was engrossed with his customer, then folded the letterhead and slipped it quickly into his pocket. "Well, I'll see you later, Matt," he called from the doorway.

"Come in any time and sit a spell." The words were controlled, but Rance could see that Everett was unduly white.

Rance left the store, crossed Main Street to the other side and entered the Delmonico Chop House. Here he took a seat near the window and ordered his dinner. A platter of ham and eggs had just been put down in front of Rance when, glancing through the restaurant window, he saw Everett's customer leave the feed store. Two minutes later Matt emerged, and after locking the door hurried off in the direction of the Morada House.

Duncan chuckled grimly. "Somethin' about that forty-five shell has thrown a scare into Matt. He's headin' as fast as he can to tell Brad Wheeler about it. Dammit! I wish I could think of some way to make them two tell what they know."

He took from his pocket the pilfered letter-head and the warning note he'd received the night previous, and closely compared the two sheets of paper. No doubt about it: the note had been composed on one of Everett's letterheads. The raw edge down one side of the note showed where Everett's heading had been torn off.

"I reckon," Rance mused, "that Matt Everett ain't as smart as he thinks he is."

He finished his dinner and stepped into the street, now blistering under the intense South-West sun. There weren't many people abroad. A few minutes later he entered the office of the Morada House to find Everett and Wheeler sitting in close conversation. Both looked startled when they glanced up and saw Duncan.

"You two hombres," Rance drawled, "are sure busy lately."

"What do you mean by that?" Wheeler asked.

"What I said." Rance nodded. He started through the door to the bar.

"I say, Rance!" Wheeler called.

Duncan paused in the doorway. "Yeah?"

"What's this ca'tridge shell you was showin' Matt? He says he never seen one like it."

"Matt's a liar," Rance said quietly.

Everett's face grew red. He decided to keep still.

Brad Wheeler said testily, "Now, look here, Rance, that ain't no way to talk."

"Better than no talk a-tall," Duncan reminded, "which remark is pointed at you two. When you get around to tellin' what you know, maybe we can do business. Come clean and I'm for you — perhaps."

They didn't have an answer to that. Duncan continued on his way to the barroom. Here he found Homer Yocum and Gus Oldfield.

Yocum said, "Nothin' in that inquest to be thankful for, eh, Rance?"

Rance shook his head, then amended, "I'm thankful Parker decided not to call Vink's daughter. She told him all she knew — which was nothin' — when he interviewed her about the killin' at Ma Jones'."

The three men discussed the inquest for a few minutes. Louie, the barkeep, served drinks on the house.

"Hugh Norris and Gillett left here a spell back," Yocum said to Duncan. "Norris says he'll have Gillett on hand any time he's wanted. I kind of felt I should hold him, but didn't have no —"

"Nothing you can do about it," Rance said. "He had Norris for his alibi, and we'll just have to take Norris' word for that, until somethin' else shows up. You seen Stinson?"

"Ward and Monte Quillan was both in here, too. They've gone down to Ma Jones' to see how Eddie's gettin' along. Ward's goin' home later. He feels plumb cut up about those remarks he made, now that he knows why Vink intended to see a lawyer."

"Quillan say where he was goin'?"

"Reckon Quillan figures to stick around Morada until after the funeral, and sort of look out for Eddie."

Duncan said laconically, "That's fine."

Gus Oldfield said, "Say, Rance, when we goin' out to the VIT and look over your beef? I ought to be leavin' as soon —"

"If the cards fall right," Rance said testily, "you can go out there with Ringbone Uhler this afternoon. He's in town, and will be headin' back to look after things. I told him to pick you up, just in case you was in a hurry —"

"But, Uhler —"

"Knows as much about VIT cows as I do. Maybe more. He ain't been my *segundo* all these years without knowin' what a cattle buyer wants to buy. Anyway, he'll take care of you. 'Course, business is business, Gus, but I should think you'd want to wait a couple of days until Vink is buried. You know Eddie's boss now, and it'll be up to her to sign agreements —"

"I understand all that, Rance, but I'm figurin' to save time. Naturally, I plan to attend the funeral, but anything I can get done before then will enable me to leave that much sooner —"

"I wouldn't be in no hurry about leavin', was I you, Gus."

"What do you mean, Rance?"

"Simply, Gus, that I want you to stick around until this murder is cleared up."

"You're crazy. You can't hold me. I'm not under arrest for anything. The verdict of the coroner's jury exonerated me from —"

"Mebbe the coroner's jury did," Rance cut in, "but I got ideas of my own. I can't hold you, legally. But you take my advice and stay in Morada for a spell. It'll be best in the long run."

Oldfield started to protest. Finally, his eyes dropped before Rance's steady gaze. "All right," the cattlebuyer muttered sulkily, "I'll stay. But not for long. I got business —"

"You'll stay as long as I want you to, I reckon," Rance said dryly. He turned to Yocum, "Let's take a walk, Homer."

"Be right with you."

As the two men descended the steps to the

street, Yocum said, "What you makin' Gus stick around for?"

Duncan said frankly, "Damn if I know, Homer. I just hate to see any strings getting away from me, that's all. 'Nother thing, Gus used to ride for the VIT before he took that job with the packing company. To me, it seemed a mite coldblooded, him being in such a hurry to get away. You'd think he'd have more respect for Vink."

Yocum popped a peanut into his mouth. "I dunno, Rance. He's got business waitin' on him, and a wife and kid back in Kansas City. Gus was telling me the sleddin's been right hard since he bought that big house and settled down. I suppose he don't want to get in wrong with his bosses. 'Sides, I think it sort of scared him to be under suspicion —"

"Oh, hell," Rance said wearily, "I'll tell him to go when his business is finished. If you see him, tell him I said so, so he'll know he ain't under suspicion with you. I'll tell Ringbone to tell him, too. Cripes! I ain't got nothin' to hold him on . . . Say, I got a hunch who it was threw that lead my way."

"T'hell you say. Goin' to gun him? Who is he?"

"Matt Everett — I think. No, I ain't figurin' to do anythin' yet. Give a man enough rope and he'll — well, he'll claim he burned himself."

149

"You're talkin' in circles, cowboy."

"I'll make it clear . . ." Duncan told of Everett's bandaged hand and of comparing the warning note to the paper on which Everett's letterheads were printed. He concluded, "They're both the same paper. Matt's headin' had been tore off, is all."

"That ain't exact proof, but it does look as if your shot scratched his hand. And then, the paper the note was made up on —"

"It ain't exact proof. That's why I'm lettin' things ride for a spell. Maybe Matt did burn his hand on a rope. Maybe somebody stole a sheet of his paper, just as I did. Here's somethin' else. Yesterday, I found an exploded forty-five shell back of the store. It's got a queer firin'-pin mark. I showed it to Matt. He denied ever seein' one like it, but I know he lied. It shocked him plenty. In fact, he had to lock up, right off, and run down to tell Wheeler about it."

"Queer firin'-pin mark. You don't mean rim-fire — ?"

"Here, take a look at it for yourself."

They were crossing Main Street when Duncan handed the shell to the deputy-sheriff. Yocum stopped short, swore under his breath. "Damn, this is queer. I don't know of any gun that leaves this kind of imprint. This is sort of triangular shape. Colt's is round and blunt, and so is —"

"It's a new one on me. I got a hunch the

150

gun that fired this shell is the one that killed Vink."

"A feller should never disregard a hunch." Yocum looked thoughtful. "I got an idea."

"That's surprisin'," Duncan smiled. "Let's have it."

"You know," Yocum went on, "we've got an ordinance in this town against totin' six-shooters. A man's supposed to deposit his gun, some place, as soon as he hits town. We've never enforced that ordinance, because we've never had any trouble. But, suppose I put it into effect for a spell, and I'll look over the deposited guns —"

"No good." Rance shook his head. "No murderer is goin' to be fool enough to pack a gun into Morada, now — not the gun he killed with."

"Reckon you're right, at that." The deputy looked disappointed. "Howsomever, we can keep our eyes peeled for such a gun. Say, why don't you ask Ernie Burks about it? He's been repairin' guns a long time now and —"

"That's what I was goin' to suggest when I asked you to take a walk. I figure Ernie will know if any man in town does."

A few minutes later they entered Burks' Gun Repair Shop, which was located in a small adobe building bearing a sign over the door. Guns of all calibres and shapes were to be seen about the small room. Burks, a lean, grizzled man, was found bent over a vise, filing a piece of gun mechanism.

He glanced up over his glasses as the two deputies entered, and wiped a smear of oil from the end of his nose. "Howdy, boys."

Without comment, Rance handed him the cartridge shell. Burks looked it over a moment, then straightened suddenly and carried it nearer a window. "Hmm," he grunted at length.

"Ever see one like it before?" Duncan asked.

"Ain't seen one in a good many years."

"But you've seen 'em, eh?"

"Some," Burks admitted. He studied the shell a moment longer, then handed it back to Rance. "Yes, quite a few — a long, long time back."

"What make of gun has that sort of hammer?"

"The make don't count," Burks commenced. "Colt's was quite frequent —"

"You're crazy, Ernie!" Yocum bust out.

"That ain't no way to talk to your elders, Homer," Burks stated severely. "If you'll let me explain —"

Duncan said, "Keep your trap shut, Homer. I don't understand it myself, but if Ernie says a single-action Colt's has this sort of hammer, I'm open to conviction."

"The hammer that exploded this shell," Burks explained, "was a Stebbings hammer. For a good many years now you fellers and a

152

lot of others have carried only five loads in your Colt cylinders, with your hammer on an exploded shell or empty chamber. That's for safety purposes, of course, in case your hammer should get knocked. You pack a six-shooter, but you only load it to five cartridges. Am I right?"

"C'rect as hell," Rance nodded.

"All right. For a long spell folks experimented around, tryin' to fix their six-shooters so they could load all six chambers and still not have the hammer restin' on a primer. One feller got up a pretty good idea by cuttin' an extra bolt notch in his cylinder. That worked, of course. However, Stebbings — Coteau Gene Stebbings, he was known by — devised a neater scheme. He filed his firin'-pin to a sort of V-shape, so it could come down and wedge between two ca'tridge rims —"

"By Cripes!" Yocum exclaimed. "That's an idea." He yanked out his Colt's forty-five and studied cylinder and hammer for several moments. "Well, what do you think of that? Plumb simple."

"Stebbings got a lot of praise for his idea," Burks nodded, "consequently there was a heap of gun toters altered their hammers so they could load cylinders to capacity. The only ones that objected to it was them that done a heap of shootin'. They claimed the firin'-pin wore down too quick. Some

153

adopted the idea and carried spare hammers. Anyway, for a man that ain't burnin' powder all the time, it's a right idea."

"This Stebbings had a head on him," Rance nodded.

Burks said, "That's the first time I ever hear of a shell like that in this country. Who owns the gun?"

Rance shrugged his shoulders. "I found the shell — some time back. Been carryin' it. Got curious. Figured you'd know about it if anybody did."

"Up North," Burks went on, "particularly in the Dakotas, there was quite a few usin' Stebbings' idea at one time. The idea spread around, of course, but like I say, I ain't heard of one in years, now."

"Where's Stebbings now?" Duncan asked.

"Haven't the least idea," Burks replied, "but wherever he is, he's tellin' folks the square facts where guns are concerned. Last I heard he was operatin' the Flyin'-Horseshoe, up in the Dakotas some place."

"Well, much obliged," Rance said.

"Don't mention it."

On the street a few minutes later Yocum said, "What now, do we get on the trail of this Stebbings?"

"I don't reckon," Rance smiled. "Don't forget, Burks told us there were quite a few guns altered to make a Stebbings hammer. But we've got to find the gun, if possible, that fired this shell. One thing I figure is, if alterin' a firin'-pin in such fashion was done years ago, the killer might be about Vink's age."

"You figure that clears Oldfield and Gillett? They're a heap younger."

"I didn't say that. I said the killer *might* be about Vink's age. Or he might have got the gun from a man Vink's age. Anyway, from Vink's time. Oh, hell, Homer, I hardly know where to start next."

"I'm on the same range, waitin' for you to give me a lead. I just happened to think that Stinson, Wheeler and Everett are about Vink's age."

"That don't prove a thing. As a matter of fact, Brad and Matt come to the Crazy River country with Vink. Stinson came in a short time later. Well, we'll have to think it over a spell."

"What you goin' to do now?"

"I'm up against a blank wall. Some time to-day I should go out to the ranch — or to-night. First, though, I want to go down to the undertaker's and see what arrangements have been made. I don't want any more than necessary left to Eddie — and I can't trust Quillan to do the right thing."

"A feller in love," Yocum observed philosophically, "ain't capable of straight thinkin', so don't blame Monte too much. Love's like the Grand Canyon — fine to think about, but I'd hate to fall in. . . . Well, I'm goin' over to the hotel porch and sit a spell. I hear a lot of things just sittin'."

He moved across the street in a leisurely slouch. Duncan stood looking after him. His lips barely moved, "A feller in love," he repeated Yocum's words, "ain't capable of straight thinkin'." A wistful smile crinkled his features. "Homer, you sure called the turn. . . ."

CHAPTER XII

Big Vink Thorpe was laid to his last rest the day following the inquest. Residents of the country for miles around came into Morada to attend the funeral. With that matter over and settled, Rance concentrated in an effort to dig up clues.

The next several days he spent in saddle from early morning until late at night. Rance hadn't forgotten that Vink Thorpe had shot at a rustler the day of his death. With this in mind, Rance scoured the range in all directions from the VIT ranch-house in the hope of uncovering some clue as to the rustler's identity. With something of the kind established, he'd have a point from which to commence.

He came jogging into the VIT ranch-yard one night a couple of hours after supper. Horse and man were dog-tired. Ringbone Uhler, Rance's *segundo* at the ranch, met him at the saddlers' corral. Uhler was a lean veteran of many cow-trails, with eyes narrowed from perpetually squinting against the South-Western sun, and skin the color and consistency of rawhide.

"You know, Rance," Uhler's voice complained through the darkness, "you're wearin'

157

yourself out — and your hawsses, too. You ought to go a mite easy. Rome wa'n't built in a day, as the Bible tells us. This chasin' all over the hemisphere ain't goin' to —"

"Sometimes, Ringbone," Rance said wearily, "I'm inclined to agree with you. But if I could only find just one small clue to start from —" He left the sentence unfinished and stepped down from the saddle.

"I'll strip your rig off, and put up the hawss," Ringbone said. "You go over and get your supper. Cookie's keepin' it warm."

Rance laughed tiredly. "A cook that'll hold supper. He's priceless, Ringbone."

"You'd see, if you were here days, that all the boys are workin' hard. They're tryin' to show you, Rance that they're with you to the last ditch, even if you aren't here every minute." He loosened Duncan's saddle cinch. A minute later and he had lifted off saddle, blanket and bridle.

"Reckon a lot of credit is due you, Ringbone," Rance spoke quietly, "for keepin' things runnin'."

"Huh!" Ringbone snorted. "Me, I'm just a brokedown wrangler that's got sense enough to carry out your orders. You're the boss — by the way, Eddie's asked for you a couple times."

"I'll eat supper, then see what she wants." Rance hesitated, then, "Quillan been here to-day?"

Ringbone opened the corral gate, struck the pony a resounding whack on the rump, and closed the gate before answering, "Yeah, he was here. Been here ever' day an' almost ever' night. Sure is ridin' close herd on Eddie."

"You don't take to Quillan, do you?"

"Who, me? Well, now, I wouldn't go to say I disliked him. Good enough cowman, I reckon," grudgingly. "But I do get all-fired sick of them fancy togs. Always a-wearin' scarlet neckerchiefs, sometimes it's green or yeller. And *fancy* shirts. An' them *bat-wings* he sports. What's the sense of 'em? All right in brush country, or when a feller's workin', but why in hell he should pull on leather pants for a ride under the hot sun, beats me — had on a white sombrero to-day too. Biggest hat I ever see. *White,* mind you. I asked him why he didn't buy a tent. Reminded me of a circus rider —"

"What'd he say?" Rance grinned wearily through the gloom.

"Told me what he wore was his own business. I answers him that he mingled business and pleasure, looked like. *Paugh!*" Ringbone spat a long brown stream of disgust. "Oh, well, everyone to his own taste, as the old woman said when she kissed the cow. But why Monte Quillan thinks he was born to golden raiment like the Bible says —"

"I don't remember that quotation."

159

"Me, neither," Ringbone confessed cheerfully. "That's just a habit of mine to credit everythin' from hell and high water down to stock prices, to the Bible — say, Eddie wouldn't accept that pinto hawss from Quillan. I heard 'em talkin' about it. Eddie allowed as how she already had enough hawsses."

"Reckon she has," Rance answered quietly. "It was a right pretty horse, at that."

"Pretty, yes, but shucks, I never yet saw a pinto that was wuth a hoot in hell for work purposes. Me, I wouldn't own one."

"Reckon you're right. Anythin' new?"

"Not much. Oldfield left to-day. Dickered for more cows than I expected, but he didn't kick none on your demands. Eddie and me took care of the papers —"

"I'll get the details later. Anythin' else?"

"Oldfield left his address with me in case you ever want to get him — say, here's somethin' that looks sort of funny. I sent Tommy in for the mail to-day. He came back with word that Everett and Wheeler has took to packin' their hardware. Them coots ain't thrun down on anythin' for ten year, I'll bet. What do you make of it?"

Rance's eyes narrowed. "It does look queer. I don't think I ever saw either of 'em pack a gun before. Well, there's just one conclusion to come to. When a man starts strappin' on his gun, he's expectin' trouble."

"That's the way it looks to me. But where them two expectin' —"

"That," Rance cut in, "is somethin' that will prob-bly show up one of these days. . . . I'm goin' to get my supper."

"Run along. I'll take your rig to the bunk-house."

Rance strode off through the night, beckoned by the cheery yellow light that shone from the mess house. On his way he passed the bunkhouse and called a greeting to the six cowhands inside.

After washing up he ate his supper in a silence that was broken only now and then by growled reproofs from the ranch cook relative to "hombres that can't never get to meals on time." But knowing such complaints constituted a prerogative of all cow camp cooks, Rance didn't deign to answer.

Supper finished, Rance made his way across the ranch-yard to the house, a rambling one-storied structure of rock and adobe, with 'dobe plastered outer walls.

Eddie answered his knock at the door. "Rance! It's about time you called on me."

"Been right busy, Eddie — though I've accomplished nothin'."

"Come in. Ringbone tells me you're doing your best to wear out your string."

"Been travellin' some," he admitted, "but I get no place."

The girl gestured toward a big chair across

the table from her own. The living-room was wide and spacious with several black and gray Navajo rugs spread on the plank floor. Both chairs faced a fireplace of native stone now crackling cheerfully with mesquite knots. A deer head was mounted at one end of the room, a buffalo head at the opposite end. On the table between the man and girl was spread a white Angora pelt. Two or three books and newspapers were placed around a large oil lamp.

Rance took out his sack of Durham and brown papers, rolled a cigarette and felt for a match. His pocket was empty. He had started for the fireplace when Eddie lifted her voice, "Coseffa! The Senor Duncan wants some matches. *Rapidez!*"

Rance resumed his chair as the clatter of dishes being washed in the kitchen ceased abruptly. A moment later a stolid-faced Mexican woman waddled into the room, deposited a handful of matches on the table at Duncan's left, and took her departure.

Duncan lighted his cigarette, glanced across the table to Eddie. "Everythin' goin' all right? Gettin' back on your feet again?"

"As well as I can expect, Rance. You know, a feller doesn't recover from a shock like that in a hurry. I'm all through with tears, though."

"Plannin' on doin' anythin' special?"

"Nothing much for me to do, except stay here and let you run the outfit. From the

162

point — well, I have my choice of getting married, or growing into a sour old maid."

"Which last is out," Duncan smiled. He added carelessly, "When's your weddin' take place?"

"I haven't decided that — yet." She looked quickly at Rance, then added, "You don't like Monte Quillan, do you?"

Duncan evaded her glance. "Can't say I dislike him, kid."

There was a moment's silence between the two. Eddie said, "That's something else, Rance. Don't you think I've outgrown being a kid?"

Rance smiled gravely. She'd been a kid to him for five years now. Scrutinising her sober features it suddenly occurred to him that she had grown up — especially since Thorpe's death.

"Reckon you're right, Eddie. I plumb forgot you were sole owner of the VIT and a grown lady —"

"Rance Duncan. A body'd almost think you were made of wood. You don't see a thing. Don't you like this dress? I made it myself. Monte noticed it to-day right off."

"Monte would," Rance said jealously. The dress was a dark blue creation of some light material. Rance admitted to himself it suited Eddie from top to toe. "You see, Eddie," he smiled at last, "it's not your clothes I look at. It's you — your hair and your eyes and your lips" — he laughed softly — "mostly your hair. I like red hair."

"If you were up-to-date, Rance, you'd call it auburn."

"A man doesn't have to be up-to-date to appreciate it."

"Oh, thank you, Mister Duncan, is that meant for a compliment?"

Rance felt his face crimsoning. "Reckon it is, Eddie. I sort of forgot Monte Quillan took care of that business —"

"Rance!"

He said weakly, "Yes'm?"

"Oh, never mind," impatiently.

Rance frowned. Now, what was wrong? He steered the conversation to safer channels. "You figurin' to stay on here, Eddie, with just Coseffa for company?"

"For a time, anyway. Why?"

"Sort of seems like you ought to have a woman here — I mean a woman who could be a friend — well, more of a companion."

"I'll have to think that over first. Coseffa is all I need, though, really."

"Uh-huh, you know best. . . . Say, Ringbone said you wanted to see me."

"Did he tell you I rode into town yesterday?"

"No, what for?"

"I wanted to talk to Judge Alvord, see if he could throw any light on Dad's sudden decision to make a will. You know, Dad always talked such things over with me. But that's once he didn't."

Rance nodded. "That's somethin' I'd like to know myself. What did Alvord have to offer?"

"The judge hadn't the slightest notion to explain Dad's sudden decision. He only knew that Dad said he wanted a will drawn, right away — one that couldn't be broken."

"Shucks! You'll get all of Vink's property, anyway, won't you?"

"Yes, now — that is, as soon as the estate is probated. Judge Alvord is taking care of that for me, up at Capitol City. He's seen to it that I have enough money to operate on, until everything is settled."

"There's nothin' to worry you, then."

"Just the same, I wish Dad had left that will, before he died."

"What difference does it make, so long as —"

"Just this, Rance. You see, Dad told Judge Alvord that he intended to leave you one-eighth of his estate. I was to have the remainder —"

"Me? Me?" Rance's mouth fell open. He half-rose from his chair, then dropped back. "Well, of all the —"

"Watch your blood pressure, Rance," Eddie laughed softly. "I've known for a long time he intended to do something for you some day. He figured to keep you here as long as he lived — and afterward. You've worked hard for the VIT. Dad thought a heap of you, Rance. You deserve something of the kind —"

"You're crazy, kid."

"Thought we agreed to forget that *kid?*"

"All right, you're just crazy, then. Now, look here, Eddie —"

"Rance, I don't want any objections, but just the minute things are settled in my name, I'm going to make an eighth of the estate over to you."

"I refuse to take it. I never heard of anythin' so — why, Eddie, it don't make sense. Vink paid me good wages —"

"If it's Dad's wish, Rance, you can't refuse," the girl said quietly. "If it was something he really wanted you to have? Aw, Rance, don't make things too hard for me. I'm only trying to carry out Dad's wishes —"

"Just the same," Rance growled, "I ain't a-goin' to —"

"We'll talk about that later," Eddie said firmly. "Come on, Rance, try and be a little cheerful. I've seen you scarcely five minutes the past week."

Rance shot his cigarette butt into the fireplace. He grinned, "What do you want me to do, tell you jokes?"

"You know that's not what I mean, Rance."

"Sure, Eddie, I was only ribbin' you." His grin widened. "I just happened to think of somethin'. You say Vink intended to leave me one-eighth of his estate. Roughly speakin', estate means belongin's — ?" He hesitated, chuckling.

"Yes, Rance."

166

"Well, now," Rance eyed the ceiling and rubbed his chin. "Would a daughter," he asked gravely, "come under the headin' of possessions?"

Eddie laughed. "Good grief, Rance Duncan! You proposing to me?"

He eyed the girl steadily. "For two cents I would *marry* you and cut out Monte Quillan."

Eddie's blue eyes danced. "You're not putting a very high value on me — but go ahead, I dare you."

Rance laughed abruptly. "What? An old gaffer like me marry a girl that's still in her teens?"

"Old gaffer!" Eddie said scornfully. "If you're thirty, I'll eat my Stet hat."

"Better make it an old hat, then, Eddie —"

Duncan sobered suddenly, noticing a letter on the table. The address side was up where he could read it plainly. Although addressed to "Edith Thorpe," it was the same handwriting he'd seen on the letter which had so upset Thorpe that day on Lookout Ridge.

"Eddie!" Rance exclaimed. "Who's that letter from?"

"My golly, don't scare a person to death. What's wrong? Do you have to be dramatic about it?"

"Reckon I do," he nodded. "Who's it from?"

"I was going to speak to you about it,

167

Rance. The VIT is scheduled to entertain a visitor."

"Who is he?"

"It's a she. Rance, did you ever hear Dad speak of anyone named Belle Thorpe?"

Rance looked thoughtful. "Can't say I did. Relation, I suppose."

"So she says. I've never heard of her. However, Dad's family was a large one. She may be some misplaced aunt or cousin, or something. To tell the truth, I don't like the tone of her letter, but I don't suppose I can do anything about it, if she chooses to pay me a visit. Here, read it for yourself."

The girl tossed the envelope across the table. Duncan drew out the single sheet of paper, and opened it.

"Dear Miss Thorpe," he read below the date line, *"I was planning to visit your dear father when I read in the papers about his death. Vink and me have always thought a lot of each other, but we have not seen each other for years, even if we are close related. I guess things must be settled by this time, so I will leave here the morning of the 9th. I expect you to meet me at the stage in Morada.*
Your affectionate relation,
Belle Thorpe."

Rance slowly refolded the letter, thrust it back into the envelope and sat gazing off into space.

Eddie said testily, "She's blunt, if nothing else. Takes it for granted I want company. 'Your affectionate relation' my eye! How can she be affectionate when she's never seen me? Good gosh, why do people have to force their way — ?"

"You better let me meet her," Rance said, somewhat grimly. "If she don't look so good, I can head her off —"

"We can't do that, Rance. I wouldn't want to turn down any of Dad's relatives. But I don't like the sound of her letter. I'll bet she's some cantankerous old maid that will boss me around. Good grief!"

"What's the matter now?"

Eddie looked frightened. "I just happened to think that she might want to make her home with me. Wouldn't that be awful? Golly, I'll bet she'll want to chaperone me when Monte calls."

"Mebbe I'm goin' to like Belle after all," Rance drawled. "No foolin', though, Eddie; I don't like this woman no more than you do. You better let me meet her and send her back."

Eddie shook her head. "No, we'll have to face the music, Rance. She's leaving on the morning of the 9th. Her letter doesn't give her address, but it's postmarked at Capitol City. The 9th is to-morrow. She'll be on the noon stage. But I don't want to meet her. Rance, it's up to you. Maybe, if the road's rough enough, you can tame her down by the time she arrives here. Golly, I'm almost afraid to have her come. I don't know why I should feel that way either — Rance, you looked startled when you first saw that letter."

"Reckon maybe I did," Rance said slowly. "You see, Eddie, Vink received a letter in this same handwritin' the day he was — the day he died. That was the letter mentioned in connection with Brad Wheeler. You heard about the inquest —"

"Dad did?" Eddie's eyes widened. "How do you know? I wasn't at the inquest, Rance. I didn't even want to hear about it —"

"I gave Vink the mail that day on Lookout Ridge. I remembered that letter, because I could see it upset Vink plenty. He dropped the envelope. I picked it up. I didn't mention it at the inquiry. Wheeler saw the letter. Vink showed it to him — say, I wonder just what Brad Wheeler might know about Belle Thorpe?"

"Are you sure, Rance? Have you the envelope now?"

"It's in my pocket." Rance produced the envelope. Heads together they compared the two envelopes. Finally Eddie looked up. "It's the same writing, Rance." There was a wail in her voice. "Golly, Rance, what will I do?"

"I don't know, Eddie," Rance said soberly. "But don't you worry. Maybe there's nothin' to worry about. It's a cinch Vink didn't take to what was said in that other letter, but that may be nothin' against this Belle woman." He scrutinized the postmark on the envelope addressed to Vink Thorpe. "I never could make out this blurred postmark. Looks like it was El Paso — then again it might be El Toro. Reckon it doesn't make much difference, though."

"The letter to me says she planned to visit Dad. Maybe that's what her letter to him was about."

"Judging from the way Vink acted, I'd say he didn't experience no pleasure in the idea." He folded the envelope and placed it back in his pocket.

Eddie tossed the letter and other envelope across to him with a grimace of distaste. "Keep this letter with your envelope, Rance. For some reason I can't bear the sight of it. Gee golly gosh darn it! I feel there's trouble ahead."

"Look here, Eddie," Rance said earnestly, "there's no use worryin' until we see what happens. Maybe everythin' will be all right. Shucks! There ain't nothin' to get fussed about, just because a relation's goin' to visit you. Maybe you'll like her. For all we know, Vink liked her. Maybe she just sent him some bad news that riled him. Now, just let matters ride for the time bein'."

Eddie remained silent. Rance rolled and

lighted another cigarette. Eddie said at last, "You haven't been able to uncover a single clue, have you, Rance — that is, anything definite?"

"I've got leads," Rance replied, "but I can't seem to get any place with 'em."

"I was just wondering," Eddie said, "if there were any strangers in town the day Dad was killed. I mean, somebody who might have come in on the night stage, and left for Breenville on the stage the next noon."

"I'm ahead of you on that one. There were two drummers stopped in town overnight. They were soliciting orders for hardware and liquor. Homer Yocum and I both checked into 'em. Also, I compared their handwritin' in the hotel register, with the writin' on the envelope. The writin' wasn't the same at all. Those two are beyond suspicion, I think."

Eddie sighed. "Just another blank wall, eh, Rance?"

"Just another blank wall," he nodded.

He blew the ash from his cigarette and prepared to leave. "Gettin' late. You better trot off to bed, Eddie. I'll leave early in the mornin', with the buckboard, so's to be in Morada when the stage rolls in."

"That's somethin' I wish didn't have to happen. At least, though, I'll know where you are. When you're away, like you've been the last few days, I don't know what to think."

"Why think, then?" he said carelessly, getting to his feet.

Eddie rose, too. "Don't you think I worry?"

"Any reason why you should?"

"Yes, there is," Eddie stated definitely. "You didn't tell me, Rance, but I heard in town, yesterday, that somebody shot at you the night before the inquest. Why didn't you tell me?"

"Haven't had much chance to talk to you," he evaded. "Not until to-night. To-night, I — well, I just forgot it."

"Why didn't you tell me?" the girl persisted, holding his grey eyes with her own blue ones. She was standing close to him.

"Shucks!" he lied, looking away. "There wasn't anythin' to tell. It was just somebody shootin' wild —"

"You're a right poor liar, Rance Duncan. I suppose when you ran through the alley back of the Morada House, after this man, you were shooting wild, too?"

Rance chuckled. "Got the whole story, eh?"

"A thing like that isn't kept quiet, Rance. You've got to be careful —"

Rance said, "Any particular reason I should?"

The girl looked away. Duncan's arms raised a trifle, then fell. He made his voice hard, "You're tired, kid. You run along to bed. Don't worry none about me. I'll take care of myself and Monte Quillan'll be lookin' out for you —"

"Oh, Monte Quillan!" she flamed so suddenly that he drew back. "Certainly he will if I want him to. But, Rance Duncan, do you think your safety means nothing? You're running risks for me and the VIT. After all, you were closer to Dad than Monte ever was. . . . Good-night!"

And with that, she whirled and walked swiftly out of the room.

"Good-night," Rance called awkwardly.

There was no answer. "Now, what in time have I done?" he asked himself, shaking his head. He caught the sound of murmured voices from the back of the house. A few minutes later, the Mexican woman came waddling in. "I'll gon lock door, now — no?" she said stolidly.

"Reckon it's about time, Coseffa," Rance nodded. He opened the door and stepped outside. *Adios.*

"*Buenos noches,* Senor Duncan."

For some time after Rance had rolled into blankets in his bunk, he lay wondering why Coseffa had had such a reproachful glance in her dark eyes. Finally he gave it up. His thoughts turned to other channels. Thorpe's desire to leave him an eighth of the estate. A lump entered Rance's throat when he thought of that. Suddenly he sat bolt upright in the dark.

From the other bunks came a varied assortment of snores, but Rance wasn't noticing that. Something else gripped his mind: Thorpe's death had prevented the drawing of the will that would have left one-eighth of all he owned to Rance Duncan.

"I wonder," Rance asked himself, "if Vink was killed to stop him makin' a will? Who could have known his intentions? . . . I wonder . . ." Finally, he stretched out again. "No, I don't reckon that had anythin' to do with it."

And with the coming of that decision sleep also came. . . .

CHAPTER XIII

Ringbone Uhler stopped the buckboard as Duncan was driving out of the ranch-yard the following morning. Duncan pulled the horses to a halt.

"Why the buckboard?" Ringbone asked.

"The VIT is due to have a guest," Duncan told him. "I got to meet the stage at Morada."

"Sho', now, who's comin'?"

"Relative of Vink's. Eddie had a letter yesterday."

"Huh? I don't remember as I ever heard Vink mention any relatives. What is it — a he or a she?"

"Woman. Eddie's never heard of her either."

"Female, eh? Shorthorn, I reckon."

"Don't know whether she's a tenderfoot or not, Ringbone. I kind of reckon to marry her to you, if she gets under foot too much. Wasn't it old Ben Franklin that stated, 'After three days, fish and visitors stink'?"

"Seems like that quotation's in the Bible," Ringbone answered seriously. "Well, I'll look her over. If she's got good points and is gaited, I may take her off Eddie's hands."

Rance chuckled. "Yes, you would — not. Still, I'd like an excuse to throw rice and old shoes at you, Ringbone — mostly old shoes. . . . By the way, I was lookin' over that chuck wagon this mornin'. Looks like it could use some new tires on those wheels."

"I never noticed that. Reckon that's why you're foreman of this outfit, 'stead of me. I'll get Red busy in the blacksmith shop right pronto. Beef round-up will be here before we know it."

"I ain't criticisin', Ringbone. I know you got your hands full as it is. Well, I'll be slopin' along."

Gripping the reins, Rance spoke to the horses, and the buckboard went rolling out of the yard on the road to Morada. . . .

The west and south-bound stage from Capitol City on its way to Breenville was due to reach Morada at twelve o'clock noon. It wasn't quite eleven-thirty when Duncan tooled the team down Main Street and drew up at the Morada House corner, the regular station for the stage, where tired horses were exchanged for fresh animals, and travellers alighted, or ascended into the coach. Rance jumped down to the road and tied the team at the hitchrack.

Deputy Homer Yocum called from the Morada House porch, "What's the matter, Rance, gettin' too old to hairpin a bronc?"

" 'Mornin', Goober Face," Rance laughed. He clumped up the steps to the shaded porch, and dropped into a chair beside the deputy. Matt Everett and Brad Wheeler were seated a few feet away from the deputy and Rance. Rance spoke to them as he took his seat, and noticed that both were wearing guns.

Yocum said, through a mouthful of peanuts, "What's the idea in the buckboard, Rance? Gettin' in supplies?"

"The VIT is expectin' a visitor on the noon stage. I got to drive her out."

"Her? Female?"

"Some relation of Vink's. Eddie never heard of her."

Wheeler and Everett straightened in their chairs. Wheeler was rubbing the side of his nose with a vigorous forefinger. "What's that you said, Rance," he leaned forward, "female relative of Vink's goin' to visit Eddie?"

"Yes, why?"

"Just wonderin'." Wheeler settled back in his chair, trying to assume an expression of unconcern, an act in which he wasn't wholly successful. He and Everett exchanged quick glances.

After a time, Yocum said, low-voiced, "Did you notice them two was wearin' their guns, Rance?"

Rance nodded. "They must be expectin' trouble of some sort. Hear anythin' new?"

"Not a damn thing. I did get a look at their guns. They're reg'lar hammers. You heard anythin'?"

"Nothin' that counts." Rance paused, then,

"I'm sort of wonderin' who this female relative is."

He was suddenly aware that Everett was talking louder than usual: ". . . it'll r-r-raise hell, Brad," the man was saying.

Wheeler said something in an undertone. Everett quieted down.

Duncan asked quietly, "What'll raise hell, Matt?"

Everett grew red. Wheeler cut in, "A drop in stock prices. It would ruin trade from coast to coast."

Rance laughed softly, scornfully. He hadn't been deceived by the reply. He rose, walked over and stood before Everett. "How's your hand gettin' along, Matt? I note you've removed the bandage."

Everett raised his hand for a momentary inspection, then thrust it out of sight. "All r-r-right," he mumbled.

"Is it?" Duncan smiled. He caught at Everett's sleeve. "Let me see that burn a minute, Matt."

Reluctantly Everett allowed Rance to inspect the healing scar. Rance tried to make Everett meet his eyes, but determinedly the man kept his gaze glued to the wound. More than ever now Rance was convinced the angry red mark had been made by a bullet and not by a rope.

"That was a bad burn, all right, Matt," Rance said softly. "You ought to be more

179

careful handlin' *ropes*. You might get hurt serious sometime."

Everett jerked the hand out of sight. "N-N-Never mind me, Rance. You take care of yourself —"

"I always have," Rance smiled agreeably.

He turned away, looked at his watch, which said eleven forty-five. "I'm goin' to drift over to the store," he told Yocum.

Descending the porch steps, he crossed the street and entered the store to find Alonzo Wheeler behind the counter.

"Hello, 'Lonzo. I got orders to bring Cookie a sack of flour and ten pounds of Arbuckle's. Want a couple of sacks of Durham for myself, too. . . . Where's Clem, gone to his dinner?"

"Left about five minutes back," young Wheeler nodded. "Say, Rance, could you fix it for me to get a full-time job here in the store?"

"Don't see's that's necessary, 'Lonzo. You'll have to be satisfied with fillin' in such time as Clem's off duty."

The boy's face fell. "Shucks! I won't never get enough money saved to go to New York. Day and a half a week and spellin' Clem at meal times don't bring me no real money. And now Clem's figurin' not to go up to Capitol City no more, since you've quit sendin' the money. He says Sundays off is enough. I need the money, too. I just finished writin' a play last night, and if I could get to New York —"

"What? Another play?"

Young Wheeler nodded. "This is the best yet. I'm callin' it *Faro Fred's Fateful Flush, or The Mystery of the Poisoned Deck.* In the second act the villain —"

"Gosh, 'Lonzo, that sounds real interestin'," gravely. "Ain't nothin' happened lately, is there, that would give you the idea to write about playin' cards?"

"Yeah — that 'dead man's hand' sort of inspired my mind to it —"

"Your what?" incredulously.

"My mind. If I could get to New York, I just know I could sell this play. Might as not I'd be asked to trod the boars in it, too."

"I'll bet. You mean, trod the boards. You and Mr. Shakespeare?"

"That's right. The Board of Avon, they call him. He writes purty good plays, too. But he uses a lot of high-toned words folks don't care for, though. He ought to write something about the cow country, to be real pop'lar."

"You've read some of his works, eh, 'Lonzo?"

"Yeah, some. *The Merchant of Venison* was one I read. Then there was another — somethin' about eggs. Oh, yeah, it was called *Hamlet.*"

"Eggs? *Hamlet?*" Rance looked blank. Suddenly he said sternly, " 'Lonzo, you give me my flour and coffee — and the makin's. I got to be on hand when the stage arrives."

"Yessir, Rance." Startled into action by Rance's tone, Alonzo hurried to carry out the order. Duncan shoved the tobacco into his vest pockets, and carried flour and coffee across the road and deposited it in the buckboard.

At that moment somebody yelled, "Stage is comin'!"

By this time quite a crowd had gathered before the hotel. The stage arrival was a twice-daily event, attended by as many as could spare the time to be on hand. Fresh horses from the livery waited just around the corner.

The stage coach rolled up in a swirl of dust and jangling of harness equipment. A long "Who-o-oa-a!" from the driver, as he footed the brake, brought the panting, foam-flecked horses to a sliding halt. The guard laid his sawed-off shotgun across the seat and climbed down to stretch his legs. Driver and guard exchanged greetings with the crowd. A sack of mail was tossed from the top of the stage, and the driver followed it to the ground.

"Got a passenger for me, Zeke?" Rance asked the driver.

Zeke shifted his cud to the opposite cheek, eyed Duncan coldly, then squirted a thin brown stream. "I only got one passenger aboard. If she's yores, yore welcome to 'er."

The coach door banged open. A large,

flamboyant woman past middle age was just stepping down. Duncan caught an impression of sagging, rouged cheeks, artificial blonde hair, and hard black eyes. Her mouth was a thin, scarlet slash. Thirty years before she might have been a striking woman, but now in her dress of cerise silk and loud "picture hat" covered with cloth violets, all traces of a former beauty had vanished, leaving in its place a blatant harridan.

"Driver!" the woman shrilled. "There should be somebody here from the VIT Ranch to meet me."

"That, ma'am," the driver replied tersely, "ain't my problem."

Snickers of amusement ran through the crowd. The woman glared around. The amused ones suddenly sobered. Here was a vindictive woman if ever one existed.

Duncan stepped forward, hat in hand. "Reckon I'm who you're lookin' for, lady. You Miss Thorpe?"

"I'm Belle Thorpe." She looked at Rance with cold, hostile eyes. "Who're you?"

"Rance Duncan — foreman of the VIT."

"Why didn't Vink's girl come to meet me?"

"I came in her place, ma'am."

"I got eyes to see that. I asked a question."

Whether it was from choice, or whether he had been overcome by the reek of cheap perfume, Duncan didn't answer. He said firmly, "My buckboard's just a few steps from here, ma'am. I'll take you to it."

Belle Thorpe sniffed haughtily. "Lead the way, Duncan."

Duncan bowed and started toward the buckboard. Belle Thorpe walked awkwardly at his side, as though her feet, squeezed into high-heeled patent leather, were a source of extreme discomfort. Disdaining the offer of his hand, the woman climbed to the seat of the buckboard, unaided.

"That's my trunk a-top the stage," she ordered. "Don't go 'way without it."

Duncan's heart sank. A trunk! That meant a long stay in all likelihood. He kept the exasperation out of his voice, "I'll be back with it in a jiffy."

The driver of the stage was unlashing the trunk when Duncan returned.

"I'll take that trunk when you get it untied," Duncan said.

"Yo're damn right you will," the driver snapped, "and I don't never want to see it again. Such a trip as I've had. It was bad enough pickin' up a lamed off-wheeler at Aubrey, without hearin' complaints ever since we left the capitol, from that female Christmas tree. The road was too rough, the coach should have new cushions so she could nap comfortable. 'Bout every hour I had to stop and see if her goddam trunk is tied tight." He swore a lurid stream at a stubborn knot.

Rance cast a glance toward the hotel. He noticed that Matt Everett and Brad Wheeler

184

were standing in the office entrance, peering around the corner of the doorway in Belle Thorpe's direction. The expressions on their faces bespoke volumes of consternation.

Homer Yocum sidled up to Rance, "I was to a circus once before —" he commenced solemnly.

"Aw, go chew your peanuts," Rance growled.

Yocum said, "You got my sympathy on that ride to the VIT, Rance. Let's see, how many miles is it — ?"

Rance said glumly, "It'll seem like a thousand to-day."

"Say, Rance, why don't you drive that painted hen over Lookout Ridge? Like's not you'd spill the wagon and kill yourself, too, but it would be better than takin' *that* home to Eddie. Ain't she had enough trouble?"

"Too much," Rance grunted savagely. "And your remarks don't bring any relief to *me,* either —"

"There's your damn box," the stage driver panted from above. He gave the trunk a resentful shove. Duncan caught and lowered it to his shoulder. Luckily, it wasn't heavy. He made his way through the crowd to the accompaniment of many low-voiced suggestions regarding the best manner in which to handle the situation on the way to the VIT.

Yocum was walking along at Rance's side. "Take my advice, Rance," he said seriously, "and don't give in too easy. These honkytonk babes are apt to be a mite impetuous —"

"Homer," Rance snapped, "if I wasn't carryin' this trunk, I'd knock your face from under your hat."

"I'd feel the same way in your boots, Rance," Homer said serenely. He added fervently, "Thank Gawd I ain't in 'em." The deputy fell back as they neared the wagon.

Rance dropped the trunk to the buckboard, untied the horses and climbed up beside Belle Thorpe. Wheeling the team, he sent his whip cracking over the horses' heads. The wagon lurched into motion. Belle Thorpe seized the side of the seat with one hand, while the other, covered with cheap jewelry, flew up to save her big hat from the rush of wind. Behind him, Rance heard a faint cheer ascend. The muscles at the corners of his mouth tightened. Again he sent the whip-lash snapping through the air.

The buckboard had reached the outskirts of Morada before Rance realized it would do no good to kill the horses. Much as he hated the job, it was up to him to bring this creature safely to the VIT. It would be mighty tough on Eddie, but there seemed no way, short of murder, out of the difficulty. In time he straightened out the horses to an easier gait.

Belle Thorpe got her breath at last. She gazed resentfully at Rance's straight, grim profile. "Seems like," she said, "you might have asked me first, before jerkin' me out of town this way —"

"Figured you wanted to get to the ranch," Duncan grunted.

"Or you might have offered a lady a drink before we started —"

"I might have," and added under his breath, "a lady. Or would I?"

"What's that?" sharply.

"I said I wasn't in the habit of offerin' *ladies* drinks."

"Bet you go to church, too," sarcastically.

"I've been."

She drew a package of *Sweet Caporals* out of her cerise silk bosom, thrust one of the cigarettes between her lips. "Got a match?"

Duncan handed her four or five matches, drove on in silence, and was disappointed when she succeeded in igniting the tobacco in her first try. It required more than a strong breeze to prevent Belle Thorpe from lighting a cigarette.

Two miles were covered without a word being spoken between the two. Then Belle Thorpe said, "You don't act like I was welcome."

Rance grunted, "That's too bad."

"Now, look here, mister," bridling, "take my advice and be decent to me. When I get settled, you may keep your job and you may not. That depends —"

"— on Eddie," Rance finished.

187

"Eddie? Oh, Vink's girl, Edith. I read somethin' about her in the papers. The papers didn't say much about his death, just that he'd been murdered. Catch the man that done it?"

Rance shook his head. The woman wanted more details. Rance gave them briefly. An hour passed with the woman asking questions. Rance replied with a short "yes" or "no," some queries he ignored altogether. He kept his eyes straight ahead on the road, or on the panorama of sage, cactus and sand that bordered each side of the wagon-ruts.

"What's those hills ahead?" the woman asked suddenly.

"Santos Hills. If we were ridin' in the saddle, we could have cut over 'em and saved time — over Lookout Ridge. But a wagon has to cut around the lower end of 'em."

"Good Gawd! I thought we must be nearly there."

"Got close to two hours' ride yet."

The woman said, "Good Gawd!" twice more, and resigned herself to another cigarette. "If I'd known it was this far, I'd have bought me a bottle, s'help me I would."

Another hour drifted slowly past in a silence broken only by the dull, monotonous regularity of thudding hoofs. Now and then a wheel screeched shrilly as it skidded across a rock imbedded in the roadway, jostling the occupants of the buckboard, but eliciting no word from either.

188

The mesquite was growing taller now. To the right, as the trail circled wide to the south, were the low-lying swells of the Santos Hills, dotted with yucca. Ahead lay a clump of cottonwoods, dusty under the hot sun.

"Crazy River," Rance announced half to himself, and with some relief.

He tooled the horses through the shadows of the cottonwood trees. The wagon lurched as he directed the animals down the bank and into the shallow, gravel-bottomed stream. The river spread out at this point. The team stood knee-deep, drinking in great cooling draughts.

Ten minutes later, Rance picked up the reins, wheeled the horses up the bank again. Water dripped from the wheel-spokes and disappeared in the sand. They left the shade of the cottonwoods and emerged into brilliant sunlight again. The buckboard jolted and swayed until the wheels found the ruts of the trail. Then it went on at a faster pace.

Far ahead in the distance, the Sangre de Santos Range lifted rugged peaks to the sapphire blue sky. Overhead sailed a pair of buzzards, wheeling and dipping on motionless wings. Rance eyed the scavenger birds a moment and glanced toward the woman at his side. He twisted a brown-paper cigarette and lighted it.

The sun grew hotter. A warm breeze brought odors of sage mingled with alkali.

Wind devils quivered and whirled on the road ahead.

Perspiration commenced to streak the layer of fine gray dust that had settled on Belle Thorpe's flabby cheeks. Her rouge wasn't standing up under the ordeal. Rance looked at her once and couldn't suppress a grin. The woman saw him smile.

"That's right, mister, laugh," she snapped. "I just guess you ain't used to the society of ladies like me."

"Nope, I ain't," Rance answered frankly.

Belle Thorpe took that as a surrender to her charms, and tried to open a conversation. "What sort of girl is Vink's kid?"

"Darn nice," Rance replied. "Pretty, too. Got a good head on her."

"Ain't married, is she? The papers tellin' about Vink's death didn't say, but I figured she wasn't."

"No, she ain't married."

"If she's all you say, that's a surprise. Suppose half the country is courtin' her."

Rance said slowly, "It's pretty much settled down to one man."

"Who's he? Got any property?" Something mercenary in the tone.

"Monte Quillan — owns the 8Q-Barred-Out." He added a trifle viciously, "Maybe you could take him away from Eddie."

Belle Thorpe displayed a row of gold-filled yellow teeth. "Oh, I wouldn't do anything like that. I reckon, though, I'll have somethin' to say before she marries him. . . . How'd she feel about my visit?"

"Well," Rance drawled. "Eddie didn't express any enthusiasm in my presence."

"She better not get uppity with me." The words carried a hidden threat.

A hot retort rose to Rance's lips, but he checked it. "Well, you can't blame her," he reminded. "She'd never heard of you before."

"That ain't my fault. Vink never let me know where he was — 'course, maybe he couldn't be expected to, under the circumstances. I ain't seen him since I was a girl. Then one day I seen his name in the paper for attendin' a Cattlemen's Convention. It gave quite a piece about him. Said he was right wealthy. That right?"

"Reckon he was."

"It took me a mite of time to get around to it, but I finally wrote to him from El Paso I was comin' to see him. Didn't he get my letter?"

"Never told me about it, nor Eddie either."

"He should have told her. Wasn't my letter found among his papers, after he was killed?"

Rance shook his head. "Ain't heard of it." He wondered if he sensed a certain relief at his negative reply.

Belle Thorpe said, "Funny nobody found it. Anyway, before I could get packed, I saw in the El Paso papers where he'd been killed

— say, did he leave a will?"

"No," shortly. "Eddie'll get everythin' he left."

"Maybe there'll be somethin' for me, too."

"That's up to Eddie."

"I reckon," very emphatically, "she'll be reasonable."

Rance didn't like her tone. He felt his temper rising. Who in hell did this strumpet think she was, anyway? He gripped the reins together, guided the team around a bad chuckhole in the road, and said, "Eddie was wonderin' just what relation you are — aunt, or cousin, or what?"

"I'll explain things when I see the girl. I'm related to Vink through marriage."

That explained it to Rance. He wondered on which side of the family she claimed relationship. On second thought he realized it would be the Thorpe side, of course. Probably some Thorpe had married this old Belle — well, what ever her name was before she was married . . .

He said, "Your letter come as a surprise to Eddie."

"It wouldn't done no harm for her to come and meet me —"

"I can't see any reason for that. She'd never heard of you before. No use her makin' this trip for a stranger."

The woman looked shrewdly at Rance from her hard black eyes. "Like Vink's girl, don't you?"

"Sure. She's a darn nice kid. She's had a heap of sorrow —"

"I don't mean that way — not just 'like her.' You don't fool me, mister. You're gone on that girl."

Rance felt the color creeping into his cheeks. That was his secret. Damn this Belle Thorpe! To have her of all people uncover the thing closest to his heart. . . .

"This Quillan feller is too much for you, eh?" Belle Thorpe taunted. " 'Course, he's got his own outfit, and you only got foreman's wages. Listen, mister, you be decent to me and I'll fix you up. I'm li'ble to need friends. The time is comin' where Vink's girl will do as I tell her —"

Rance jerked the team to a savage stop. For a moment the woman thought he intended to strike her. When Rance's words came they were brittle hard, "I'm askin' you, Miss Thorpe — or Mrs. Thorpe, whatever your name is — to 'tend to your own affairs. I don't know why you've come here, but I'm tellin' you frank, I don't like it. You ain't here for no good, that's certain —"

"Look here, mister, you can't talk to a lady in that fashion —"

"Shut up!" Rance said savagely. "I'm not talkin' to a lady. You take my advice and move plumb circumspect. I don't aim to have Eddie harmed in any way — not in any way, understand!"

The woman cringed before his blazing eyes. Rance abruptly cooled off, felt a little ashamed of himself for employing such language to a woman. He gave his attention to the team. The buckboard rolled on.

Gradually color came back to Belle Thorpe's face. She lighted a cigarette, blew the smoke defiantly toward Rance. "You talk mighty high, mister," and her tones were threatening. "We'll see what your Eddie has to say about that, when I've talked to her."

Rance set his lips tightly, shook the horses to a faster pace. Belle Thorpe settled to a grim, menacing silence that was matched only by the scowl on Rance's tanned features. From then, until the VIT ranchhouse was reached, no word passed between the two.

The wagon rolled in a little after three o'clock that afternoon. Rance spied Eddie and Monte Quillan seated on the broad porch that fronted the house. Ringbone Uhler was also sitting there. Monte's horse was tied to one of the porch supports.

Rance wheeled the team to a stop before the porch, saw the amazed looks that came into the eyes of his audience. He jumped down from the vehicle, seized Belle Thorpe's trunk and slammed it fiercely up on the porch.

"Why, Rance — !" Eddie looked dumbfounded.

Belle Thorpe was out of the buckboard

now, and approaching Eddie. She raised her arms dramatically, "My poor child, how you must have suffered. You must be terrible broke up —"

Eddie retreated a step. "I'm not your poor child," she said stiffly. "I presume you are Belle Thorpe. I didn't know — father has never spoken of you — oh, I beg your pardon —" She introduced Quillan and Ringbone Uhler.

"I've heard about Mister Quillan," the woman was shaking Monte's hand with some vigor. "The foreman — this man that drove me — told me you was to be congratulated."

"Much obliged," Quillan said awkwardly. "Well, I got to be goin' now." He moved off the porch.

Belle Thorpe scarcely noticed Ringbone. She turned back to Eddie, "You got a room ready for me, miss?"

"That back bedroom on the right, Rance," Eddie said nervously. "Will you put Miss — er — Mrs. — will you put the trunk back there?"

"Surest thing you know," Rance nodded.

He picked up the trunk, carried it into the designated bedroom. When he returned to the porch, Monte Quillan was riding out to the road. Ringbone had disappeared. Belle Thorpe had dropped into a chair and was fanning herself with her handkerchief. Eddie was still standing, an expression of disbelief in her blue eyes.

195

Belle Thorpe said, "Well, my dear," and her tones commanded the situation, "you might show me where my room is."

"Of course." Eddie forced a feeble smile.

Rance said, "I'll take the buckboard down to the barn, Eddie. If you want anythin', sing out."

"I'll do that, Rance —"

Belle Thorpe's raucous tones cut in. "Eddie ain't goin' to want you for a while, Duncan. We got a lot to talk about."

Eddie looked at Rance, noted the angry red in his cheeks, and shook her head slightly. Rance nodded, climbed into the buckboard and drove around the corner of the house.

At the barn he was met by Ringbone Uhler. "You don't marry me to that," the *segundo* stated emphatically. "My Gawd! What is she, Rance?"

Rance shook his head. "A virago from hell, I reckon, though she claims relationship to Vink."

Ringbone looked uncertain. "We-ll, I never heard tell of that breed of animal before, but if this Belle Thorpe woman don't remind me of a burleycue queen from a show that I saw once in Kansas City, may I be strung up for a hawss-thief!"

"Ringbone," Rance said grimly, "you never did have horse-thief tendencies."

CHAPTER XIV

Four days passed in which Rance scarcely saw Eddie. An abrupt change had come over the girl. For some reason, uncomprehendible to Rance, she avoided him. When it became necessary to confer on ranch matters, Eddie sent Coseffa for Ringbone Uhler and imparted her information through the *segundo*. Rance felt hurt. After the first day of this condition, he again took to riding the range, his mind awhirl with speculation concerning the girl's changed attitude. There was little doubt in Rance's reasoning but that the change was in some way due to Belle Thorpe's presence at the ranch, but just how the woman had affected this was beyond Rance's comprehension.

It was shortly after noon of the fourth day that Rance rode into Morada. Nearing the deputy-sheriff's office he saw Homer Yocum tilted back in a chair against the front wall of the building. As usual, Homer was meditatively crunching peanuts.

Rance reined his mount over to the hitchrack and dismounted. Homer's chair came down on all four legs. "Long time no see you, *amigo*," the deputy greeted. "I was

197

commencin' to think that female Medusa had petrified you."

"Female who?"

"Medusa. A snake charmer I read about once. This Medusa was so plumb ugly, every hombre that looked at her got turned to stone."

"Mebbe that's what's happened to Eddie."

"Come and tell daddy about it." The deputy rose from his chair and led the way to a bench on the shady side of the building. "Cripes! Rance, if your face gets much longer you'll be steppin' on your chin."

Rance dropped down at the deputy's side. "There's a reason for that, too."

"You don't have to tell me. You look like you was ready to let down your hair and have a good cry."

"Homer, did you ever hit a woman?"

"Some women affect me that way, too. Did she yell much?"

"I caught myself in time."

Yocum said disappointedly, "You strong-willed men are always makin' mistakes. I been wonderin' how you and her got along on that trip to the VIT the other day."

Rance related the circumstances, ending with, "Now, I don't know what to think. Eddie's gone plumb haywire. If she wants anything, she gets it from Ringbone, instead of askin' me. I've only seen her twice since that damn woman arrived, and I could see she'd been crying. Her eyes were red as blazes. I asked her the first time if anything was wrong. She said, 'Nothing you can help,' and ran into the house, leavin' me standin' there with the back door slammed in my face. I've been leavin' Ringbone to run things day-times and stayin' away. Ringbone tells me he had to drive that she-hellion in town twice —"

"I saw 'em. Eddie on her horse, and Ringbone and the woman in the buckboard. Ringbone looked like he was escortin' a puma cat took violent with hydrophoby."

"This Belle Thorpe claims the ranch ain't lively enough to make it pleasant for her, but she insists on stayin'. . . . What did she do in town?"

"If you asked *who* did she do, it'd be more 'propriate. I sort of sashayed around on their trail. It looks to me like she was makin' Eddie escort her around, introducin' her as a 'dear' relative of Vink's."

"Dear relative hell!"

"Yes, ain't she? I was talkin' to Joe Myers. He says she and Eddie come into his Empor-ee-um and this Belle she-cat she bought a couple of new dresses, which same Eddie had to sign for. There was other things bought in other stores, too. Eddie signed to pay for all of it, near's I can learn."

"Damn robber!"

"Yes," Homer continued, "this town is sure conscious of her presence. She seems to be trying to get acquainted with everybody. But she won't get no invitations to tea from the women of Morada. She let drop a hint that she might join the Busy Bee Sewin' Circle, but I reckon everybody that could give an invitation was deaf. She wanted me to arrest old Lucas —"

"What in time for?"

"Claimed Clem sassed her when she criticised the store."

"Good for Clem."

Yocum nodded. "I bought him a drink on it last night. What do you think? — he took lemonade. Yep, I don't crave no truck with Belle Thorpe. One man's meat is another's poison, and I know *I* ain't her man."

"What did she say to you?"

"Told me the Thorpe store didn't carry nothin' a lady would buy. Wanted me to arrest Clem 'cause he told her to get her peppermint lozenges some place else when she claimed they weren't fresh." A funereal grin creased the deputy's solemn features. "I swore to her them peppermints was state inspected and that Clem was bonded by the Gov'ment. And that I couldn't arrest him without a warrant, which had to be got at Capitol City. Mebbe she knew I lied. Anyway, she shut up and went back for more peppermints later."

"What did Eddie have to say about it?"

"Eddie wasn't with her. She'd got tired

traipsin' around and was waitin' at the hotel until Belle got ready to start home. Belle, she flitted in and out of stores, on her lonesome, like —" Yocum groped for a simile, " — like a buffalo cow makin' a round of wallows."

"What else happened? You seemed to be trailin' Belle right close."

"She's the talk of the town. Yeah, I followed her around some. She stopped Ward Stinson on the street. Don't know where she made his acquaintance."

"Stinson made the VIT a neighborly call the evenin' she arrived. What'd she say to Ward?"

"That's what I asked Stinson. He told me none of my business. You know, he's short and grumpy sometimes. I heckled him some, and finally he admitted she had asked where she could find Brad Wheeler."

"What did she want with Brad?" Rance showed fresh interest.

"I dunno. I reckon Brad didn't want anythin' to do with her, 'cause I'd seen him duck out the bar exit of the hotel, when Belle first arrived, like the woman was smallpox infected. Well, Ward Stinson had seen Brad in the Cowmen's Rest Saloon, and he told Belle where her prey was. Belle flounces off to the Cowmen's Rest, sticks her head between the swingin' doors and calls Brad out."

"T'hell you say."

"You should have been in town, Rance. It was rich. Brad comes out, his face like the color of raw beef. They talked a few minutes, then Brad walked Belle, reluctant, down to the hotel. I followed along and see her and Brad sittin' on the porch. She had a glass in her hand, and it wasn't lemonade either. Brad looked like he was bein' tortured, or had ants in his pants, or somethin'."

Yocum crammed some peanuts into his mouth, chewed loudly, and went on, "Just then, who should come along Main Street but Mrs. Brad —"

"Good Lord!"

"You said it. You know how Brad is — scairt to death of his missus. Brad ain't weak-spined one bit, but he lacks man's judgment in negotiatin' the speaker sex. Brad got red and white by turns, like somebody turnin' the heat on and off. Missus Wheeler stops like she was shot when she sees them two sittin' on the porch. "Brad-lee!" she shrieks. "Who is that woman?""

"What'd Brad do?"

"What could he do? His knees was knockin' together when he came down the steps. He tried to quiet his missus, but Missus Brad was talkin' louder every second about men that neglect their family and business to go gallivantin' with strange females. That was too much even for Belle. She got up and hurried into the hotel. Brad tried to

202

explain that Belle was a relation to Vink, but Missus Brad wouldn't shush two-bits worth."

"I'm glad somebody put the kibosh on Belle."

"Me, too. I'd bought Missus Brad a drink, only she's Christian Temperance. While Brad was trying to explain things to his better seven-eights, Eddie come out of the hotel. She saw me and asked me to look up Ringbone Uhler and tell Ringbone they wanted to go home. Her chin was up, but there were tears in her eyes. Missus Brad had Brad laid out to a frazzle when I left to locate Ringbone, which same I accomplished in the Cowmen's Rest. When I come back, Missus Brad was flouncin' down the street with her nose in the air like she'd smelled a bad odor. Brad looked limp as a dishrag. That was the first day Ringbone drove in."

"What come off the second time?"

"It was a mite quieter," the deputy said disappointedly. "Brad lit out for home the minute Belle arrived in town, and wasn't seen until she'd left."

"Matt Everett talk to Belle?"

"Matt had sense enough to lock up his store and go to his boardin' house both times she was here. She didn't talk to him that I know of, but I'll bet she knows Matt if she knows Brad."

"It's sure a fine fix for Eddie. Wish I could do somethin' about it."

"Why don't you?"

"Eddie acts as if she wanted me to mind my own business."

"Maybe Monte Quillan will take a hand —"

"I've been hopin' he would. By the way, speaking of Quillan, this morning I roped one of his cows that had drifted on our range."

"Figured you'd get to the business that brought you in pretty soon."

Rance nodded. "This was a yearlin'. I only dropped in to look at the brand. It had caught my eye as I rode past. Careless job of brandin'."

"Stamp iron?"

"No. Probably a critter that had been missed at calfbrandin'. The brandin' had been done later with a runnin' iron. Now, I ain't saying that everythin' ain't all right, but that sloppy job of brandin' started me to thinkin'. As I remember it, I've heard that outfit used to be called the 8-Barred-Out."

Yocum nodded. "Up to six years ago, when Quillan bought the outfit from old Abe Ripley. Don't know where Quillan came from originally, but when he hit the Crazy River country he was well heeled with money — enough to buy the ranch, anyway — which, as I heard, had been left to him by some relative. Quillan just added his initial to the brand."

"Ever give it a thought how easy it would be to work over a VIT brand into an 8Q-Barred-Out? It would have to be done with a runnin' iron, of course."

Yocum's eyes opened wider. "You hintin' that Quillan is — well, enterprisin'?"

"Mebbe. Look here. The VIT brand is made with the three capital letters, set alongside each other. Quillan's is a figure 8 and a capital letter Q, with a bar runnin' through the upper part of the 8 and Q."

"I know that," impatiently, "but I don't see how the VIT could —"

"Look, I'll draw it."

Rance leaned forward from the bench, picked up a small stick of wood near his feet, and drew in the sandy earth a large VIT. "Now," he paused a moment, "it could be worked into an 8Q-Barred-Out in this fashion."

With quick deft strokes he added further lighter lines to his drawing, thus converting the Thorpe symbol into the Quillan brand. He glanced grimly at the deputy.

Yocum's eyes seemed glued to the drawing.

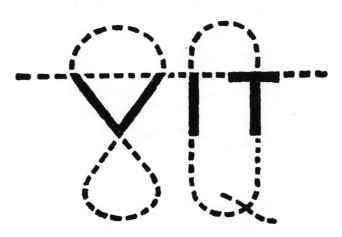

VIT brand converted into an 8Q-Barred-Out.

"Sufferin' rattlers!" the deputy exclaimed. "Rance, that's evidence — wait a minute! How about earmarks?"

"Earmarks dovetail, too," Rance said grimly. "It looks as if Quillan planned plumb through. The VIT splits the right and left ears." Again he drew a swift design in the sand, depicting the right and left ears of a cow.

VIT earmark: Split right and left.

Rance went on, "The 8Q-Barred-Out swallow-forks the left ear, and under-half-crops the right. All Quillan would have to do, after altering our brand, would be to cut off a little more ear on either side, completely disposin' of our ear-marks. Here, let me show you." He rubbed out part of the design on either ear, then glanced up for the deputy's approval. "How's that?"

8-Q-Barred-Out earmark:
Swallow-fork and under-half-crop.

Yocum nodded slowly, his lips tightening.

Rance scuffed out the sand drawings with his foot. Neither man spoke for a few minutes.

Finally Yocum said, "Want me to make an arrest? — I forgot, you're still a deputy. You takin' action?"

"Not right away."

"On Eddie's account, eh?"

Rance looked away without replying.

Yocum said, after a minute, "You been expectin' either Quillan or Norris to tip a crooked hand one of these days. I reckon this settles the question as to which one it is."

"Maybe not," Rance pointed out. "Maybe things just happened this way. It might be pure luck —"

"Quincidence, eh?"

"Coincidence is the word, Homer."

"You can settle that easy enough."

Rance looked at the deputy. "You mean kill the cow and skin out the brand?"

Yocum nodded. "That's the idea. From the underside the hide would show where the new brand joined the original burn. Don't tell me you didn't know that."

"I know it all right," Rance said glumly, "but I ain't just ready — well, to be frank, Homer, I don't know whether I want definite proof or not."

"You're a fool about that girl," Yocum stated bluntly. "A person would think you was in love with her yourself."

Rance winced. "Oh, hell, I'm just tryin' to do

what's right by Vink Thorpe's daughter. . . ."

"Well, I ain't forgot Vink took a shot at a rustler. It wouldn't be doin' right to let her marry —"

"Unless I had actual proof said rustler was responsible for Vink's death I wouldn't do anythin' at once. I'd rather go slow for a spell, and see what else shows . . . Homer, do you think Quillan would listen to reason?"

"You mean, give him a hint to go easy?"

"Somethin' of that kind."

"Well, I would — in his boots. It might work. Damn his ornery hide! I can't see why he wants to steal stock, when he'll be runnin' the VIT anyway one of these days."

Rance's voice was harsh when he answered, "We don't know yet — for certain — that he is stealin' VIT stock?"

"Don't overlook any bets, Rance. Vink shot at somebody that day. If you could go deeper into this matter, no tellin' what you might uncover —"

"Homer, I never said anything about this to you before, but that day Vink saw that rustler, I went down to give a look-see for myself after I'd left Vink. The cows had drifted out of sight by the time I got there, but I could see a horse's hoof-marks real plain. It was a toss-up whether I should trail the cows or the horse. The horse won —"

"What'd you find?"

"The sign led me through the Santos Hills

toward the trail that runs from the Star-Cross to Morada. The prints crossed the trail and ended in a box canyon. I found Hugh Norris' paint horse — dead."

"Dead — you mean it —"

"It had been shot through the head. Forty-five, I guessed, from the hole the slug made. The saddle and bridle had been stripped off."

"That don't prove it was Norris that Vink saw."

"No, it don't Homer. You remember that day Norris announced that somebody had stole his pinto. Now let's pretend, just pretend, mind you — that it was Norris. When Vink shot, Norris high-tailed it for the trail that ran to his place. We'll say he was afraid his horse had been recognized and wanted to get rid of it. From the box canyon in the hills to the Star-Cross ain't more than a three-four-mile walk. He could have run his pinto into that canyon — which is off the trail — killed the horse and then walked to his ranch."

"Never knew a cowman yet that liked walkin', but the thing is possible. Then, he saddled another horse and burned the road into town, eh? Still, I was sittin' at the hotel that day he arrived. His bronc didn't look like it was fagged. On the other hand, I can't say I remember noticin' it to amount to anythin'. I do know he said that day that

209

somebody had rustled his pinto."

Yocum looked thoughtful and continued, "Yeah, it could have been done. Howsomever, don't forget that Quillan was ridin' a paint that same day. He's got several pintos on his spread. If I ain't mistaken, Norris bought his paint animal from Quillan."

"I don't think it was Quillan, Vink saw that day. I checked with Ringbone on the time Quillan left our place. It was nearly an hour after Vink pulled out —"

"And it was an hour later than Vink that Quillan pulled into town. There's just a chance, Rance, that Quillan rode like hell, got to the spot where Vink saw him —"

"You're dreamin', Homer," Rance cut in. "It would have to be a damn speedy horse —"

"Sure it would," Yocum agreed. "But don't forget that Monte would be ridin' on comparatively level ground, and goin' fast. Vink would just be loafin' along, pro'bly, and besides would lose quite a bit of time on that steep trail leading to the top of Look-out Ridge. It could be done, Rance —"

"I think you're mistaken, Homer — or I may be the one that's mistaken. If there was any way to prove it, I'd bet money that of two men, Norris or Quillan, it was Norris that Vink saw that day."

Yocum shook his head in disapproval. "Build up a case against Quillan, and then you try to protect him. In the face of you

210

showin' me how a VIT can be altered to read 8Q-Barred-Out, I'd say it was Quillan —"

He broke off as Rance suddenly lunged to his feet and disappeared around the corner of the building.

"What the hell!" Yocum sat open-mouthed a moment, then hearing voices jumped to his feet and followed Rance.

Within earshot, standing close to the corner of the deputy's office on Main Street, stood Bert Gillett. His face was working angrily.

". . . and I tell you," Gillett was insisting, "that I wasn't listenin' in on your talk, Duncan."

"You lookin' for me — or Homer?" Rance snapped angrily.

"Not none. Hell! I didn't even know you were sittin' there until you came chargin' around the corner."

"What you doin' here?"

"Just walkin' along. It's a free street, ain't it? Do I have to get your permission to take a walk?"

"Walkin' for exercise or pleasure?" Yocum drawled skeptically.

Gillett glanced insolently at the deputy. "I don't know as it's any of your business, Yocum, but I got a nail stickin' up in my boot. I'm headin' to Heinie Schwartz to get it fixed."

He gestured toward the neighboring building, a few yards distant from the jail, where a sign announced to anyone interested that the building was occupied by the H. Schwartz Boot Repair Shop.

"All right," Rance nodded. "If *I'm* wrong, I apologize. If I find *you* are — well, you're li'ble not to have any chance to do your apologizin'."

"Either way," Gillett rasped, slapping his holstered gun, "this hawg-laig will do my apologizin', if necessary. Don't you get so proddy with me, Duncan."

Rance smiled scornfully. "You been drinkin', Gillett. Better get along with your business before you get into trouble."

"It ain't nothin' to you, if I take a drink."

"No, it ain't," Rance conceded, "so long as you don't step on my toes." He turned a contemptuous back on the man and returned to his seat on the bench. A moment later he was joined by Yocum. Together they watched Gillett enter the Boot Repair Shop.

After a moment's silence Yocum said, "Speakin' of boots, you didn't see any bootprints near the spot where you found Norris' dead pinto, did you?"

"Nothin' definite. All hardpan and rock. The pony's hoofs bit deeper and were easy to read."

In a short time they saw Gillett emerge from the boot repair shop across the street, and head back toward the centre of town.

"You should have fired that hombre long

before you did," Yocum observed.

"I wanted to give him his chance. He's a good worker when he stays sober."

"And then," Yocum added, "he's plumb ornery. Lookin' for trouble the minute he gets some red-eye under his belt. For two cents I'd jam him in the cooler. Ain't had a prisoner in so long I'm gettin' lonesome."

"Let him ride," Rance said grimly. "If he's locked up he can't start anythin'."

Yocum nodded. "I see your patience is gettin' short. Well, that's a good way to look at it." He rose to his feet. "I'll be back *pronto*."

The deputy entered the boot repair shop and again emerged almost immediately. There was a look of surprise on his face as he returned to Rance's side. "Do you know, that hombre actually did have a heel-nail that needed poundin' down. Heinie Schwartz said it was right sharp and should have been taken care of before this."

"Provin'," Rance laughed, "that you shouldn't convict a man on circumstantial evidence."

"It don't prove that Gillett didn't hear what we said, though."

"There ain't any argument about that, Homer. Lucky, I heard him there."

"Do you suppose he heard what we said about Norris and Quillan?"

"I wouldn't be surprised."

Yocum cracked a peanut, flipped the shell

thoughtfully through the air, popped the kernel into his mouth.

"Well," he said at last, "I don't reckon it would do any harm in the long run. Matter of fact, it might bring things to a head."

"Exactly my view. I'm gettin' plumb tired ridin' the range in search for a cow with an unhealed brand —"

"Shucks! The burn would be healed and the hair growed out by this time, like's not —"

"I'm through lookin' for the particular cow Vink saw branded. I'm lookin' for others."

"Likely a cow-thief would herd 'em out of sight."

"That's possible, too. Well, I'm goin' to head for the VIT, and eat supper with my crew to-night. Cookie will be fit to be tied if I make him keep my chow warm another night. Besides, I want to see if I can't have a talk with Eddie, and learn just what's wrong."

Rance walked to his horse, climbed into the saddle. "*Adios,* Goober Face."

"Give Belle my sweet regards," Homer said, and added, "from the twin barrels of a scatter-gun."

CHAPTER XV

It wasn't quite dark when Rance rode into the VIT ranch-yard. He glanced at the porch, but saw no sign of Eddie or Belle Thorpe. Lamps were already lighted in the house. Rance jogged his pony on down to the corral. While he was unsaddling, he noticed a paint horse in the enclosure. That meant Monte Quillan was visiting the VIT.

Rance turned his pony into the corral, and picking up his equipment started toward the bunkhouse. It was empty, except for Ringbone Uhler, who was just starting through the doorway.

"Hi, Rance! You're just in time for supper."

"I heard Cookie beatin' his dishpan as I rode in." Rance set his saddle inside on an empty canned-goods box. He unbuckled his gun-belt and hung it on a peg in the wall. When he came back to the doorway the *segundo* was waiting for him.

"I see Monte Quillan's here," Rance said.

"He's up to the house. He was invited to stay for supper."

"I want to see him before he leaves."

"Anythin' special?"

"Sort of, yes." Rance rapidly sketched the

talk he'd had with Yocum that afternoon, explaining how the VIT brand could be changed into an 8Q-Barred-Out.

Ringbone swore, low-voiced: "That dirty cow-stealin' son!"

"Maybe it just happened that way, Ringbone," Rance warned. "I'd hate to spread such a story if that brand of Quillan's was just due to coincidence."

"Coincidence, hell! Howsomever, I won't say a word, but —"

"How's Eddie acted today?"

"Damn that Quillan for a low-down buzzard —"

Rance repeated his query. Ringbone frowned.

"T'tell the truth, Rance," he said, "she's actin' short of queer. The poor kid looks beat out. Somethin' has jolted her plenty, looks like. She seems sort of lifeless, and that Belle woman orders her around like Eddie ain't no spirit of her own. Damned if I understand it."

"Me, neither . . . Did Eddie tell you what happened in town that first day you drove 'em in?"

"Eddie didn't mention it, but I got part of the story from Yocum when Eddie sent him to find me in a hurry."

"Belle got Brad Wheeler to buy her a drink, and Brad's wife come along. You can guess what happened. . . . Let's eat, I'll tell you about it later. There's too few laughs these days to keep a good one to myself."

"I'll bet there was hell to pay," Ringbone chuckled. "By the time Brad's wife got through him, Brad pro'bly thought a cyclone had struck." Abruptly he growled, "Next time I take that female hellion into town, I got a notion to make the horses run away and tip the wagon."

"Go as far as you like."

The sun was already low behind the Sangre de Santos range. Dusk crept down, remained for a moment, and then it was dark. Silhouetted against the yellow frame of the mess-house door, the cook yelled, "Better come in and get it, Ringbone. There's only one hombre draws pay on this spread that gets a warm meal held over —"

"And he's on time to-night, Cookie," Rance called through the darkness.

"Miracles has come to pass," the ranch cook growled. He disappeared inside. Rance and Ringbone entered the mess-house and found seats at the long table. Rance nodded to the half-dozen punchers already busy with beans, steak and "spuds," and filled his own plate.

The men noticed that Rance was unusually quiet all through the meal. Supper over, Rance rose to his feet and twisted a cigarette. "If any of you men happen to see Monte Quillan pullin' out," he said, "tell him I want to see him before he goes — I mean, in case

I don't see him myself."

He left the messhouse and returned to the bunkhouse, where he lighted an oil lamp suspended on a bracket on the front wall, and looked through some old newspapers in an absent-minded manner.

The punchers entered from the messhouse a few minutes later. Four of them gathered about a table and commenced a game of seven-up. The other two busied themselves with dog-eared magazines. Ringbone discussed the probabilities of putting up a new corral with Rance. Rance heard him through in an almost total silence, nodded, and withdrew to his own abstractions.

Twice two of the hands rose from the card-table and went outside, to return with the report that Quillan's horse was still in the corral. Half an hour later Rance got to his feet, buckled on his gun and belt and stood in the bunkhouse doorway, lost in thought. After a time he came back into the room, removed his weapon and again hung it on the wall. The other men watched him without comment.

Ringbone said finally, "Anything I can do, Rance?"

Rance shook his head. "This is my headache."

He passed silently through the doorway, rolling a cigarette with steady fingers. Ringbone cleared his throat uneasily, started up from the bunk on which he was seated, then sat down again. The four card-players watched Rance until he had disappeared outside, looked significantly at one another. The game continued.

One of the punchers suddenly dropped his magazine, strode to the open doorway and stood there looking out into the night. The glowing end of Rance's cigarette paced restlessly back and forth near the corral.

Ringbone said reprovingly, "Tommy, seems like I heard Rance say he'd 'tend to things."

Tommy looked uneasy. "Rance," he pointed out, "ain't got his gun."

Ringbone repeated, "I heard Rance say he'd 'tend to things." He got up, lighted a lantern and placed it on the floor near the doorway. Then he sat down again.

Tommy returned to his magazine . . .

The back door of the ranch-house opened after a time. Momentarily Monte Quillan was framed against the oblong of light. He said "good-night." The door closed again. Quillan came striding through the darkness. Near the corral he saw a pinpoint of dull crimson described a brief arc through the gloom, and strike the ground in a scattering of quickly-extinguished sparks. Cigarette.

Quillan said, "Hello, there."

Rance answered, hard-voiced, "I'm waitin' to see you, Monte."

Monte wasn't missing Rance's tone. He

said, "You, eh, Rance?" He moved to the corral where he had left his saddle atop the uppermost bar. His gun and belt hung from this saddle-horn. Monte strapped on the weapon before adding, "What's up?"

Rance took as long to reply. He came close enough to make out Quillan's features in the faint star-light. "I want to talk to you, Monte. It's a job I hate worse'n poison. But it's got to be."

Quillan stiffened. "If it's about Eddie, Duncan —"

"It's not about Eddie — though it concerns her. That's why it hurts —"

"Cripes!" Quillan said, bridling. "Let's get it over with."

"Monte, you rustled any VIT stock?"

"Huh!" Silence, then, "What you mean?"

Rance caught a new tone in the darkness. Whether one of surprise or guilt, he couldn't determine. Maybe both. He said, level-voiced, "My words were direct. They don't need explanation."

Quillan laughed harshly. "Duncan, you got a sort of habit of nosin' into trouble —"

"That's not what I asked. I want a plain 'yes' or 'no'."

"No — a hundred times — no!" insolently.

"I hope you ain't lyin' —" Rance commenced.

"I don't give a damn what you hope. You can't tell me —"

220

"I'll tell you plenty, Quillan." Rance was level-voiced, patient. "To-day I picked up a cow wearin' your iron. It was a sloppy brandin' job. Somebody'd been in a hurry."

"If my brandin' suits me, it ain't your concern."

"No? You're wrong, Quillan — especially if that particular 8Q-Barred-Out happened to have been worked over from a VIT."

"You're crazy, Duncan." Quillan started to reach for his saddle.

Rance caught him by the arm. "Wait — you'll listen to what I got to say."

"You're crazy," Quillan repeated angrily. "How in hell could a VIT be worked into my brand —"

"Do I have to tell you?"

"I'm waitin'," Quillan snapped. He swung around, facing Duncan.

Rance held his voice to normal as he explained, "Burn a loop on the bottom of the V, enclose the top of the V with a half-loop. There's your 8. Connect bottom and top of the IT with half-loops. Continue the crossbar of the T to make your barred-out burn. Put the little tail on, to make the Q. Now, do you know what I'm getting at?"

A full minute passed before Quillan answered. Finally, he nodded. "It could be done, couldn't it?" thick-voiced. "Never realized that before. But, it's just a coincidence, Duncan —"

"Is it?" Rance's voice was cold. "That's what I want to know?"

Quillan suddenly turned belligerent. "Look here, Duncan, you callin' me a cow-thief?"

"That's what I want to know," Duncan repeated.

"You're crazy as hell!"

And a third time, "That's what I want to know?" Duncan said. He was holding steady for whatever came. "If your answer is 'no,' I don't aim to go any farther with this business, except to tell you to go easy. There's too many VIT cows missin'. Vink was inclined to let that slip, but so long as I'm roddin' the VIT I'm earnin' my wages."

Abruptly, Quillan lost his head. "Duncan, you say another word insinuatin' I'm stealin' VIT beef and I'll —"

"I'm still waiting for your answer. You're goin' to give it before you leave —"

Quillan swore at him, raised his clenched fist. Rance swayed back as it struck his shoulder. He righted himself and hit Quillan. Quillan staggered. Rance hit him again, and Quillan crashed to the earth.

He rolled over, gained his feet, came up, cursing and clawing at his holstered gun. Rance closed in, seized Quillan's right wrist, bent it sharply back. A sudden jarring report carried a flash of smoke and flame through the darkness.

Rance put on additional pressure, wrenched

the weapon from Quillan's hand. His right fist struck savagely at Quillan's jaw. Quillan's knees buckled and let him to the ground, where he lay still. Rance stood over him a moment, breathing heavily. Then he backed away, still holding Quillan's six-shooter in his left hand.

A yell sounded from the bunkhouse. Punchers came pouring out. Ringbone hurried up with the lighted lantern. "You hit, Rance!" he called anxiously.

"Not none," Rance answered. "The shot went wild."

The men gathered around. Rance sent one of them back for a bucket of water. When it arrived he dashed it over Quillan. Quillan groaned, swore, and sat up, feeling his jaw with exploring fingers.

The back door of the ranch-house banged open. Eddie called, "What's the matter? Anybody hurt?"

Rance answered her, "Nobody hurt. A gun went off by accident."

Eddie raised her voice again, "Ringbone, please come up to the house a minute."

Rance answered for the *segundo*. "Ringbone is busy now. I'll be there *poco pronto*."

The ranch-house door closed again.

Rance said to the punchers, "You fellers drift back to the bunkhouse. Everythin's all right. I ain't hurt. Ringbone and me'll attend to this."

The men departed reluctantly. Ringbone saw in the yellow light from the lantern that Rance's face was white and drawn.

Ringbone said, "He tried to gun you, eh?"

"Guess it was a mistake," Rance answered quietly. He still held Quillan's gun. "I had to hit him."

"It was Quillan's mistake all right. Going to take him in to jail?"

Rance shook his head. "I'll give him his chance. He's had his warnin' —"

"I think you're crazy."

"That's what Quillan said."

Rance drew back the hammer of Quillan's six-shooter, examined it in the light of the lantern. After a moment he let the hammer down, and gave the gun to Ringbone. Ringbone stuck it in the waistband of his overalls and looked at Rance with questioning eyes. Quillan had clambered to his feet by this time and stood swaying uncertainly before the two men.

Rance said, "Ringbone, saddle up Quillan's horse. There's his saddle atop that corral bar." He moved over to Quillan, "You can have your gun next time you come here, Quillan, but not to-night. We've each had our say — each in our own way. From now on, govern your actions accordin'."

Quillan mumbled through split lips, "I tell you, Duncan, it's just chance that my brand can be worked thataway —"

"On the strength of that, I'm giving you the benefit of the doubt. But don't try to explain anythin' else — not with your Colt gun. Next time I might be packin' my own iron."

Quillan's eyes dropped to Rance's hips, then lifted again. He stared at Rance uncertainly, continued to stare at him when Rance brushed past and started toward the ranchhouse. Rance didn't speak to him again that night.

Ringbone led up the saddled pony. He watched Quillan climb up with shaky legs.

"You goddam fool," Ringbone said. "Pullin' on a man that ain't got his hardware."

"How was I to know he didn't have his gun? He come, makin' war talk —"

"It wasn't war talk, Quillan. He was tryin' to warn you to go easy. He's givin' you your chance — on Eddie's account. It's a damn sight more than I'd do —"

"I'll admit I lost my head."

Ringbone snorted. "You damn near lost your life. Rance had figured you might blow up. But he refused to put on his gun —"

"But, Ringbone, I ain't rustled any VIT beef. That brand is pure luck, workin' out the way it does —"

"So you told Rance. I'll back his play. Better get goin', Quillan."

"But I tell you, I —"

Ringbone spat disgustedly, turned an abrupt back on the owner of the 8Q-Barred-

Out, and walked grimly toward the bunk-house.

Quillan looked after the *segundo*, frowning. He felt his jaw tenderly, swore low-voiced, then dug in his spurs. The horse leaped ahead. At the back door of the ranch-house Quillan pulled to a halt. Exploring his bruised features with light fingers, he decided to go on. A minute later he was loping across the range, wondering what Duncan's next move would lead to.

CHAPTER XVI

Rance had found Eddie in the ranch-house kitchen. The girl was reluctant to talk, but she was frankly curious about the shot she'd heard. Coseffa had retired for the night. Movements from the front of the house told Rance that Belle Thorpe was still up.

"Why didn't Ringbone come when I called him?" Eddie asked.

"I had other work for him. Any objection to me comin'?"

Eddie didn't reply at once, then she said, "You should know there's not. Why do you say that?"

"Why do you act the way you do?" Rance countered. "You act like you don't want to see me —"

"Well," Belle Thorpe's harsh voice from the inner doorway, "a gent would know enough to take a hint." She came into the kitchen and sat down. Eddie was seated near the kitchen range. Rance stood with his back against the rear door.

He said to Belle Thorpe, "I don't know as I asked your opinion."

"You got it, mister, just the same."

Rance eyed the woman disgustedly. She

wore a flowered kimona, and her hair lacked the appearance of having been combed that day.

"Please, Mrs. Thorpe —" Eddie commenced.

"You leave him to me," Belle Thorpe snapped. "Eddie, you need to be more firm. This feller had his chance. He didn't choose to be friends with me. I said I'd show him."

Eddie sighed and remained silent. Once she looked appealingly at Rance. Rance said, "You asked what happened out there. It isn't anythin' to worry about. A gun went off, unintentional —"

Belle Thorpe's raucous laughter cut his words. "I'll bet it was unintentional. Mister, I could hear Monte Quillan cussin' you to beat the band, 'way up here. I called Eddie to listen."

"You would," Rance growled. "Can't you mind your own affairs without worryin' Eddie plumb to death —"

"I ain't worryin' Eddie. You can ask her."

"It's true, Rance," Eddie nodded. Her eyes didn't meet Rance's. "I don't see why you should object to Mrs. Thorpe being here. You wanted me to have a companion. That's not the question, though," and again she looked directly at Rance, "What was the trouble between you and Monte?"

"No trouble at all, Eddie —"

"Don't put me off, Rance. I heard — I heard Monte denying he was a cow-thief —"

" 'Course he denied it," Belle Thorpe cut in, smiling nastily. "Duncan don't like Monte. He's tryin' to stir up trouble. If we could get at the truth of the matter —"

"Look here, Eddie," Rance asked, "can't I talk to you alone?"

"I want to know what happened," Eddie persisted. "We heard your voices. It was something about brands. Surely Monte hasn't been stealing. Monte's not a thief, whatever you may say."

"Sure not, kid, it was just chance, that's all."

"What was chance?" Eddie persisted.

Rance's hands gestured hopelessly. He floundered through an answer. ". . . but you see, kid," he ended, "that don't prove a thing against Monte Quillan. I'm sure he's all right."

Eddie's eyes were wide. "And can a VIT be worked over into an 8Q-Barred-Out?"

Rance nodded dumbly. Word by word Eddie finally forced the whole story from him.

Belle Thorpe slapped the table. "I don't believe it," she snapped. "Quillan's no thief. This foreman of your'n, Eddie, is just makin' up the whole pack of lies —"

"That same foreman," Rance said grimly, "is itchin' to slap your face, Belle Thorpe. I don't know what you're doin' here, but when I find out I'm goin' to send you packin' on your way in a hurry. Maybe you can bluff

Eddie, but you can't bluff me —"

"Hear that, Eddie!" Belle Thorpe shrieked. "He's tryin' to run out your own kith and kin. I won't stand for it. Either that man goes, or I do. If I have to leave, you know what —"

"Wait, wait!" Eddie was on her feet now. "Please, Rance, forget this whole business —"

"If he don't, I'll turn this country upside down," Belle Thorpe threatened.

Rance said, "Eddie, what do you mean — forget this whole business?"

"Just let things slide for a while," Eddie begged tearfully. "Monte and — and everything. We can afford to lose a few cows. Please, Rance, drop your investigating. I'm sure Monte will be able to explain —"

"But — but, Eddie, you don't want me to stop lookin' for Vink's murderer?" Rance was aghast at the thought.

Eddie turned away, looked back at Rance, then toward Belle Thorpe. The woman jerked her head in the affirmative. Eddie said to Rance, "I think it best if you drop even that for a time, Rance —"

"Eddie, I can't do that!"

She faced him, tears streaming down her cheeks. "You've got to, Rance. Please, just drop everything. I'll — I'll explain it all some day, but don't ask me now. You'll see I'm working for the best. What if Monte did take a cow or two. That doesn't matter —"

"Eddie," Rance exclaimed, "you've lost your head."

"You see," Belle Thorpe said triumphantly. "I told you, Eddie, you didn't have any control over your foreman."

"But I have," the girl cried wildly. "You'll see . . . Rance, you'll do as I say, won't you, please —"

"Eddie, I can't do that. I'd do anythin' — but that — girl." His voice was miserable. "You don't know what you're sayin' —"

"I do, I do!" Eddie panted excitedly. "You've got to give up the search. Later, perhaps — but now —" The words broke abruptly in a flood of tears.

Belle Thorpe said, "My Gawd! If he was my foreman, he'd obey orders or get out —"

Eddie's chin came up. "Please, Mrs. Thorpe, I'll 'tend to this —"

"Well, 'tend to it, then. I'll help you out," the woman snapped. "If Duncan stays on here, he obeys your orders, or I'll have a thing or two to say."

"You'll shut your mouth, that's what you'll do," Rance said hotly.

"Tell him his business, Eddie," Belle Thorpe screamed. "I ain't got much more patience. I've warned you what to expect. Now, you give him his orders, or —"

Eddie raised one trembling, protesting hand. Her voice was quavery. She gulped, "Mrs. Thorpe is right, Rance. If you stay

231

here you must do as I say."

"You can't mean that, girl." Rance looked shocked. "I'll do what you say, of course — except that I won't give up this search for Vink's killer —"

"That settles it, then." Something dead and lifeless about Eddie's words. "You'll have to leave the VIT, Rance. I'll send — send you your check."

"But, Eddie, I don't understand —"

"That's not necessary," Eddie said blindly. "For the last time, Rance, won't you do as I say —"

"I can't, Eddie," Rance protested. "If you'd only explain —"

Eddie faced him, her lips ashen. "It's good-bye, then, Rance." Tears commenced to trickle down her cheeks. "I think I —" Sobbing, she turned away and hurried from the room.

Rance gazed dumbly at her. Belle Thorpe laughed triumphantly. "You see, mister, you ain't got any influence. You just thought you had. You can't buck me and —"

Rance whirled savagely across the floor. He towered above Belle Thorpe, his hands trembling. "I'd like to pound hell out of you, you she-cat. If you were a man —"

Belle Thorpe's laugh taunted him. She leaned back in her chair, her hard black eyes glistening boldly, secure in the knowledge he wouldn't strike her.

Rance leaned close. "So help me, God," he said, low-voiced, tense, "if I learn for sure this is your doin's I'll kill you, Belle Thorpe!"

Whirling back, he jerked open the kitchen door and plunged into the ranch-yard. The woman's cold laughter followed him until the door swung closed."

Ringbone Uhler met Rance half-way to the bunkhouse. Rance said grimly, "It's up to you to run the outfit from now on, Ringbone."

"Howcome?" incredulously. "You ain't cuttin' your string?"

Rance's voice was bitter. "Eddie's just cut it for me."

"You don't mean it!"

"Surest thing I ever said."

"I don't figure it, Rance. What happened — not on Quillan's account?"

"I reckon," Rance nodded soberly. "I tried to slide over the matter, but that damn Thorpe woman took a hand. Eddie insisted on details. I give 'em — against my will —"

"And you mean to say that Eddie — ?"

"In plain words she told me I'd have to give up my investigatin', or my job."

Ringbone swore an oath. "Me, I been thinkin' you was a fool, but if Eddie fired you for uncoverin' a lousy, two-bit rustler, she's a bigger fool."

"Eddie's all right, Ringbone. If it was anybody but Monte she'd be different."

"Oh, hell! . . . Rance, you go roll into your bunk. Mebbe, come mornin', Eddie'll change her mind."

But when morning came Eddie called Ringbone to the house, then sent him to Rance with a check for a month's pay. Disconsolately, Rance saddled up and started for Morada. He knew now he'd never give up the search for Vink Thorpe's murderer.

CHAPTER XVII

It wasn't more than eight-thirty when Rance loped his horse into Morada. There were a few horses and vehicles on the street, and the town was stirring to life. Rance noticed several men talking in doorways, or before houses, and while he noted their sober expressions he was too engrossed with his own affairs to give them a thought.

Entering Morada from the west, the first building of any importance was the combination deputy's office and jail. To Rance's surprise he saw Homer Yocum seated before the office, glumly chewing peanuts. The deputy got to his feet as Rance rode up.

Rance said, "Didn't know but what you'd be at your breakfast when I arrived."

"I been up since early," Yocum said shortly. "Just tryin' to get up enough ambition to ride to the VIT and see you."

"See me?" Rance smiled ruefully. "You won't have to go to the VIT any more when you want to see me. I been sacked."

"Huh!" Yocum looked his surprise. "My Gawd! Everythin' comes at once —"

"What do you mean?"

"I see you ain't heard." Homer Yocum was

the type that likes to hold his audience in suspense. He spat out a peanut shuck: "You'll sure blow up when you hear it."

"Don't hurry on my account," sarcastically.

"Matt Everett's dead."

"No!"

"There's definite proof at the undertaker's. I'm givin' you facts."

Rance scrutinized Yocum's features, saw the deputy wasn't joking. "I'm askin' for more facts — quick."

"You'll get 'em — much as I know, which same ain't much. It was done yesterday, while you and me were sittin' here, talkin' —"

"What was done?" impatiently.

"The murder. They found Matt —"

"Good Lord, Homer! Was Matt murdered? Who done it?"

"We don't know. He was stabbed to death."

"Lord! That's hard to believe. Who found the body?"

"Ward Stinson. Stinson dropped into the feed store around five o'clock last evenin' and found Matt on the floor, beside his desk. He was layin' on his face, with the handle of a knife stickin' up between his shoulders. Doc Parker says he died instanter."

"Well, I'll be damned." Rance got down from his pony and leaned against the hitchrail.

"You'll be damned more when you hear the rest of it. Matt wasn't holdin' cards, like

Vink Thorpe was, but the dead man's hand was strung along his back, face up, when the murderer left 'em —"

" 'Dead man's hand'! You mean the same five cards?"

"Not the *same* cards we found on Vink, no. I got those in my desk, holdin' 'em as Exhibit A, B, or X, or somethin'. But, ordinary playin' cards like Vink's — ace of spades, ace of clubs, ace of hearts, eight of clubs and eight of spades."

"My gosh, Homer! It's hard to believe. That looks like the same murderer —"

"— that killed Vink Thorpe? We ain't no argument on that, Rance, but who is he?"

Rance looked grim. "We'll get him this time, sure. No killer can pull two murders like this and not leave some sort of clue to be followed. Had Matt's gun been fired?"

"Still in his holster," Yocum shook his head. "Matt never had a dawg's chance, I reckon."

"The fact it was done in broad daylight is what stops me. Somebody's got plenty nerve."

Yocum nodded. " 'Course, in a way, that can be explained. Doc Parker says Matt died about three o'clock — mebbe a little before or after — and you know it's right hot at that hour. The sun's beatin' down, and folks ain't movin' around much. A good deal of the town takes a *siesta*. 'Nother thing, Matt's store has only got one window in the front and one in the rear. Neither of 'em has been washed since the Sangre de Santos Range was a valley. It's sort of dark and gloomy in the store."

Rance said, "It could be done, of course. A man might come down the alley without bein' noticed and enter Matt's back door. Across the alley is that barn Matt owns. Next door to the feed store is an empty buildin'. But, by gosh, Homer, there must be someone under suspicion —"

"The coroner's jury didn't bring in no indictment."

"Doc Parker hold his inquest already?"

"Last night. I wanted to delay it until you got here. Figured to ride and bring you. But Parker 'lowed as how you'd wanted Vink's inquest held in a hurry, so you couldn't have any objections if he rushed Matt's through *pronto*. Parker said, like's not, you wouldn't have any evidence to offer anyway —"

"He was right for once."

"Anyway, the inquiry was held and the jury returned a verdict of 'killed by an unknown. Motive also unknown.' There were a few dollars in Matt's desk that hadn't been taken. . . . There you are. Just like Vink's murder — done by an unknown. Parker had just about instructed the jury to bring in an indictment against Ward Stinson, too."

"Why Stinson?"

Yocum crammed a couple of peanuts into his mouth, shrugged his shoulders. "You got me — still, I dunno. Doc Parker is madder'n a rattler skinnin' itself, because there's been two murders and nobody caught. I reckon he feels his jury ought to offer somethin' final and definite —"

"But just because Stinson found the body is no sign that he —"

"Stinson had been there before — either about three, or two forty-five. There seems to be a difference of opinion about it —"

"Whose opinions?"

"Clem Lucas' and Stinson's."

"Darn you, Homer," Rance said with some exasperation, "I wish you wouldn't always tell your stories backwards. What's Clem got to do with it?"

"He was on his way to dinner when he saw Stinson come out of Matt's store. Clem claims it was about three o'clock. Stinson says it was probably fifteen minutes earlier."

Rance's eyes narrowed. "And Matt died about three o'clock. Stinson admitted bein' there, then?"

"Yes, after Clem told of seein' him come out of the store. Didn't mention it before. But he admitted it finally. Says he went to see Everett about orderin' some cottonseed cake. Ward figures to feed cake to some of his stock this winter. Stinson claims Everett couldn't give him a quotation on the cake,

239

because Matt couldn't locate the price-list from his wholesaler. Accordin' to Ward, Matt told him to come back later, when he'd had an opportunity to look through his desk for the missin' price-list. Stinson returned about five o'clock and found Matt dead. That's Stinson's story."

"How'd Stinson act when he was being questioned?"

"You can guess, knowin' how hot-tempered he is. Flew off the handle a couple of times and swore a blue streak. Acted damn indignant at bein' suspected. It made him mad as hell when Clem insisted it was around three o'clock he'd seen him — though Clem wasn't positively sure of the exact minute."

"Clem's usually pretty accurate. . . . What was he doin' goin' to dinner at that time?"

"I told Doc to ask Clem that same question. Clem explained it. He and 'Lonzo Wheeler were takin' inventory. It's the end of the store year, or somethin' of the kind. 'Lonzo went home to eat at noon. When he got back Clem finished addin' some figures before he left. Clem thinks it was just about three when he came down Main Street. Lookin' across the road from the corner of Main and Thorpe he saw Stinson comin' out of Matt's store —"

"Hell! Can't George Kohler tell what time Clem come in the restaurant?"

"Clem didn't eat at the Delmonico Chop

House. He just goes there for supper. He ate dinner at the Chink's restaurant, across the street from Kohler's place — just three doors from Matt's store. He must have passed Stinson close enough to recognize him and be sure. 'Course, I suppose Clem's eyes are gettin' old —"

"Did they speak?"

"Clem says he spoke, but didn't get replied to. Stinson says he don't remember seein' Clem. 'Course, Stinson always walks along wrapped up in his own thoughts."

"How about Quong Kee? Don't he remember what time Clem came in to eat?"

Yocum said, "You remind me of Doc Parker. He was doin' his best to fasten the evidence on Stinson, too."

"I'm not tryin' to do that. I'm tryin' to get facts clear."

"Well, Quong Kee didn't notice the time. Alonzo Wheeler didn't notice the hour Clem was away either, and it seems nobody else noticed either Stinson or Clem. You know — *siesta* hour. Folks catch cat-naps. There's your facts. Matt was killed around three. Stinson found the body at five. Stinson was in the shop either at three or fifteen minutes before. Parker didn't release his jury until two this mornin', tryin' to get them six jurors to arrive at somethin', that would fasten the murder on Stinson. It was no go. Hell! You can't indict a man on such evidence."

Rance ran quickly through his mind the names of those suspected in the Thorpe murder. He said, half-aloud, "Quillan was at the VIT when I arrived. I don't know how long he'd been there, though. . . . How'd Brad Wheeler take the murder?"

"Brad's pretty well broke up. He was sittin' on the hotel porch with Gus Oldfield around three o'clock, he says —"

"Oldfield back in town?"

"Come in by buggy yesterday noon. I didn't know it until after you'd left, though. After the stage pulled out, I came back to my office. Oldfield had missed the stage at Capitol City, and hired a buggy —"

"What's Oldfield back for?"

"Says he's straightened his affairs around so he could get leave to come back here for a spell, until you get it out of your mind that he had anythin' to do with Vink's death."

"Well, that's somethin' in Oldfield's favor," Rance said grudgingly.

"I'd say it cleared him."

"I wonder if those cheques he gave Vink ever showed up?"

"I asked Gus that last night. He says they didn't."

"If Oldfield had 'em, they wouldn't. It's funny him showin' up the day Matt Everett is killed."

"Get him out of your mind. He's got Brad Wheeler for an alibi, and Brad's got him.

That clears 'em both."

"I reckon it does, Homer. . . . Just to complicate matters, Hugh Norris should have been in town yesterday —"

"He was," Homer interrupted. "Gillett, too — as you know. Norris had come in to get a bill of goods. Gillett to get that boot nail pounded down, though I don't see why he couldn't have done that himself. Doc questioned both of 'em. Norris was gettin' his order made up at the store, when 'Lonzo returned from dinner. Both Gillett and Norris was sore at bein' held for the inquest. I didn't see much sense in it myself. They didn't know anythin'. Testified they'd been around town all afternoon, in and out of the Cowmen's Rest and the Morada Bar — though nobody, includin' themselves, could say with any certainty exactly where they were at three o'clock."

"Must have been close to three when we caught Gillett listenin' to us, wasn't it?"

Yocum shrugged his shoulders. "I ain't any idea what time that was. Middle of the afternoon sometime. You see how it is?"

"They still in town?"

"Pulled out this mornin' early, after the inquest."

Rance looked thoughtful. After a time he said, "The Cowmen's Rest is on the corner, just across from Matt's feed store corner."

"Yep, both of 'em on Main. I thought of that, too, but it don't add to any sort of total."

243

Rance sighed. Suddenly a frown creased his forehead. "Homer, can you imagine Norris or Stinson or Brad — any of those fellers — usin' a knife?"

Yocum shook his head. "Cold steel seems more like a greaser. On the other hand, the murderer might not want to use a gun in broad daylight. A knife is noiseless. That was proved yesterday. Besides, I don't think there's a Mex in Morada that ain't a pretty good hombre."

"What sort of knife was it?"

"Ordinary huntin' knife — wait, I got it inside. I'm holdin' it as one of those alphabetical exhibits — I ain't sure which letter I'll tag to it."

Yocum entered his office and returned with the knife responsible for taking Matt Everett's life. It was a keen-bladed affair with a wooden handle. Rance glanced at the maker's name engraved on the shining steel.

"This knife hasn't been used much," he said. "It likely come out of the Thorpe store. I remember when Vink ordered them. That was a year or more ago. No tellin' now who these knives were sold to —"

"I just happened to think," Yocum said, "that the murderer could have walked past the feed store and hurled this knife through the open door. Say Matt was standin' with his back to the door. There's a good chance the killer wouldn't be noticed."

"I sort of doubt that. It's more likely the man entered the store, from the alley, through Matt's back door —"

"And Matt just stood there and let the killer stab him, eh?"

Rance shrugged helpless shoulders. "It's got me down, Homer."

"I'm glad you're in town to help untangle it — say, what's this about gettin' sacked from your job?"

Rance related the circumstances. When he had finished, Yocum said, "So you slapped Monte Quillan down, eh? He always was too flashy to suit me. The women fall for those handsome types, though. Damn! You ought to have brought him to jail, even if Eddie —"

"Let's not talk about that Homer."

"Just as you say." The deputy returned the knife to his office, then asked from the doorway, "You want to see them playin' cards that were found on Matt's body?"

"Anythin' out of the ordinary about them?"

"Ordinary playin' cards, Bicycle Brand, red backs. I'll bring 'em out."

Rance looked over the five cards. Contrary to the ones found in Thorpe's hand, these were brand new and showed no sign of ever having been used.

Rance handed them back. "The 'dead man's hand' don't liven my thoughts any. Might as well put 'em away. Call 'em Exhibit X. I've heard that X stands for unknown somethin' or other."

Yocum went into his office, then rejoined Rance at the hitchrail. The two men conversed for a few minutes. A hail reached them from across the street. They turned to see Doc Parker emerging from his office-residence which was situated almost opposite the deputy's building on Main Street.

The doctor advanced soberly, nodded to Yocum and said to Rance, "I suppose Deputy Yocum has told you about Matt Everett."

"I just got the story from him. It's a hell of a note, if you ask me."

"Awful, Rance. We went over all the evidence we could collect last night, but my jury failed me."

"I wouldn't say that, Doc. You can't expect your jury to indict without proof — leastwise more proof than was offered."

"But I have a feeling Ward Stinson is the guilty man."

"The evidence doesn't show it, as I get it from Homer. Maybe Homer overlooked something. Do you mind going over the facts for me, Doc?"

Parker complied with Rance's request. When he had finished, Rance saw that Yocum had thoroughly covered the ground.

"There's this much to it," Parker said at last, "Morada needs a deputy in the Crazy River country that can ferret out these murderers. If something can't be done about finding Everett's killer, I think I'll have to petition Sheriff Cannon to appoint a new deputy here."

"Why not do that right now, Doc?" Yocum said belligerently. "Mebbe Windy Cannon will come down here and take personal charge —"

"Now, don't get mad, Yocum," Parker said testily. "But you must admit you haven't accomplished one definite thing —"

"Hell, Doc, I ain't no Surelock Holmes."

"I'm commencing to think," Parker snapped, "you aren't capable of anything, except eating peanuts from dawn until dark."

Yocum kept his temper, laughed good-naturedly. "Peanuts go to build up my nourishment, Doc, and hold down my temper. Shucks! There ain't any use of you and me tanglin'."

Rance said quietly, "Homer's got the right idea, Doc. He's doin' the best he knows. This whole business is a mystery to me."

The doctor turned on Rance. "You're supposed to be a deputy. Can't you do something?"

"Maybe I will."

"Well, I hope it happens soon," Parker answered gruffly. He turned and crossed the street to his office.

"Plumb petulant, ain't he?" And Yocum popped a peanut into his mouth.

"He's worried," Rance pointed out. "After

all, he don't make so much money in this town, even if he is a damn good doctor. What little he gets from the county, actin' as coroner, helps, I suppose. He wants to get the job again, when election comes this fall. If his juries don't produce indictments, folks is li'ble to vote against him."

"I suppose. Me, I'd resign right now, if it would help matters any — where you goin'?"

Rance had moved around to his horse. "Reckon I'll drift down the street," he said, climbing into the saddle. "Talk to a few folks here and there. I might pick up somethin'."

"Good luck. Want me along?"

"I'll let you know if anythin' turns up."

CHAPTER XVIII

Rance walked the horse along Main Street, turned at the corner of Hereford, and dismounted before the entrance to the Morada House Bar. Ascending the steps he found Brad Wheeler and Gus Oldfield in the barroom. The morning shift bartender was just putting out glasses and a bottle of Bourbon.

At Rance's step, Wheeler started nervously. A look of relief crossed his features as he saw Rance. "Hello, Rance," he greeted. "You're just in time to join us in a mid-mornin' drink. Suppose you heard about Matt?"

Rance nodded. Wheeler looked worn out and drawn as though the previous night had been a sleepless one. Brad Wheeler was worried, no doubt about that.

Rance said, "Yes, Homer Yocum told me the story. It's a hell of a note. . . . Hello, Gus. I heard you were back."

Oldfield flushed angrily. "Yes, and I'm here to stay, Duncan, until you feel free to tell me to go. I don't like being under suspicion. I've got my business affairs arranged, so I'll stay as long as you need me here."

"Don't know as I do, Gus, but I'm glad to see you back. Right good of you to come."

Rance shook his head at Wheeler's repeated invitation to drink. "Nope, too early for me, Brad. Go ahead and have your drink, then I want to augur with you a mite —"

Wheeler put down his glass. "About what?"

"We'll go into that later. Finish your drink."

"Want to talk to me, too?" Oldfield asked. There was a hint of a sneer in the words.

"I'll let you know if I do," Rance said calmly. "But I do want to talk personal to Brad — wait, don't hurry your liquor. Brad and I'll go out on the porch. Reckon we can talk there without bein' disturbed."

Wheeler put down his glass, wiped his mouth with his handkerchief. He was pale, his bloodshot eyes were questioning. Without a word he followed Rance out to the porch, and around to the Main Street side. Rance pulled up a chair and elevated his feet on the railing. Wheeler sat down beside him. Rance rolled and lighted a cigarette. Wheeler shifted uneasily, opened his mouth to speak, then closed it without having made a sound.

Rance blew the ash from his cigarette. His eyes were on the street as he said quietly, "Brad, you helped kill Matt Everett. Why?"

Wheeler leaped to his feet, eyes blazing. "Good God, Rance! Am I under suspicion of that —"

Rance looked up at him. "You're not entirely free of suspicion where Vink Thorpe is concerned either."

"But, good God, Rance! I wouldn't do that, even if I had reason. And I didn't. Matt and Vink were my best friends. You ought to know that as well as I do. We've been friends ever since — since — well, it's almost too many years to remember. Why do you say that?"

Rance shoved his sombrero to the back of his head, looked gravely at Wheeler. He said, almost gently, "I'm sorry, if I threw a shock into you, Brad. But you need shockin'. I know *now* that you ain't a murderer. I was never convinced that you were."

Wheeler gingerly resumed his chair, his face streaming with perspiration, though it was cool on the porch. "That's a hell of a thing to say to a man, Rance — even if you were just joking."

"I wasn't jokin', Brad. I said you helped kill Matt Everett. I still think you did — indirectly. If you'd come clean, Matt's death might have been avoided, I think, though I ain't got anythin' but a hunch to go on. Don't you want to see justice done the murderer?"

"More than I want anything else, s'help me."

"You know who killed Vink and Matt, Brad." It was a direct statement of fact. Rance felt sure of his ground.

Wheeler was silent. Rance took the Stebbings-marked six-shooter shell from his pocket, showed it to Wheeler, then put it away.

"That shell gave Matt a scare, Brad. He

251

told you about it. You both knew who fired it, you knew the significance of the five cards called the 'dead man's hand.' Both of you saw that letter Vink received. You both know Belle Thorpe. I could see that in your faces the day she arrived —"

"Damn that woman!" Wheeler growled.

"We're agreed on that, anyway. Brad, if you'd come across when I first asked you to, Matt's death might have been prevented. I can't say for sure, of course. You know better than I do. Enough harm has been done already. Don't you think it's about time you talked?"

His voice didn't carry above normal. It was quiet, steady, with something of pleading in the tones. Wheeler kept silent, gazing out in the street with unseeing eyes. Once he started to speak, then changed his mind.

"Brad," Rance persisted, "what's the idea behind the killin' of Vink and Matt?"

"Revenge," Wheeler said impulsively in a hoarse voice.

Rance nodded. "Two's been killed. Anybody else on the murderer's list?"

"Reckon I am." Wheeler essayed a feeble smile.

"Figured as much, when you took to wearin' your gun. But wearin' a gun didn't save Matt. Figure it'll save you?"

"I . . . don't . . . know . . . Rance." The words came hard.

"Who's the killer?" Wheeler didn't answer. Rance pursued, "Who is he, Brad — Stinson, Norris, Quillan, Gillett? — not Oldfield or is it? Or is it somebody else? All of those named have been under suspicion one time or another."

"I don't think . . . any of them," Wheeler cleared his throat uneasily, "though I ain't sure, dammit, I ain't sure. They may be mixed into it as accomplices —" He broke off, considering. Impulsively he said, "Hell! I might as well tell you. If Nickie Zane ain't back of these killin's, I don't know who is."

"Nickie Zane? Never heard of him."

"Mostly we called him Nick. No, I reckon you never did, Rance. It's a long yarn. I wish I'd given it to you before. Mebbe a heap of trouble could been avoided —"

"We all make mistakes, Brad. It's too bad you didn't, though."

"You'll understand, when I tell you, Rance. Hell! I just couldn't tell it. I was hopin' things would blow over. If the facts were known it would create a hell of a rumpus. Look at me. My reputation's good in Morada. I had to protect my family. I couldn't afford a scandal. There's Alonzo, just growin' to manhood. Do you think I want him to learn his father was a stage robber?"

A surprised exclamation left Rance's lips. Wheeler nodded grimly, "It's true, Rance. God knows I've regretted it more than once.

And you know how my wife is. Never a better woman made, but — and there was Matt's reputation, too — and Vink's daughter to think of." He shook his head. "Poor fellows. Well, if the truth ever comes out, I'll just have to face the music." A wan, sheepish smile touched his lips. "Annie will raise plumb hell. As I say, there was never a better wife lived — but her belongin' to the church and all. She'll never let up on me —"

"If anythin' you tell me can be kept quiet, Brad," and Rance tried to keep the impatience out of his tones, "I'll do my best to keep your wife from hearin' about it."

"It ain't only Annie," Wheeler said. "The scandal would hit Eddie Thorpe worst of all. I tried to keep still on her account, most of all —"

"What's Eddie got to do with it?" Rance stiffened.

"She's most affected. And now that damn Belle Thorpe has let the cat out of the bag. It nigh killed me when Eddie asked me about it, but I had to admit the truth. I didn't give her details, though. Maybe we'll be able to get rid of Belle before things get out."

"Truth about what? Get on with your story, Brad. I'll be listenin'."

Wheeler nodded. "I'll have to go back to the beginnin' — back to the days when Vink Thorpe, Matt Everett and myself met in a gold camp up in Colorado. That's thirty years ago. The three of us was prospectin'. Vink was the only one that struck anythin', and his pay streak didn't last long. But he cleaned up somewheres around six thousand dollars, before his claim petered out. This was in a town known as Spade Gulch. Spade Gulch was rich diggin's for a few months."

"I was through there once," Rance nodded. "Nothin' but a ghost town now."

"You're right. The gold didn't last. But the camp had opened with a bang. Most of us thought Spade Gulch was destined to develop into a real city. You know how these boom camps are. They attract every sort. Honkytonks, saloons and gamblin' parlors. Folks of all kinds pourin' in daily. The town even erected a church, though the sky-pilot never did do what you'd call a rushin' business.

Wheeler rubbed the side of his nose reminiscently with forefinger, as though to marshal old memories to his tongue. "Among them that come to Spade Gulch was a brother and sister named Zane — Nickie and Belle Zane —"

"Wait," Rance jerked around. "You don't mean to tell me that Vink was related to —"

"I'll get around to that part presently, Rance —"

"Go ahead, I interrupted." Rance sat back, his mind seething with speculation.

Wheeler went on, "Belle Zane was a right

255

smart looker those days. She took a job dancin' in the Golden Girl honkytonk. That'll give you a clue to her character — wild and woolly as they come, but all the same, a sight for sore eyes. Nickie was a right wild sort, too. Him and his sister had come out from some place in the east, a couple of years before, where Nickie had got into trouble over his loss of memory as he jokingly called it."

"Loss of memory?"

"Forgot his name," Wheeler explained with grim humor, "and took to writin' other names on cheques. Some people call it forgery. He'd got out of the scrape without goin' to jail somehow. Probably let him off because of his youth. He was younger than me and Matt — about the same age as Vink. For a time he tried to make an honest livin'. He prospected with Matt, Vink and me. Belle worked in the dance-hall. Vink and Matt and me bunked together in a tent. Belle and Nickie rented a cabin near our claims. Vink never did take much to Nickie Zane, but he got hard smitten with Belle —"

"I been expectin' that."

"Don't jump to conclusions, Rance. . . . Anyway, we all knew, except Vink, that it was Vink's money that Belle was after. She got it, too. Vink wouldn't listen to reason, and, one night, him and Belle eloped to the sky-pilot's house and got married. You see, Rance, we were younger those days, and didn't have much sense. Vink was crazy about Nickie's sister, though. The sky-pilot, seein' a chance of makin' an honest woman out of Belle, didn't have the brains to refuse to marry 'em —"

"And Vink got a divorce later, eh? Or I suppose he'd let her get it?"

"We'll come to that part in short order. Let me tell this in my own way, Rance, so I won't get my facts mixed." Wheeler seemed to be finding relief in telling the story to someone.

He continued, "Naturally, that marriage raised hell. Nick Zane got indignant and pulled a gun on Vink, yellin' some trash about how Vink had ruined his sister. There wasn't nothin' left to ruin by the time Vink married her, and nobody knew that better than Belle's own brother. Even Vink knowed it, but bein' in love, he thought everythin' would be all right. Anyway, me'n Matt prevented a shootin' between Nick Zane and Vink, and took Nick's gun away until he'd cooled down."

"Was that gun equipped with a Stebbings' firing-pin?" Rance asked.

"You know it's called a Stebbings, eh? Matt recognized that exploded shell the minute he saw it, and so did I. Where'd you find it?"

"Back of the store — but get on with your story."

"As I said, Nick was sore as hell because

Vink married his sister. Didn't think Vink was rich enough. He admitted later, Nickie did, that he'd been hopin' Belle would tie up to one of the millionaire claim owners in Spade Gulch. But at the time he was pretty peeved. Belle took him to one side and talked him out of his peeve somehow. Then she made Vink and Nickie shake hands. The upshot of the matter was that Nick come to live with me and Matt in the tent. Belle and Vink took over the cabin. Nick didn't like givin' up the cabin either, but Belle told him to take his cot and get. Belle always could control him. I reckon that's why Nickie liked her and felt so put out when she married Vink. Or maybe it was because he wouldn't have the benefit of her dance-hall earnin's any longer."

Wheeler drew out a cigar, chewed meditatively on the end, lighted it and went on, "The marriage only lasted a couple of weeks. By that time Belle had got all of Vink's money. With that accomplished, she ran off with a slick faro dealer who was workin' the town. Vink took it pretty hard, and turned to drinkin' for a spell. In fact, we were all punishin' the bottle pretty steady. A couple of months slipped past, and Vink realized he was makin' a fool of himself. He sobered up and went back to prospectin'. But me'n Matt and Nickie didn't have his sense. I reckon we were pretty tough cases."

Rance said, "Sometimes boom-camps make tough cases out of the best of 'em."

"You're right, it does. We weren't any exception to the general run that hit Spade Gulch. One night when we were pretty drunk — Matt, Nick and me — Nick suggested we hold up the stage which was due to leave camp early in the evenin'. At the moment, it seemed like a mighty smart idea to us. We were practically broke — and drunk, mind you. I left the tent, and found Vink buckin' a weel in one of the gaming houses. I put it up to him. He wouldn't have anythin' to do with the scheme, and advised me not to. But I was too oiled to pay attention to sound advice. To cut a long story short, Nick, Matt and myself went through with our plans, held up the stage and got a strong box containin' around nine thousand dollars, which was being shipped through Spade Gulch for a payroll in another town."

"Reckon I can understand," Rance smiled thinly, "why you don't want this story to leak out."

"That's the truth, Rance. Can't you see what Annie would say? I'd suffer to my dyin' day. . . . Well, next mornin', me and Matt didn't feel so proud of our job, when we realized what we'd done. We'd pulled the holdup neat and clean, without no killin', and covered our trail back into Spade Gulch neat. The express company offered a reward.

Me'n Matt were worried, but Nick Zane just laughed. Finally I told the whole story to Vink, and asked him how we could get out of the scrape. Vink promised to try and fix it up."

"That sounds like a man-sized job."

"Vink was man-size, even in those days. He went to the stage agent in Spade Gulch and told him if he'd agree not to proscute, he'd see that the money was returned. The agent agreed, which was a heap better than spendin' the company's money to prosecute. Arrangements were mane, Vink not thoroughly trustin' to the agent's word, that the agent was to send a representative to Colby, a town twenty miles west from Spade Gulch, at which time Vink would see that the stolen money was turned over to the representative. Colby was named as a meetin' place, just in case the agent didn't keep his word. It was in the next county and would give me and Matt and Nick a chance to make a getaway, if plans went wrong. Nick was against returning the money right from the first, but me and Matt forced him to agree by takin' his share of the split-up away from him."

Again Wheeler hesitated in his narrative, his face cloudy at old memories. Rance prompted him, "Was the money returned?"

Wheeler nodded. "The agent's representative — a man named Kellicut — met us in Colby. Vink explained that we three pulled the hold-up as a joke more than anythin' else. We had drinks all around — Kellicut was a pretty good fellow — and laughed over the matter. Kellicut put the money in his valise most of it bein' in bills, and got ready to catch the night stage back to Spade Gulch. Meanwhile, Kellicut havin' a couple of hours to wait for his stage, Nick Zane suggests a poker game.

"Vink and Matt and me didn't feel like playin', so Kellicut sat down to a two-handed game to pass the time, with Nick. We never dreamed what Nick had in mind, nor that he'd dare try anythin', there in the saloon where we'd met. Vink, Matt and me went out to get somethin' to eat. The last thing as we left I remembered Nick was suggestin' big stakes, and Kellicut refusin' to play more than two-bit ante —"

"Zane's scheme bein' to try and get Kellicut in deep and then win the stage money, eh?"

"You guessed it, Rance. But Kellicut didn't need to draw on the stage money, even if he'd been tempted to. But he did succeed in trimmin' Nick down to his last four-bit piece. We got the story from the swamper and the barkeep, the only other two in the saloon at that time. Nick lost his temper along with his money. He got up from his chair, after dealin' a hand, with the excuse that he wanted a drink. Walkin' behind Kellicut, he shot him in the back, grabbed Kellicut's valise with the money, and after throwin' a couple of wild shots at the barkeep and swamper, ran out to his horse.

"Vink and Matt and me were down the street a spell, when we heard the shots. Next we saw Nickie Zane ridin' hellbent out of town. We ran to the saloon, and found Kellicut dead. In his hand, when he died, was the ace of hearts, ace of spades, ace of clubs, eight of spades and eight of clubs —"

"The dead man's hand!" Rance exclaimed.

Wheeler nodded. "We never did forget that hand, especially some years later when Bill Hickok was killed in Deadwood, it was found he held aces and eights, too. After that, aces and eights were often termed the 'Dead Man's Hand' in the western country. A combination of black aces and eights got to be a sort of gamblers' superstition. Some sharps hated to hold 'em, even if they proved to be winnin' hands."

"I've heard of that," Rance said, "though I didn't remember it right off when we found Vink holdin' the cards. But I'm interruptin'. What happened next?"

"Vink said to square ourselves, me and Matt would have to help him capture Nickie Zane. The three of us took Nick's trail, and caught him about a month later. Got most of the money, too. Nick had been afraid to try and spend it. The trail ended up in Wyoming, where Nick made a stand in an abandoned cabin. He put up a terrific fight. Matt and me were both wounded slightly. The fight ended when Vink got impatient and went into the shack after Nick. One of his slugs struck Nickie in the shoulder and the fight was over.

"We brought Nick back to trial when he'd recovered. He cursed the three of us somethin' awful. Swore he'd deal us all a dead man's hand before he was finished with us. Matt and me were scared plenty for fear we'd be implicated, but the law was fairly lax in Spade Gulch those days. Nick made a mistake of swearin' Vink had helped in the hold-up of the stage. Vink had several alibis, of course, and when Nick got around to tellin' about the part Matt and I played, the judge thought he was still lyin', and wouldn't allow the testimony. Matt and I were plumb lucky to get out of it that easy."

"Weren't you, though?"

"It was hard to believe our luck. Nickie Zane should have been hung then and there, but some of the jury wasn't actually convinced that Matt and I hadn't had a part in the holdup. But as Nick was on trial for murder, and not for the hold-up, the matter wasn't gone into very deep. In the end Nick Zane got a life sentence, and went to the Colorado penitentiary to serve it."

"But now he's out, eh?"

"It looks that way. I've been thinkin' maybe some relative of Nick's has took up the feud. You see, when Nick was sentenced, he flew into a rage and cursed judge and jury — Vink, Matt and me worst of all. He said we'd double-crossed him, and he swore by every oath he could lay tongue to that some day he'd kill the three of us. He meant it, too. He was a revengeful cuss, and it makes my blood run cold to this day just to think of the look in his eyes when he swore to get us."

"Have you tried to learn if he is out of the penitentiary?"

Wheeler shook his head. "I've been tryin' to avoid any publicity in the matter. From time to time, after Nick Zane first started to serve his sentence, he'd manage to get letters out to us, remindin' us that he'd get us some day. But after a couple of years we didn't hear anythin' more of him. In fact, I reckon we'd just about forgot Nickie Zane, until Vink was killed. When Matt and me heard about that 'dead man's hand' we *knew* a showdown was at hand. When I saw that shell with the Stebbings' firing-pin imprint, I was more certain than ever — and so was Matt. We were positive then that the cards Vink held weren't in his hand due to just coincidence."

"Must have jolted you plenty."

"It sure did. Hell! Think of it — over thirty years afterward. The three of us had come down here to settle for life. Our wild days were over. I had a successful hotel property. Matt had his feed business. Vink had built up a big ranch, married, buried his wife, and raised a daughter. Morada was on the grow. Do you wonder we forgot about Nick Zane and those former days?"

"I'm still wonderin' where Belle Zane — or Thorpe — comes in?"

Wheeler swallowed with difficulty and nodded. "Vink had always thought she was dead. At the time Nick entered the penitentiary, she had showed up there to say good-bye to him. I never dreamed she had that much feelin' in her heart, but I suppose blood is thicker than whisky in the long run. Or maybe she thought he had some money he could turn over to her before he stepped behind the bars. Anyway, when she'd said good-bye and Nick had passed through the prison gates, Belle left Colorado and headed East. The train she was travellin' on was wrecked. The papers carried her name as bein' among those killed in the accident. Vink was plumb relieved when he read how she'd finished —"

"But didn't Vink ever divorce her?"

Wheeler slowly shook his head. "That's what is raisin' hell, Rance. Vink didn't see any need of that. He thought she was dead."

"Then — My God!" Rance came to his feet, eyes burning down into Wheeler's. "But, Brad, I — why, Brad, the Belle Thorpe that's out to the VIT now is Vink's legal widow!"

"You're not tellin' me a thing, Rance," Wheeler said brokenly. "Now, can you understand why I've refused to talk, why I've tried to keep things quiet? Belle Thorpe bein' alive makes Vink's marriage to Eddie's mother illegal — gives Belle Thorpe first call on the estate —"

"Not only that, Brad. It makes Eddie an illegitimate daughter. That poor kid. Not that illegitimacy makes any difference to me, but — Hell! No wonder Belle Thorpe is runnin' things with a high hand."

"Do you wonder I been worried nigh sick over the whole business?" Wheeler gulped. "Matt and me did our damdest to keep this from gettin' out. It just wasn't in the cards to be kept quiet, I reckon. Do you realize what I've been through tryin' to protect Vink's daughter, and my own family, too, of course? If I'd told what was in that letter, at Vink's inquest —"

"Hell, yes! That letter must have hit Vink hard — fact, I know it did, but I didn't know why. No wonder he looked upset, that day on Lookout Ridge."

"He'd settled down some by the time he got into Morada," Wheeler said. "He showed me the letter —"

"Do you remember the wording?"

"Not exactly — Belle just wrote Vink that he'd probably be surprised to learn she was

266

alive, and that she intended to pay him a visit. She stressed the point that she needed money. Vink kind of cooled down after a spell, and figured to buy her out. He knew she'd do most anythin' for money. He showed me the letter, and Matt, too. Vink told me that day he wouldn't send the store receipts to Capitol City as usual. He didn't know but what Belle might be in on the night stage. The postmark on the letter was blurred. Vink couldn't tell whether it had been mailed at El Paso or El Toro. If it was El Toro, Belle might have come in that same night. If she'd arrived that night, Vink figured to offer her the store receipts just to get her away. He knew she'd want more later, of course."

"This explains why Vink was suddenly so anxious to have a will drawn, too. He wanted to protect his money from Belle, so Eddie would get it."

"That was the idea, Rance. Vink had figured to go to Capitol City to see a lawyer the next morning. Me and Matt were to keep an eye out for Belle, in case she arrived before he got back, and hush her down before she had a talk with any strangers. While I was worried about my family learnin' things, our first thought was to protect Eddie. That's why Matt and I lied about that letter at the coroner's inquest. I've had to give Annie a cock-and-bull story about that letter, too. Matt and I figured things might quiet down, and that we'd keep mum about Belle just as long as humanly possible."

"Why did Belle Thorpe wait all these years before lookin' up Vink?"

"She didn't know where he was, or that he had money. Just learned that recently in readin' about some Cattlemen's Convention Vink attended. . . . Oh, yes, I've talked to her. She's been flyin' around the country all these years doin' suckers, I suppose. But she's getting too old for that now. She's still got her old marriage license to Vink, though. Smart enough to hang on to that. She brought it in that day I talked to her. I tried to talk her out of her plan, but she says if I put anythin' in her way she'll raise hell around town and tell everythin' she knows."

"What's her plan?"

"She's offered to get out of this country and keep her mouth shut if Eddie will give her seventy-five thousand dollars. Eddie's goin' to do it, but until Vink's estate is probated she can't get the money. It may not be quite legal goin' through with that probatin' the way things stand now, but I ain't said a word and I guess Eddie ain't thought of it. Eddie's so worried she can't think straight for fear you'll turn up some evidence that will spill the beans. Meanwhile Belle is runnin' Eddie to suit herself, and threatenin' to tell her story all over Morada if anybody crosses her. Belle knows, of course, if she wants to go through with it she can get her legal share of the estate, but I reckon she prefers gettin' seventy-five thousand and goin' her own way, if it can be done."

"So that's why —" Rance commenced, then stopped. "That poor kid. And like a dumb packmule I thought —" Again he stopped and asked, "What's to prevent Belle Thorpe from returnin' when her seventy-five thousand is gone and tryin' a little blackmail on Eddie and you?"

Wheeler shook his head hopelessly. "Not a thing we can think of. We've just got to chance that."

"You're absolutely sure, eh, Brad, that Belle Thorpe at the VIT is the same one that married Vink. No chance of her bein' an imposter, is there?"

"Not a chance." Wheeler shook his head emphatically. "I knew her right off — and so did Matt. Matt kept out of her way. I tried to, but she caught me. Annie saw us together. I haven't been able to explain that yet. And did I catch hell! I'm gettin' so I'm afraid to go home. . . . No," in answer to Rance's query, "Belle says she hasn't heard from her brother since she said good-bye at the pen. She's not interested. For all she knows he is dead."

There was a few minutes' silence between the two men. Rance's mind was awhirl with thought. After a time he said, "Brad, it was

Matt who sent that warnin' note and shot at me that night, wasn't it?"

A rueful smile crossed Wheeler's face. "I told Matt he hadn't fooled you with that talk about burnin' his hand on a rope —"

"Why in time did he do it, Brad?"

"He didn't try to kill you, Rance. Matt had a fool idea that if he sent you a warnin' and followed it with a shot, he might scare you off."

"But, why?"

"You'll remember, Rance," Wheeler explained, "that you was ridin' Matt and me pretty hard about that letter Vink showed us. We were afraid of the story comin' out — on Eddie's account. I told Matt you weren't the sort of hombre who scares easy when you wanted to turn up evidence, but Matt figured to try, anyhow. He shot wide, a-purpose. Matt wouldn't have hurt you for the world —"

"Cripes! I might have killed him," Rance muttered.

"Your shot grazed his hand when you were chasing him through the alley. He reckoned from the noise that you had stumbled and fallen down. You were gaining on him up to then. Once he got through to Thorpe Street he ran into the barn back of his feed store, and waited until things had quieted down. Later he heard a buggy comin' along the street. He guessed it was Yocum bringin' old Lucas from Capitol City. After the buggy passed Matt went on to his boardin' house, and let himself in without bein' seen or heard. He was plumb disappointed that his scheme hadn't worked."

Rance sighed. "I wish you'd given me all this story before, Brad."

"Wish I had, too — now. But don't you see how it was, Rance? We didn't want that story about Vink and Belle to get out. We done our best to prevent it, but our best wasn't good enough — and now Matt's gone."

"Everybody makes mistakes at one time or another, Brad. What's done is done. Your story has cleared the atmosphere some, but we're still as far away as ever from the killer who finished Vink and Matt. Got any idea when he'll try to kill you — ?"

"Wish to God I had," Wheeler said fervently. "Matt and I always felt safe durin' the day, but now that Matt was killed — Hell! It's gettin' on my nerves at the thought of Nick Zane ridin' into Morada and killin' as he pleases — if it is Nick, personal. Maybe some relative of his has took up the argument. I can't sleep nights. I'm jumpy as a cat. For God's sake, Rance, if you know of anythin' —"

"I don't," Rance said grimly. "But with what you've told me to go on I've got a startin' point."

"What you aimin' to do?"

"Get my dinner, then line out for Capitol City and send a telegram to the warden of the Colorado Penitentiary —"

"And find when Nickie Zane was released, eh?"

"Either that, or see if I can get a line on who he's in the habit of writin' to. We don't know — he may have been in touch with Belle Thorpe. I wouldn't trust to her word. . . . Brad, you look up Homer Yocum and tell him the story you've told me. Tell him where I've gone."

Wheeler looked dubious. "Shucks! I don't want that story spread all over town —"

"It's li'ble to be spread anyway in time if we don't get busy. Tell Homer to keep his mouth shut — and his eyes open. He'll keep still if you tell him to, and the knowledge you give him might help him to play his cards better if anythin' new comes up. And I don't need to warn you to keep your mouth shut about my whereabouts."

"All right," Wheeler sighed, "I'll tell Yocum."

Rance nodded, rose to his feet, and walked around the side of the porch. Here he descended the steps to his pony and mounted, swinging into Main Street. He stopped at Quong Kee's restaurant for a hurried meal, then pounded out of town on the road that led to Capitol City.

CHAPTER XIX

Two mornings later Rance loped his horse along the trail that led from Capitol City to Morada. It was still early, the sun wasn't yet up. A streak of pink suddenly flamed along the horizon at Rance's back, then widened and spread into the gray of vanishing night. Abruptly the blaze of vivid pink melted into gold. Overhead the sky was transformed to a cloudless blue.

Rance had left the capitol during the night, and stopped twice to rest and water his horse. The previous day had been a hard one. He had sent, all told, three wires to the warden at the Colorado penitentiary and received answers to each, but the wires had been slow, the first two replies inadequate. Information was difficult to procure at such long distance.

Two hours passed to the accompaniment of the staccato drumming of hoofs. Rance pushed on. Topping a rise in the road he could see still far ahead of him the rooftops of Morada, with beyond the low-lying Santos Hills, whose one and only high-level was Lookout Ridge. Beyond the hills the climbing sun was commencing to pick out pink high lights on the jagged peaks of the Sangre de Santos Mountains.

Ten miles east of Morada, Rance pulled his steaming pony to a slower gate. It was growing warm now. The chill of early morning was dissipated. Rance considered, "Better keep goin' to the Star-Cross. Nothin' like strikin' while the iron is hot."

He kicked his pony in the ribs and pulled off the stage-wheel-rutted road to head directly across the range. An hour later he passed Morada, which lay a few miles to the south. The pony was nearing the Santos Hills now and getting into rolling country.

Occasionally Rance swung his mount wide to avoid an abrupt outcropping of granite or a huge clump of prickly pear. Ahead lay the Santos Hills, their grasses burned brown under the torrid South-West sun.

Rance was into the hills before he realized it almost. Swinging a half-mile to the north he struck the hoof-marked trail that ran from Norris' Star-Cross outfit to Morada. It wasn't far from here he had found Norris' dead paint horse.

For another fifteen minutes the pony drummed on. They were getting out of the hills now. For a mile the trail bordered a series of precipitous buttes of red granite. The buttes were slashed deep with draws and canyons. It suddenly occurred to Rance that these buttes would make mighty good hideouts for stolen cattle.

Unconsciously, he drew rein to a slower gait. He was commencing to see small bunches of stock now branded on the left ribs with the Star-Cross design — a five-pointed star with connecting lines from point to point, with, in the center, two straight shorter lines crossing at right-angles to constitute a crude cross. Like the VIT, practically all of the Star-Cross cows were Herefords.

From far ahead through the clear morning air came a frantic bellowing. The sound had come from beyond a rise, and to Rance's right, near the vicinity of the butte walls. Rance pulled to a halt and listened.

He hadn't long to wait: a white-face yearling steer came lumbering clumsily over the rise. Seeing Rance, it swerved and headed for open range. Rance spurred close. The cow increased its speed. This suited Rance.

A quarter of a mile Rance pursued the animal into open country before he reached for his lariat. A moment later he had shaken out the rope, built his loop, and was closing in swiftly on the cow. He had already noted it bore the Star-Cross brand. The pony's drumming hoofs carried him closer. Rance's rope whizzed through the air. The loop flew straight and true to its mark. . . . The next few moments were busy ones. At the end of ten minutes Rance, having completed his examination of the newly-burned brand, released the cow and ran to his waiting pony. The steer clambered to its feet indignantly. It lowered its head, looking angrily at Rance and the pony for a few seconds. Then it trotted stiffly off to join others of its species a short distance away.

Rance settled in his saddle, his face hard. "That's the way Norris works it, eh?" he muttered. "Damn smart, that hombre, but I've got somethin' on him now."

He turned the horse back toward the spot where he had first picked up the steer. Drawing near, he saw a second cow. This one, too, was freshly-branded Star-Cross. The cow dashed off when it saw him. Rance didn't attempt to follow it. He was after bigger game now.

Dismounting, he dropped reins over his pony's head and crept on foot toward the rise of ground over which the freshly-branded cows had appeared.

Nearing the top of the rise Rance dropped on his stomach and wiggled forward. A minute more and he was peering cautiously around for signs of the rustler who converted VIT cows into Star-Cross property.

From the top of the rise the earth fell away in a wide swale that reached to the shadows of the buttes, and was covered with a scattered growth of mesquite, chapparal, catclaw and cactus. There seemed to be a sort of trail leading deeper into the swale. There was no one in sight, but certain significant sounds were being thrown back from the butte walls.

Rance rose to his feet and descended the slope. He pushed as quietly as possible through the bush. Five minutes passed. The sounds were somewhat louder now. Abruptly peering around a tall chaparral, Rance saw a broad cleared space ahead of him. He stopped short, in sheer surprise. Here was an ideal layout for a cattle-thief.

Against the wall of the buttes had been erected a crude but effective corral. At the moment it enclosed some dozen or so Hereford cows. Twenty-five yards from Rance a man was just rising to his feet from the side of a yearling which had been thrown and had three of its feet tied together. A taut rope ran from the yearling to a saddled horse a few yards away.

The rustler's back was to Rance at the moment, but Rance had no trouble in recognizing Bert Gillett. He watched Gillett carry a running-iron back to a small fire several steps away, and thrust the straight length of iron back among the hot coals.

Gillett straightened and turned one side to Rance. He removed his gloves and wiped the perspiration from his forehead. One hand went to a tobacco tag dangling from a vest pocket. He laughed softly, spoke aloud to the prone bovine:

"Wonder how Quillan will like you now, doggie. . . . I reckon your new sign changes you some."

Rance stepped into the open and said quietly, "I reckon it does, Gillett. You're workin' early this mornin'." He started toward the rustler, hands swinging easily at his sides.

Gillett whirled around, stiffened, backed away a pace. "Duncan! Christ!" Just the two words. His right hand streaked to holstered gun, flashed up, morning sunlight glinting along the barrel. The gun roared.

Rance heard the bullet whine high overhead. His own gun was out now, but he held his fire. It wasn't a question of how rapidly he could shoot, but how accurate his aim would be. Coolly he advanced, rapidly closing the distance between them.

Again Gillett pulled trigger. This time the leaden slug came nearer. Rance waited to make sure of his mark. He'd let Gillett do all the hurrying.

Gillett swore at him, unleashed a third shot. The breeze from the bullet fanned Rance's cheek. Rance laughed grimly. Abruptly his right hand jerked, exploded a savage burst of smoke and white fire.

Gillett staggered, endeavored to raise his gun for a fourth attempt. Quite suddenly he crumpled to the earth, the weapon fell from his hand. He tried to rise, then sprawled face downward.

Rance plugged out the empty shell in the cylinder and methodically shoved in a fresh load. He walked over to Gillett and stood looking down on him. After a moment he stooped and retrieved Gillett's gun, then turned the rustler over.

The man was unconscious, his eyes closed. "Mighty near the heart," Rance muttered. "He might live long enough to talk some. Anyway, I can't leave him here."

He ripped open Gillett's shirt to see what could be done about stopping the flow of blood. . . .

CHAPTER XX

It wasn't yet eleven in the morning when Rance rode into Morada leading Gillett's horse behind him. Lashed to the pony's back was the still unconscious figure of Bert Gillett. A sudden yell carried along Main Street. Men came running from all directions.

Deputy Yocum emerged hastily from his office just as Rance drew to a halt before Doctor Parker's house. Yocum came hurrying across the street.

"My Gawd! It's Gillett! What happened?"

Rance stepped down from the saddle. "Caught him improvin' the VIT brand with a hot-iron — that is, improvin' from his point of view."

"T'hell you say. Where? Cripes! I didn't know you were back from Capitol City yet."

"Got back this mornin'. Found Gillett near those red buttes, just off the Star-Cross trail. Help me get him inside —"

"Is he alive yet?"

"Some," Rance said grimly.

A crowd had gathered. Doctor Parker came out to the road, firing questions at Rance. Rance refused to talk until the three men had carried the unconscious rustler into the doctor's house, where he was laid on a bed. The doctor sent his Mexican housekeeper for water and bandages, then turned to Rance.

Rance explained briefly what had happened, ending, "No use lettin' that crowd out there know what Gillett was doin'. . . . I'd like to talk to Gillett. Will he live?"

"I may be able to bring him around, again I may not," Parker said shortly. "I'll do my best. You and Yocum wait in my office. I'll let you know in a little while."

In the office Yocum said, "What in time were you doing on the Star-Cross trail?"

"Headin' to see Norris."

"You got somethin' on Norris?"

"I reckon."

Homer thrust some peanuts into his mouth. "My, you're talkative. But suit yourself if you don't want to furnish details. . . . Brad told me about Nick Zane — and all the rest. What did you find out from the warden of the Colorado pen?"

"I'll give you the whole story in a little while. I'm tryin' to dope out somethin'!"

"What?"

"I'm wonderin' why Gillett was workin' over a VIT cow into an 8Q-Barred-Out —"

"Huh? You said he was burnin' a Star-Cross brand. If I'd thought, though, I'd knowed that couldn't be done. Not a Star-Cross. No man can make a Star-Cross out of a VIT."

Rance laughed softly. "Yesterday I'd have said the same thing, but it can be done, Homer."

"You got to show me," scornfully.

"I'll do that." Rance rose from his chair and found a pencil and blank piece of paper on Parker's office desk. He quickly sketched the three capital letters VIT.

"Now, bear in mind," he said, "that the VIT brand is burned with a straight bar, about seven inches long, affixed to a handle. By turnin' said iron bar in the necessary positions, the letters can be made with five applications of the iron — two for the V, one for the I, and two to make the T —"

"I know all that," Yocum said impatiently.

"I suppose. Well, sometimes when we're brandin' in a hurry at calf round-up, or later on the range, when an animal that's been overlooked gets picked up, some of those lines aren't burned as straight as they should be. When Norris, or Gillett, found such a brand he herded the animal into his hidden corral until he was ready to work it over. That was done in this way."

Quickly Rance added several lighter lines to the VIT, then tossed the drawing across to Yocum. The deputy glanced at it, his eyes widened in amazement. "By cripes! It can be done, can't it? Just like you claimed! I'd never have believed it." He gazed at the sign a moment longer.

Star-Cross brand converted from a VIT.

Rance said, "It's not an absolutely perfect star, of course, but for that matter the lines in our VIT brand aren't always slapped on absolutely perfect. By the time the brand is healed and haired over it'd take more than an ordinary look-see to notice any irregularities."

"By gosh!" Yocum said suddenly. "The earmarks work out, too, don't they?"

Rance nodded. "The VIT splits right and left. The Star-Cross gotches right and left — cuts about half the ear straight off — which slashes off enough ear to completely dispose of the VIT earmark."

"My God, man! It's perfect —"

"Well thought out," Rance amended. "While I was in Capitol City I checked into the brand registration books. Norris adopted the Star-Cross brand when he got the ranch. He's probably been stealin' from the VIT for some time."

"The lousy thief," Yocum growled. "Say, what were you sayin' before, about catchin' Gillett makin' an 8Q-Barred-Out?"

"That's what's got me wonderin' — unless Gillett's workin' for both Quillan and Norris." Rance explained in a few words what he had witnessed that morning, ending with, "You see, I'd already examined the brand on the made-over Star-Cross animal I roped. After that a second stolen Star-Cross came past me. Those two told me just how the VIT could be altered. But at the time I caught Gillett he'd just finished burnin' a VIT into Quillan's brand."

"What did you do with the animal?"

"Put it in the corral with the VIT stuff that was waitin' to have its brands altered. You see, I wanted it as evidence, so I couldn't cut it loose. I couldn't leave it layin' there for fear Norris would come along. If he found Gillett gone he'd lose the cow himself, knowin' somethin' had gone wrong. And I simply had to get Gillett into Doc Parker before he died on my hands —"

"Plumb tender-hearted, ain't you?"

"I wanted him to live long enough to do some talkin' anyway. I'm hopin' if Norris goes to join Gillett he won't notice that 8Q-Barred-Out animal in the corral. Seein' Gillett's gone should make him come high-tailin' to Morada. Which same, if it happens, will save me a trip out to the Star-Cross."

"By Gawd! It looks like we got the dead-wood on Norris."

"You're damn right, we have," grimly. "You don't know half of it."

"I'm waiting to hear it all."

"That'll come later. Do you know anythin' about Norris' crew?"

"Aside from Gillett and an old cook, he only had two hands workin' for him. The way things have shaped up I'm thinkin' the two hands are honest, and that until he hired Gillett, Norris was doin' his own rustlin'."

"What makes you think his two hands are straight?"

" 'Cause they quit him yesterday. They were in town. I asked why they were leavin'. They told me they got tired punchin' for Norris. Here's what I think. They learned about that hidden corral and figured there was skull-duggery afoot. They didn't want to be mixed in it. But they wouldn't squeal on a man whose wages they took. So they cut their string and lit out."

"That sounds likely. Say where they were goin'?"

Yocum nodded. "Both of 'em left an address. They got kin-folk near Tucson. They asked me to drop 'em a line some time. Now I know they left those addresses so we could get in touch with 'em if trouble broke. They were keepin' their own boots out of the mud."

"They were wise. Hell's due to break loose

285

right sudden. I got a hunch Norris will come out to check up on Gillett to see if he's workin' all right. When he finds Gillett gone he'll high-tail it for town."

"Mebbe he'll read signs and decide somethin' is wrong."

"I thought of that. Erased prints and such before I pulled out. Rode out to my own horse standin' in one stirrup of Gillett's bronc. All Norris should see, if he stops to look, is one set of hoof-marks goin' out. I don't think he'd dare take time to do more than that —"

At that moment Doctor Parker entered the office. Rance jumped to his feet, "Is he livin', Doc?"

"He may live and he may not. Gillett's got a tough constitution, though."

"Well, can I talk to him?"

"He's still unconscious, man. Come back later and I'll let you know how things stand. . . . Have you found any clues to the murders yet?"

"Come back later," Rance smiled, repeating the doctor's words, "and I'll let you know how things stand."

Yocum snickered. Parker frowned, "All right if you feel that way about it, Duncan. You haven't told me in detail yet how you come to shoot Gillett."

"It was his life or mine, Doc. He threw down first. You'll get the whole story eventually."

Rance added to Yocum, "Let's get outside."

On the street Yocum said, "You're holdin' somethin' up your sleeve, Rance. What is it?"

Rance smiled cryptically. "Wait until Norris comes in, Homer. I'll tell you how to make your arrest then —"

"Maybe he come in while we were in Doc's."

"I don't reckon so. I kept my eye on the window all the time we sat in Parker's office. You stick around here and get reports on Gillett's condition. If he gets so he can talk come and get me —"

"Where'll you be?"

"Around town. Keep your eye peeled for Norris' arrival, too. I want to know about that."

"Right-o, Rance."

Rance climbed into the saddle. Again that cryptic smile. He reined his pony away from the hitch-rack. "Heard anythin' from Eddie?"

"Not a word. It's tough for her — what Brad Wheeler told me about Belle Thorpe."

"Ain't it hell?" Rance frowned. "That's got me worried —"

"I expect her and that Belle woman in town this afternoon.

"What makes you think so?"

"Most everybody'll be in town. Matt Everett's to be buried at three-thirty, you know."

"I'd forgotten that."

"Goin' to attend, ain't you — ? There goes Ward Stinson now."

Stinson, dressed in rusty black, rode past on his horse. He nodded crustily to Rance and the deputy, and trotted on.

Rance said to Yocum, "You seen anythin' of Monte Quillan?"

"He's in town. Dressed flashy, too. You'd think he'd tone down some for a funeral. He came in a short time before you arrived. His features sort of look like they'd been worked over."

Rance smiled, spoke to his pony. "See you later, Homer."

He moved off down the street.

In front of the hotel Rance saw several acquaintances. Brad Wheeler's voice hailed him from the porch. Rance turned in the saddle, "I'll see you after a while, Brad," he called. "Got somethin' to tell you."

He drew rein before the Thorpe store and dismounted. Alonzo Wheeler was behind the counter when Rance entered.

"Hi-yuh, Rance," the boy greeted.

"Same to you, 'Lonzo, . . . Where's old Clem? He ain't takin' the day off, is he?"

Alonzo shook his head. "Clem ain't took a day off, 'cept Sundays, since Mister Thorpe was killed. Says he don't take no pleasure no more in bein' off the job. No, he's out to his dinner."

"Shucks! Is it only dinner time? Things has been happenin' so fast I thought it must be late, though my stomach ain't complained any."

Alonzo nodded toward a clock on the wall. "Just twenty minutes to one, Rance. Say, I heard you shot Bert Gillett. Tell us about it."

"Nothin' to relate, 'Lonzo. You'll hear the story later. You lookin' for new material for a play?"

Alonzo brightened. "Everythin' that comes fishin' in my net gets caught," he misquoted.

"I reckon. . . ." Rance's eyes ran along the tobacco case. "Give me a sack of Kenmild Smokin' Mixture."

Alonzo opened the case, looked inside. "Sorry, Rance, but there ain't none here. I'm sure there's a case in the store-house though. Can't you take Durham?"

"What's the matter, you too lazy to go to the store-house and break out that case of Kenmild, 'Lonzo?"

Alonzo shook his head. "It ain't that, honest, Rance. Only, Clem always keeps the key to the store-house, and it's locked up. I always tell Clem he should leave me that key when he goes out, but he plumb forgets it lately. . . . Take Durham."

Rance shook his head. "Shucks, I can wait until Clem comes back."

A few minutes later Clem came shuffling into the store. Alonzo seized the hat hanging back of the counter and galloped away. At the doorway he paused, called back, "Rance wants some Kenmild Mixture, Clem."

"Howdy, Rance," Clem nodded. "Ain't

seen ye for a couple of days. Nobody from the ranch ain't been in, either." He doffed his coat and hat for a work apron. "Had prune pie for my dinner at Quong Kee's this noon. Ain't sure how it'll set on my innards, but a feller has to have some pleasures. Howcome ye ain't been in?"

"Ain't been in town," Rance explained. "Ridin' around, trying to pick up clues. First Vink, then Matt Everett is killed, and nothin' to show who done it."

"I'm afeared ye're up agin a hopeless case, Rance. . . . I hear tell ye shot Gillett this mornin' —"

"Yes, we had a little run-in. Gillett ain't dead, though —"

"He ain't? Way I heard it he was killed instanter. Somethin' about rustlin', wa'nt it?"

"It looked that way, but I might be mistaken — say Clem, how about that Kenmild tobacco I asked for?"

Lucas shuffled around behind the tobacco case. He opened it and looked inside, then announced, "Ain't got no Kenmild on hand. Won't Durham do? It's the best —"

"I want Kenmild. 'Lonzo said there was a case in the store-house."

"So there be. I'd plumb forgot. Don't know where my wits has flew to lately. I'll get it for ye? Won't take but a jiffy to pry open that case."

He searched his pockets for the key to the

store-house, then came around the counter holding the key in his hand. "I'll be right back, Rance, quicker'n two twists of a steer's tail."

Rance reached out and took the key from Lucas' fingers. "Shucks, Clem. No use you leavin' the store. I know that store-house. I'll find the case of Kenmild and bring it in for you. No use you luggin' boxes around —"

"No, no, Rance, that's part of my duties. I can carry that box. It don't weigh nothin' —"

"Bosh!" Rance laughed. "You stay here and 'tend your store. I'll be back *pronto.*"

He brushed past Clem Lucas' restraining hand, and despite the old man's protestations walked on through the back room and let himself out the rear door. Crossing the short stretch of yard brought him to the padlocked door of the store-house, which was in reality little more than a long shed.

Rance inserted the key in the padlock. It snapped open. He removed the padlock and thrust it into an overalls pocket. Then he swung back to the door and stepped across the threshold. It was dark and gloomy in the building, the only light entering through the doorway. There were no windows. Boxes and barrels were stacked nearly to the corrugated iron roof. A crate of shovels rested against one of the uprights that supported the roof. Just inside the doorway stood several bright-bladed axes with red handles.

Rance looked quickly around, then moved to the far end of the long shed. Here he got behind a barrel and crouched down. A minute passed. From outside came Clem Lucas' shuffling step. Lucas entered and looked around in surprise at seeing the storehouse apparently empty. He moved back to the doorway.

"Humph!" Rance heard him mutter disgustedly. "Gone off and left the door open. Took my padlock along. Dang it all!"

Rance crouched lower behind the sheltering barrel.

CHAPTER XXI

Homer Yocum rose from his tilted chair before his office as he saw Hugh Norris come tearing into town. Norris' face was cloudy with anger, his pony was streaked with sweat.

"Hi-yuh, Norris!" Yocum hailed.

Norris pulled the horse to a stop, then jerked it toward the deputy's hitch-rack. He sat frowning down from the saddle. "You seen Bert Gillett this mornin', Yocum?"

"Why, you huntin' for him?"

Norris growled, "Yes, damn his hide. I gave him a job to do. When I rode out to see how he was gettin' along, he'd gone —"

"Where was this?"

"Listen, Yocum, I ain't got no time for talk. Have you seen him, or ain't you?"

The deputy chewed meditatively a moment. "Yeah, I seen him," he admitted.

"Humph! Figured you might have. Had to come to town for a drink, did he? I should have known better than to trust him. I suppose he's dead drunk by this time."

"You're about fifty per cent correct, Norris. Leastwise, he ain't drunk, but he may be dead by this time.

"What are you hintin' at, Yocum?"

"I ain't hintin'. I'm givin' facts. Gillett's at the doctor's now. Parker says he's pretty bad."

"Huh," surprised. "He must have been took sudden with somethin'."

"Yeah. A lead slug. Rance Duncan brought him in a spell ago."

"Rance Duncan! I don't understand you, Yocum. What's this about a lead slug — ?"

Yocum scornfully spat out a peanut shuck. "Listen here, Norris, you might as well own up. Duncan caught Gillett workin' some VIT cows into Star-Crosses. Gillett seen he was caught red-handed and went for his iron. Rance Duncan took to the suggestion, and made his argument stick."

Norris looked steadily at Yocum, his eyes narrowed. There was a minute's slow silence. The deputy tensed, hand near holster.

A flash of anger crept into Norris' features. Finally he nodded and said quietly, "Gillett's at Doc Parker's now, eh?"

"Yep, unconscious. Parker is tryin' to pull him through, so he can give evidence." Yocum didn't quite comprehend this. He was puzzled at Norris' attitude. Norris hadn't displayed the expected consternation. According to custom, Norris should have vehemently denied the charges, or even reached for his gun. Why, the man didn't even attempt to turn his horse for a getaway. Something had gone wrong. This wasn't at all according to Hoyle.

Yocum said, "That's a right smart way to do it — changin' that VIT brand to a Star-Cross. But it spells your finish, Norris."

That spur didn't prod Norris to the expected action either. Norris burst out suddenly, "Don't be a total damn fool, Yocum. It's the only sensible way to fix that brand. No use spoilin' a hide by ventin', and then burnin' some more. Any damn fool could see that —"

"My Gawd!" Yocum gasped. "You ain't admittin' it?"

"Man alive," Norris smiled coldly. "There's no reason for hidin' anythin'. Certainly Gillett was workin' VIT cows into Star-Crosses. I put him to work at it. Now, dammit, Duncan has to make trouble. Yocum, what's the matter with you, anyway?"

Yocum was staggered. This was more than his brain was capable of absorbing. All he knew of cow-country ways and customs vanished. Here was a cow-thief, brazenly admitting his guilt.

"Well," he said weakly, "the VIT ain't swore to no warrant, but I reckon I better arrest you, Norris." He racked his mind, struggling to adjust it to these new conditions. "Seems like that's customary in such cases — though mebbe I'm crazy —"

"You're crazy as hell," Norris snapped. "Arrest me? What for?"

"Stealin' VIT cows, of course," Yocum

tried for a certain strength in the words but failed miserably.

"Who said I stole any VIT animals?"

"You just admitted it."

"I admit I put Gillett to work brandin' over some VIT cows, but you can't arrest me for —"

"Norris," Yocum now thought he understood, "have you been smokin' *marijuana* —"

"Certainly not. I ain't loco. I ain't stole any VIT stock. Them animals I had Gillett brandin' I paid for — bought 'em from Vink Thorpe — five hundred of 'em —"

Yocum's mouth fell open, "When was this?"

Norris considered. He said, "A month or so back."

"Damn funny," Yocum said, "he didn't tell Rance Duncan about it?"

"Mebbe he did. I don't know —"

"Rance never said anythin' to me. Besides —"

"Look here, Yocum. I ain't no time to waste. I bought them cows, all legal, paid cash for 'em. Vink Thorpe knew his brand could be changed into a Star-Cross. I showed him one night — same night I bought the cows —"

Yocum laughed scornfully, "Do you expect me to believe that?"

"I don't give a damn whether you believe it or not. I'm tellin' you. Prove I'm a liar, if you think so."

"Well, that's damn queer," Yocum muttered. "Rance Duncan never said anythin' about it — or about makin' delivery of five hundred Herefords —"

"The VIT wasn't supposed to make delivery. I arranged with Vink Thorpe to pick 'em off the range any time I got ready for 'em. I been pickin' up a few at a time for the past week or so, herdin' 'em into a corral. Christ, Yocum!" Norris said irritably, "Vink Thorpe was capable of doin' business without tellin' Duncan about it."

"Yeah," slowly, "I suppose he was — only it seems sort of funny. . . . Say, look here," suddenly suspicious, "I suppose you got a bill-of-sale for them white-faces?"

"You're damn right, I have," Norris said promptly. "Want to see it?" He reached into hip-pocket, took out a wallet, and produced a folded slip of paper, which he handed down to Yocum. "Read that, Yocum, then do some apologizin'."

Yocum unfolded and perused the bill-of-sale. His last suspicions took wing. There it was, plain in black and white, a receipt for money for the sale of five hundred VIT cows to Hugh Norris, and signed, Vincent I. Thorpe. The bill was dated a little more than a month previously.

"Believe me now?" Norris taunted.

The deputy feebly nodded his head and handed back the bill-of-sale. "Ain't nothin' else for me to believe," he admitted. "Damn if I know why Vink didn't tell Rance —"

"Your friend, Duncan, has got himself into a mess this time." Norris was suddenly angry. "Shootin' a hand of mine for doin' his work. By God! This means Duncan's finish. I'm goin' to swear out a warrant before Judge Alvord. You'll have an arrest to make, all right, Yocum. If Gillett dies, we'll swing Duncan higher'n a kite —"

"That's whatever, Norris," Yocum drawled. "But I just want to remind you that Gillett shot first. Nobody but a guilty man would do that —"

"You've only got Duncan's word for it. I don't believe Gillett shot first. Like's not, Duncan threw down without givin' him a hound-dawg's chance —"

Yocum had an inspiration. "Maybe," he suggested, "the fact that Gillett was brandin' an 8Q-Barred-Out animal at the time had somethin' to do with it —"

"What!" Norris stiffened in the saddle. "What's that? An 8Q-Barred-Out, did you say? You're crazy. It couldn't be done."

The deputy commenced to feel better. He had shaken Norris at last. There *was* something wrong. "Oh, yes, it could be done," he drawled, resuming his mastication of peanuts. "Don't tell me, Norris, that you don't know it. Y'know, Gillett overheard Rance and me discussin' that very thing one day, too.

Maybe that's where he got his idea. Also, any man smart enough to think out that Star-Cross brand wouldn't overlook a bet on Quillan's iron —"

Norris damned something under his breath, then asked, "Where is this animal Rance claims to have caught Gillett workin' over?"

"Ask Rance," Yocum said sleepily. "He's got it put away for safe keepin'."

"We-ell," Norris admitted reluctantly, "mebbe that brand could be worked over at that. I don't know anythin' about Quillan's cows. I'm only interested in my own stock. I can't understand Gillett doin' anythin' of that kind, though. It looks to me like he had thrown in with Quillan to make a little money on the side —"

"You won't back Gillett in that play, then, eh?"

"Certainly not," angrily. "I can't back a thief. . . . Reckon I'll go over to Parker's and talk to him."

"Won't do you no good," Yocum said. "He's unconscious. Doc Parker has promised to let me know if he comes to, but it looks like he'll die without regain' consciousness. I been waitin' a long spell now."

Norris was silent for a minute, his eyes narrowed in concentration. "Well, there's just this to it," he said at last, "if Gillett is workin' with Quillan to run off VIT stuff, he ought to be jailed if he don't die. He can't expect any help from me, after me givin' him work, when Duncan fired him. Damn his measly hide, anyway! Why, he might have got me into serious trouble with the VIT. Serve him right, if Duncan's shot spells his finish —"

"Got another fiddle to play your tune on, didn't you?"

"Certain. I can't back any such play of Gillett's. But I'm goin' to tell Duncan a thing or two, just the same. I got a legal right to five hundred VIT cows, and if I don't tell Duncan what's what, he's li'ble to take a shot at me one of these days. . . . Where's Duncan now?"

"Headin' toward the centre of the town, last I seen of him. You'll probably find him around the Morada House some place. If he ain't there, maybe Brad Wheeler, or some of the others, will be able to tell you where he went."

Norris nodded gruffly. "Better let this be a lesson to you, Yocum. Don't always be too ready to judge a man on circumstantial evidence."

He turned his horse and moved thoughtfully down Main Street.

Yocum returned to his chair before his office, his face a study in bewilderment.

"Damn if I understand it," he muttered. "I threw a shock into Norris tellin' about that 8Q-Barred-Out, but this sale of five hundred VIT critters is beyond me. It wasn't like Vink to transact such a deal without tellin' his foreman. On the other hand, he might have forgot, or somethin'. It's damn queer. Norris prompt forgot about havin' Rance arrested for shootin' Gillett, when I told him a few things. . . . Howdy, Eddie. Hello, Ringbone."

Eddie Thorpe had just passed on her pony, riding at the side of the VIT buckboard, which carried a frowning Ringbone Uhler and the flamboyant Belle Thorpe, triumphant in considerable rouge and a feather boa. They replied to the deputy's salutation, and Yocum settled back to exchange glares with Belle Thorpe. Horse and wagon passed on, down the street.

"Come in for Matt Everett's funeral, I reckon," the deputy mused. "You'd think that hussy would wear black on a day like this, 'stead of dressin' herself up like a circus horse."

A hail reached him from Doctor Parker, across the street, "Gillett has regained consciousness, Yocum. If you want to talk to him, you better come right over. Where's Duncan?"

"Down near the hotel, some place." The deputy crossed the street. "Want me to get him first?"

Parker shook his head. "You better come in and do your own talking now, without further delay. Gillett may die within the next ten minutes. Or he may live, if what Rance

Duncan said is true, to serve a long prison sentence. I can't decide, but I don't think we should waste any time."

"You're the boss, Doc."

Yocum followed the doctor into the house.

CHAPTER XXII

Peering around the side of the barrel, Rance saw Lucas shuffle to a stack of boxes about midway between the door and Rance's hiding place. Lucas lifted down the top box, which appeared to be weighty, and placed it on the floor, then reached up for the next box. This he hefted in his hands a moment, nodded with satisfaction, and put it back. Then, replacing the first box on top of the stack, he turned and slowly shuffled out of the store-house.

Rance waited until the footsteps had died away, then quickly moved to the stack of goods that had interested old Lucas. He lifted down the top box, marked "Canned Peaches," and placed it on the floor. The second box was lighter, and if the stencilled words on sides and ends were to be believed, contained canned tomatoes. Rance doubted this.

He looked at the box as he set it on top of the one containing canned peaches. The top boards had at one time been pried off, and although replaced, had not been nailed firmly down. Gripping one of the boards with his fingers, he pulled steadily. The nails came loose. Three quick wrenches sent the remaining boards the way of the first. The box was opened to Rance's gaze now. An exclamation of exultation came to his lips.

At the bottom of the box lay a bulky canvas sack. Rance seized two of its corners, upended it. A shower of objects tumbled into the box: gold, silver and paper money, a forty-five six-shooter, a new deck of playing cards with the cover-seal broken, and some papers.

"The store receipts and Vink's poker winnings," Rance exclaimed. He thumbed back the hammer of the gun, examined it, and laughed triumphantly. Here was the weapon he'd wanted to find — the gun with the Stebbings' firing-pin, the forty-five employed by Thorpe's killer!

The papers next caught his eye. Three of them were cheques for various amounts, made out to Vincent I. Thorpe, and signed by Augustus Oldfield. Here were the missing cheques.

The remaining paper was a folded letter. Rance opened it, saw that it was addressed to Thorpe, and signed by Belle Thorpe. This was the mysterious letter Thorpe had received that day on Lookout Ridge. Rance started to read,

"Dear Vink —

"I'll bet you will be surprised to find out I'm alive. They give me up for gone in that railroad accident. The papers all said I was dead, but I got well again. So your little Belle

is all safe and sound. I am coming to see you. Vink, I saw a piece in a newspaper about you. It said you had married again and had a daughter, but your wife had died a long time back. The paper called you a wealthy cattleman. That was good news, Vink. I can use some money in case you don't want me to take my place in your home as your legal wife —"

A snarling remark from the doorway interrupted the reading. Rance dropped the letter into the box, whirled to find Clem Lucas confronting him.

"What you doin'?" Lucas said hoarsely.

Rance laughed coolly. "Sort of figured this was the only safe place you'd hide these things, and I let you lead me to 'em. Didn't figure on you comin' back so soon, though —"

Lucas swore at him. He backed a step to seize one of the sharp-bladed axes near the doorway, then rushed madly at Rance, the axe flashing through the air. Rance leaped forward to escape the descending blow. The handle struck his shoulder, numbing it for an instant. He closed with Lucas, reaching for the axe.

Lucas fought like a madman, displaying a wiry, vicious strength that belied his appearance. The two struggled the length of the store-house, hurtling against barrels and boxes, then back again. Lucas wrapped one leg around Rance's knee, tripped him. They went to the floor with a crash, but by this time Rance had managed to wrest the axe from Lucas' grip.

Over and over the two rolled, fighting for a finishing hold, kicking and striking. Finally Rance managed to reach his feet. Lucas clung to him like a leech, cursing insanely. Rance jerked one arm free, spread his hand across Lucas' face and shoved back the man's head. Fighting desperately to retain his hold, Lucas was forced back and back. His clutching hands were torn loose.

Rance's right hand gripped Lucas by the throat. He jammed the man's head with no little force against a case of goods. His right hand went to holster. Miraculously, the gun hadn't fallen out during the melee.

"I don't want to pull this gun," Rance panted, "but, so help me, I will, if you don't talk and talk plenty. Get busy!"

Lucas' breath was wheezing through his lips. His eyes were wild with mingled hate and terror. "Don't — don't kill me, Rance. I'll tell who done it. Norris —"

"Talk!" Rance said grimly. "And don't lie!" Again he slammed Lucas' head against the packing-case.

"I'll — I'll talk," Lucas gulped. "Take your hand away from my throat. It — it was Norris that —"

"Don't lie, damn you!" Again Rance's hand

closed down. "Your game's up, Zane. I been suspectin' you some, ever since that night Homer Yocum drove you over from Capitol City. You and your rheumatics! It don't go, Nickie Zane —"

"I don't know what you mean," Lucas squirmed.

"I mean you were stiffened from makin' that fifty-mile ride from Capitol City and back. I've seen tenderfoots lamed just like you were, from ridin'. You hadn't been in a saddle in thirty years, Zane. It crippled you plenty — but it wasn't rheumatism."

"You're wrong, Rance. I been troubled with rheu—"

"Dammit! I want the truth. I'll admit you sort of fooled me. It might have been rheumatism. Mebbe I was mistaken. But when I was in Capitol City I checked up. Your room in that hotel was in the back, on the ground-floor. You knew there were horses, every night, tied under that horse shelter, back of the hotel. Always one or two with saddles on. You slipped out the window of your room, stole a horse and started here — didn't know you was stealin' Sheriff Cannon's horse, though, did you?"

"I don't know what you're talkin' about —"

"Liar! I knew that horse of Cannon's wasn't good for that whole trip here and back. Some horses could do it in the time you took, but not you, and not on that fat nag of Cannon's. I knew you didn't dare get fresh horses at Aubrey or Haslam Tanks. Somebody'd remember you. That meant you had help. Somebody had relays along the way for you —"

"I swear you're wrong, Rance. I don't understand —"

"I'm tellin' you! Who helped you? Norris? Figured to bring him here and let you two face the facts together, but it didn't work out that way. Anyway, you came here that night, killed Vink Thorpe, then went back to Capitol City. You crawled back through the window of your room and pretended to be sick. You were sick, all right, but not from rheumatism. The sheriff found his horse, two days later, wanderin' on the outskirts of the town. Didn't you tie it up again, you murderin' skunk — !"

"Don't, Rance. That hurts. You wouldn't hurt old Lucas. You're wrong as can be —"

"Old Lucas hell! Zane, you mean. Nickie Zane! You dirty killer! I can understand why Vink failed to recognize you, two years ago, when you answered his ad, in the Capitol City paper for a clerk in his store. Prison ages men. I've been in touch with the warden at the Colorado penitentiary. He thought you'd gone east. I got your description. 'Fifty-two years old, but has the appearance of seventy.' That's what one telegram said. And another, 'Bad scar on left side of face, received in riot when Zane incited prisoners to mutiny.' That scar helped to fool Vink — that and your whiskers and your glasses. And you're a damn good actor, Zane — good enough to fool the warden into thinkin' you were goin' to die when you got smashed in that riot. That's how you got your pardon. The warden didn't realize he was loosin' a mad wolf on the range —"

"It's all a mistake, Duncan. You're wrong. You got me mixed with somebody else —"

"Dammit! Don't lie to me. I've checked at Quong Kee's where you ate dinner that day you killed Matt Everett. The Chink fell asleep on his stool, while you were eatin'. Nobody else in his restaurant. You left before he woke up. It was the easiest thing in the world for you to leave by the back way, go down the alley, and then enter Matt's store — oh, hell, do you realize now it'll be best to own up — ?"

"So help me God, Duncan, I didn't —" Zane tried to rush past Duncan. Rance seized him, hurled him violently back against the stacked cases.

"I've got other evidence, too, Zane, from that Colorado warden. Hugh Norris served a term there, nearly ten years ago, for cattle rustling, didn't he? You and Norris were right thick. You're game's up, Zane, but I want the details — Norris' part."

Nick Zane suddenly wilted. "All right,

Duncan. I'll tell it all." He tried to hold Rance's eyes, but Rance saw him look up and past. Suddenly Nick Zane shrieked, "Get him, Norris! He knows — !"

Rance whirled to one side, still holding to Zane, as Hugh Norris came plunging through the doorway. Norris' six-shooter roared. Rance's movement had brought Zane in line of the shot. Zane screamed and went limp under Rance's hand, then lurched forward with great violence, pulling Rance down.

Rance flung himself sidewise, drawing his gun as he fell. One shot left the barrel before he struck the floor. Hugh Norris staggered, fell back against the door-jamb. Here he righted himself, cursing, lifted his gun.

Through the fog of smoke, Rance heard the slug thud into a barrel at his back. He twisted to his left side. His gun flashed up, then down, a streak of smoke and flame belching from the muzzle.

Norris's six-shooter dropped from his hand. An expression of acute pain contorted his features. Slowly his head drooped, his knees commenced to buckle. A queer, folding-up movement seemed to envelop the man as he dived forward and crumpled on his side.

Rance climbed slowly to his feet, sheathed his gun. Two men were down, gasping out their lives. After a moment Norris was quiet.

Rance said, half aloud, "I reckon that's all." His voice sounded flat and toneless after the roaring concussions of the forty-fives.

Norris lay without movement. Nick Zane was cursing horribly, trying to regain his feet. A crimson stain was spreading rapidly over the denim at Zane's breast.

From Main Street came startled exclamations and the sounds of running feet. Men crowded into the store-house, asking questions. Brad Wheeler's words reached Rance through a blur of voices:

"What in God's name's happened now, Rance?"

Rance said, quiet-voiced, "I've caught the man that killed Vink and Matt, Brad. He's through killin' —"

"It's Norris!" came Ward Stinson's voice.

"Not Norris," Rance corrected. "Nick Zane —"

"Where's Zane?" Wheeler's voice trembled.

Other men pressed into the long shed. Everyone talked at once. Someone announced that Hugh Norris was dead. Rance said grimly, when he could make himself heard, "Take a good look at Zane, Brad. You think he's Clem Lucas, but he's Nickie Zane."

Zane had struggled to his feet by this time, fighting hard for life. One outspread hand was placed behind him, supporting his weight against a stack of boxed goods.

"Yes, Wheeler, I'm Zane — your old pal, Nickie Zane," he snarled defiantly. His eyes glared vindictively. "With a mite more time

I'd killed you, too, Brad, you double-crossin' —
" His voice choked, he went on in a moment,
"But you'll never hang me — not Nickie
Zane. I've got mine and I'm goin' — fast.
Damn you, Wheeler, I swore I'd come back
and get you three —"

His speech stumbled and he slid to the
floor. The babel of voices was renewed. Brad
Wheeler and Rance knelt by Zane's side. The
man was still living, his eyes blazing hate at
them. After a moment he closed his eyes.

"Somebody fetch Doc Parker," Rance said.

"By God! It is Zane," Wheeler exclaimed.
"I'd never recognized him, but his voice was
familiar when he let it out. We been so used
to seein' a crack-voiced old man around —"

"That scar sort of twists his face. Prison
aged him, too — in looks, anyway. And that
beard and his glasses. He was a good actor
as well as a bad one, Brad."

Wheeler looked white. "He'd a got me,
next. . . . Did you shoot him, Rance?"

"Norris's slug got him — it was meant for
me, though —"

"But, Norris — ?"

"He's mixed in it — rustlin' VIT stock,
anyway —"

"Who rustled VIT stock?" Ringbone Uhler's
voice.

"Hello, Ringbone," Rance said. "Norris was
stealin' VIT —"

"Rance! Oh, Rance!" It was Eddie. Rance

rose to see the girl fighting her way through the press of men. "Rance, someone said you'd been killed." Her voice was full of tears. And then she was in his arms, sobbing on his shoulder. "Rance," brokenly, "why did you let me send you away — ?"

"There, there, kid, take it easy." Rance's words trembled. "Everythin's goin' to be all right." Having just witnessed Monte Quillan's face in the crowd, Rance tried to disengage Eddie's arms, but she clung the tighter to resist his efforts. For Rance it was an awkward position.

"Rance, don't you want me — ?"

"Eddie!" low-voiced. "There's Monte over there —"

"Oh, darn Monte!" Her face was crushed against his shirt. "I never said I'd marry him. Everybody jumped to conclusions. Haven't you any eyes at all? It's you who counts. Can't you understand? Have I got to say it all? You always treated me like a kid —"

"Hush, Eddie, hush —" Awe-stricken, Rance gazed around the shed. He saw Quillan, Oldfield, Stinson and others watching them.

"I won't be hushed," raising a tear-stained face to his. "You always acted like I was a kid, but now you've got to listen. You've never paid any attention to me. Just because Monte Quillan was calling —"

"Eddie — Eddie," Rance stammered, flustered. He gazed appealingly at Brad Wheeler, "Brad, for Heaven's sake, get this crowd out of here." Then he turned back, tightened his arms about Eddie's slim, yielding form. "Eddie, Eddie," he breathed softly, "I never knew —"

Wheeler, meanwhile, was getting rid of the crowd. The last man to go was Monte Quillan. Monte crossed the floor to Rance. Eddie's words hadn't reached him, but he'd guessed their import.

"Eddie's right, Rance," he said, a trifle wistfully. "I never could quite make the grade with her. And about that brand — I'm still insistin' it's coincidence. You'n me got off on the wrong foot a couple times, but you're gettin' my congratulations, just the same."

With that, he turned and stalked stiffly out of the door. Ringbone Uhler and Wheeler stayed in the shed. Wheeler pulled the door partly closed to keep the crowd out.

After a moment Eddie stepped back, her eyes shining in the semi-gloom of the building. "Rance, do you think it nice to make love to a girl with dead men around?"

Wheeler and Uhler had their backs to the couple, bending over Nick Zane. Wheeler said over one shoulder, "Only one dead man. Zane's still livin'."

The door was opened suddenly. Deputy Yocum burst in, followed by Doc Parker.

Parker glanced at Norris, then went directly to Zane's side.

Yocum stood looking at Eddie and Rance. "Darn your hide, Rance," he said, "why didn't you tell me you were comin' to a lead-slingin' shindig? When the feller came after Doc, I could hardly believe it. Thought I'd heard shots, but I was so busy talkin' with Gillett —"

"Gillett talked, eh?"

"Yes, he spilled the beans. Norris was the rustler Vink shot at that day. He was afraid his horse had been recognized, so he killed it — I hear Norris is dead."

Rance pointed to the huddled form on the floor. "It was a case of him or me, Homer."

"What's all this shindig about? Howcome old Clem is — say, was Clem workin' with Norris and Gillett —"

"You'll get that part later. Clem put one over on us. What did Gillett say?"

"Did Norris show you that bill-of-sale?"

"Don't know what you're talkin' about."

"It'll be in his pocket, then. You'll see it. It's a forgery. Norris had a story to account for the VIT cows he was rebrandin', but he wouldn't back Gillett, when he heard that Gillett had run an 8Q-Barred-Out burn. I passed Norris's words on to Gillett. When Gillett heard that Norris was tryin' to keep his own boots clear of the mud, he opened up. Gillett and Norris had planned to brand a few cows 8Q-Barred-Out, do a crude job, so we'd be sure to blame Monte for missin' VIT cows. And we did."

"I'll have to apologize to Monte about that," Rance said slowly. "His brand is due to pure chance, I reckon —"

"What happened here?" Yocum asked.

Rance told the story in a few words and returned to the matter of Gillett. "This forgery you mentioned, what was that?"

"Gillett gave me the whole dope," Yocum said. "Norris and Clem Lucas — Nick Zane, rather — had it all planned out. That forged bill-of-sale was Norris's ace-in-the-hole, in case we ever did catch him. He got Zane to write it. Zane wrote other bills-of-sale, too, in the past. Norris used to pick up small bunches of VIT cows and drive them across the Mexican Border, or into the next state, and sell 'em without changin' the brand. That was easy, with a VIT bill-of-sale to make the deal. Folks thought they were buying from a VIT representative. But that was too much work for Norris. He preferred runnin' his own brand. Norris had rustled some from Monte Quillan, too —"

"This man is regaining consciousness," Doctor Parker spoke crisply.

CHAPTER XXIII

Rance and Eddie moved nearer to the men gathered around Nick Zane.

"We've got to have more air in here, if you want this man to talk," Parker said irritably. "He hasn't long to live."

Brad Wheeler spoke over his shoulder to Yocum. "Throw that door wide open, Homer, but keep people back. You understand. Things might come out that shouldn't be spread around. Where's Belle Thorpe?"

Eddie answered that. "Last time I saw her, she was trying on dresses in the Emporium."

Nick Zane had been propped up on folded horse blankets. He hadn't long to live. Realizing he was beyond the reach of the law, the killer was willing, nay, eager, to talk of his exploits. He admitted boastfully, triumphantly, to the murders of Thorpe and Everett. Once started, the only check on his confession was his failing strength.

Rance turned suddenly to Eddie, "You better go outside, girl. You don't want to listen to this."

Eddie was pale, but her chin came up defiantly. "I'll stick," she said. "Belle's on Main Street some place, and I'd run into her.

317

That would be worse."

". . . I always swore I'd get 'em, and I done it," Nick Zane was stating vindictively. "My only regret is I didn't get you, too, Wheeler."

"Want to tell just what happened?" Wheeler urged.

A harsh smile twisted Zane's bearded lips. "Want to tell? Hell! I'm dyin' to tell it all." He cackled grimly at the grisly joke. "Ask Rance, he knows damn nigh as much as I do."

Rance said, "A lot that I know is guess-work. Zane left by the back window of his hotel in Capitol City, stole a horse and come here. But he had help — from Norris, I think. And I'm still wonderin' why he waited all this time before committing the murders."

Zane explained, a gloating something in his voice, how he had wanted to prove himself trustworthy, against the day when Thorpe established a bank in Morada. In such event, Zane had been promised a position of trust, and he had figured to postpone his revenge until, through having access to the bank's funds, he could augment it with a "real clean-up."

Zane went on with his confession.

One day, when getting the VIT mail from the post-office, Zane had recognized, on one envelope addressed to Thorpe, a handwriting that looked familiar. That night he had steamed open the envelope and learned with surprise that Belle Thorpe was not only alive but was coming to the VIT to see Thorpe.

Fearing that Belle's arrival might in some way disrupt his plans, Zane decided to kill Thorpe as soon as the matter could be arranged: "I knew Belle would want money, so I didn't send her letter to Thorpe until the day when the store receipts were in. Thorpe was due in town that day, and I figured he'd get it from Rance, when Rance took the mail. I thought that letter would cause Thorpe to hold the store receipts, in case Belle arrived on the night stage, and I guessed right.

"I'd seen Norris, and told him to have relay horses on the trail. Told him I'd come back and take the store receipts. I didn't reckon that Belle would be in that night, regardless what Thorpe might expect, though she hadn't stated when she'd arrive. Norris had the horses planted the day before Thorpe got Belle's letter. Norris didn't know that I planned to kill Thorpe. He just thought I was after money. . . . He and Gillett both agreed not to say anythin' about the killin'. I'd been forgin' VIT bills-of-sale for Norris for some time. He needed my penmanship. If I do say it myself, I can forge any hand written."

He closed his eyes and sank back, fighting for breath. Tiny flecks of crimson foam were blowing out on his beard now, as he said, "I got headed back. Gillett followed and brought back the two relay horses. You all

319

know what happened . . . next day . . . and at the inquest. When Wheeler refused to tell about that letter, I knew I was safe from any check-up with the warden. I had half a notion to leave the country then, but decided to stick. . . ."

The story was pieced out with frequent pauses for breath. Bloated with conceit at the success of his first killing, Zane had decided to stay and finish Everett and Wheeler as well. After Belle Thorpe's failure to put in an appearance in the first days following Thorpe's death, Zane had grown more confident than ever.

"Look here, Nick," Wheeler said sharply, to arouse him to life, "didn't Belle Thorpe recognize you —"

Parker interrupted with surprise, "Why should she? I don't understand this connection with Belle Thorpe. What has that woman — ?"

"Keep still, Doc," Wheeler cut in. "There's a story back of this you don't know."

Zane was speaking again, "Yes . . . Belle recognized me. Somethin' about my voice . . . give me away. She accused me of killin' Thorpe. We argued . . . me denyin' it . . . but she knew all right. Somebody come in the store . . . we pretended to be . . . arguin' about stale . . . peppermint candy . . ." His voice died to a whisper, then failed him.

From outside, there came a sudden interruption, "Eddie! You come out here." Belle Thorpe's voice.

Eddie moved back into the store-house, seized Rance's arm and clung to it. "Rance," her whisper was a wail, "I should have told you before. That woman married Dad."

"Don't let it worry you, Eddie," the man's voice just reached the girl. "I know about it. Brad Wheeler told me the story —"

"I wonder how Brad happens to know her?"

"There's a lot of story you haven't heard yet, Eddie. What does she say?"

"She won't give me any details, but she's got a marriage license to prove she married my father. Rance, I'm a — a —"

"Don't say it, kid." Rance led her away from the others, kissed her. "Now, smile, Eddie."

"But I can't smile, Rance. It's too terrible."

"It's not terrible at all. What if she did marry Vink? Vink was young. It's nothing against him. Folks will think just as much of him and you. Now, let's have that smile. There — that's better. That's Vink Thorpe's girl. He always said your nerve was good. Now — there! — you're provin' it with a smile like that —"

From the doorway came Belle Thorpe's voice, "Eddie! Did you hear me? Come out here!"

There came the sounds of a struggle at the door, then the slap of an open hand against Yocum's face as he protested, "Nope, ma'am, you can't come in here."

"Stand aside, deputy, I'm goin' in," Belle snapped.

"Let her in, Homer," Brad Wheeler said.

"Just as you say," Homer said wearily. "It'll have to be your problem, though." He felt of the white fingermarks on his face, and swore under his breath.

Belle Thorpe sailed into the room, resplendent in a wide hat covered with pink roses. She glared at Rance, then said to Eddie, "No use you stayin' here, girl. Come outside."

"I'm staying," Eddie retorted firmly. "I've stood just about enough from you."

"Well, of all the unnatural creatures!" the woman puffed up angrily. "After all I've done, keepin' my mouth shut about —" She broke off as her eyes fell on Norris's body, then on the group about the dying Nick Zane. "Prefer lifeless bodies to the society of your mother, do you —"

"That'll be enough of that talk," Rance said savagely. "You keep your mouth shut, Mrs. Thorpe, or so help me, we'll put you in the cooler —"

"I'll handle this, Rance," Brad Wheeler came forward. "Belle, why didn't you tell us Clem Lucas was your brother? It would have saved Matt Everett's life."

"Brother?" Eddie exclaimed. No one heard her.

Belle Thorpe stiffened. For a moment she

was silent, then a harsh, unnatural laugh fell from her lips. "So you discovered that, eh?" she sneered. "Well, why should I squeal on my own brother, Brad Wheeler?"

"You're guilty of aiding and abetting a criminal, Belle," Wheeler said sternly.

"Well, what about it, Brad?" the woman said contemptuously. "You ain't the nerve to make any charges, and you know it. I'd be a fine sister, wouldn't I, to turn up my own brother?" She peered over Wheeler's shoulder at Nick Zane, whose eyes were half-open, glassy. Parker arose.

"Dead, eh, Doc?" she said harshly.

Wheeler said, "It was your duty to tell us, Belle — brother or no brother. I'll see that you pay for this."

The woman's chin came up defiantly. "Oh, you will, eh? Well, listen to me, Brad Wheeler, you oppose me and there'll be trouble. My situation here ain't changed a mite. I know what I'm here for, and so do you — and I'm going to get it. One peep out of you, because I didn't tell on Nick, and I'll spill everythin' I know. Then we'll see what Morada thinks of you and Vink Thorpe. I'll blast your reputation from —"

"Look here, Mrs. Thorpe," Doctor Parker said grimly, "you're under certain obligations, if this man is your brother. You'll have to tell us how to dispose of the body. It will be necessary to make funeral arrangements —"

Belle Thorpe laughed shrilly. "What if he is my brother? I don't care what you do with the body. He's nothing to me. He always was a murderin' blackguard. Good riddance, I say. You ain't goin' to saddle my good name with responsibility for him. I don't care what you do with the body. Suit yourself." Again that shrill laugh.

Some spark of life was left in Nick Zane, a flicker that was fanned to resentful flame by Belle Thorpe's scornful words. His eyes opened wide. Unassisted, he jerked his body to one elbow, pointed a shaking, revengeful finger at the woman.

"A murderin' blackguard am I?" he croaked vindictively. "Good riddance, eh, Belle? You're playin' a big game, Belle. I was all for you lettin' you get away with it, but not after those words —"

"Nick! Don't you —" Belle Thorpe cried. She had suddenly gone ashen.

Nickie Zane's laughter was horrible. His blazing eyes searched out Wheeler's face. "I'll tell you, Brad, why she didn't tell you I was her brother," his cracked voice grated through the room. "She didn't dare squeal on me, that's why — or I'd have told what I know. Brother, hell! We only posed as brother and sister . . . back in Spade Gulch days . . . so she could fleece the suckers!"

"It's a lie!" the woman screeched.

"It's the truth," Zane contradicted. "Brother

and sister hell! She's my wife! Go in and get my coat. You'll find our marriage license in the . . . inside pocket. I've always . . . carried it. . . . Thought you'd lost it . . . long time back . . . didn't you, Belle? You always were a double-crossin' female. I was a fool . . . to love you the way . . . I did. But you were my wife two years . . . before you met Vink Thorpe. Your marriage to him . . . was never legal. Good riddance, eh, Belle? I'll show you! I've dealt you a hand you . . . never will play out. It's better'n aces and eights . . . better'n aces . . ."

Zane's head suddenly rolled to one side, his mouth dropped open and he fell back. Parker knelt by him. In a moment he looked up. "Dead," he announced grimly.

Belle Zane tried to speak. Words wouldn't come.

"This finishes you, Belle," Brad Wheeler stated coldly. "You better make yourself scarce."

Rance had raced into the store and found Zane's coat hanging behind the counter. There were several papers in the inner pocket. He sorted an old envelope from the rest, opened it and drew out a folded document, yellowed with age.

He came dashing back into the store-house. "Here it is," he yelled. "Eddie, this makes everythin' all right, do you hear, girl?" He showed the license to Eddie, then handed it to Brad Wheeler.

Wheeler examined the date first, his face lighted up. He turned to Belle Zane. "It's all here, Belle — 'joined in matrimony to Nicholas Zane on August 23rd —' "

"Hell!" the woman sneered. "I know the date. You don't need to read it. I reckon that paper is mine, though —"

"I'll keep it, Belle," Wheeler answered sternly. "It's too late for you to catch the noon stage, but I'll gladly hire a man to drive you to Capitol City or Breenville."

"The cards are stacked against me, Brad. I'll wait at the hotel for your driver. Well, so-long, folks. I'll be seein' you in Sunday school one of these days."

They heard her harsh, contemptuous laugh at the doorway as she faced Homer Yocum, then she passed on through, head high, pink roses nodding on her hat in a final defiant gesture.

There was no comment for several moments. Rance turned to Eddie. The girl was radiant.

"C'mon, let's get out of here," he urged, grinning. "This isn't any place to — to —"

He didn't finish the sentence. Further words weren't required, any more than was a reply from the girl. They were at the doorway now, then outside, pushing through the crowd, with no thought for anything except the great love that had come to them.

The employees of Thorndike Press hope you have enjoyed this Large Print book. All our Thorndike and Wheeler Large Print titles are designed for easy reading, and all our books are made to last. Other Thorndike Press Large Print books are available at your library, through selected bookstores, or directly from us.

For information about titles, please call:

(800) 223-1244

or visit our Web site at:

www.gale.com/thorndike
www.gale.com/wheeler

To share your comments, please write:

Publisher
Thorndike Press
295 Kennedy Memorial Drive
Waterville, ME   04901